# Breathe

# Breathe

## Abbi Glines

SIMON AND SCHUSTER

First published in Great Britain in 2013 by Simon and Schuster UK Ltd
A CBS COMPANY

First published in the USA in 2013 by Simon Pulse an
imprint of Simon & Schuster Children's Publishing Division

1 3 5 7 9 10 8 6 4 2

Simon & Schuster UK Ltd
1st Floor, 222 Gray's Inn Road
London
WC1X 8HB

Simon & Schuster Australia, Sydney
Simon & Schuster India, New Delhi

A CIP catalogue record for this book
is available from the British Library.

eBook ISBN 978-1-4711-1743-5
PB ISBN: 978-1-4711-3470-8

Printed and bound by CPI Group (UK) Ltd, Croydon, CR0 4YY

www.simonandschuster.co.uk
www.simonandschuster.com.au

*To my mother, Becky, who has been reading my "manuscripts" since I was nine years old and encouraging me every step of the way.*

## ACKNOWLEDGMENTS

My husband, Keith, always comes first on this list. Without his help I couldn't write the first word. He has supported me completely throughout this wild and crazy ride.

My three kids, who can order takeout like champs. They don't complain about their mother's lack of culinary skills and they tell me often they're just glad I know how to write. My middle child gets a special shout out for this book. Annabelle's obsession with teenage musicians inspired the idea behind Jax Stone. So thank you, baby girl. You started this whole ball rolling.

Jane Dystel, my agent. She is a rock star. I swear it. I'm so thankful I made the decision to work with her. It was one of the best decisions of my life.

Lauren Abramo, my foreign rights agent who is making sure my books are all over the globe.

Bethany Buck, Mara Anastas, Anna McKean, Carolyn Swerdloff, Paul Crichton, and the rest of the Simon Pulse team. They're all amazing. They are a fantastic bunch of people to work with.

My FP girls. This world wouldn't be nearly as much fun without y'all in it. I love all your faces.

# Prologue

**SADIE**

Life has always been a struggle for me. From what I could tell, it wasn't daisies for everyone else, either. But I never let go of the fantasy that one day I wouldn't feel so alone and isolated from the rest of the normal world. My dream was what kept me going many nights when I fought the desire to just disappear. It would be easier if I'd never been born.

I'm positive my mother sees things the same way. I know what you're thinking, and no, she never said those words, but my entrance into the world dramatically changed the course of her life.

My mother had been a beauty queen in the small Arkansas town where she'd grown up. Everyone said she would make it big someday. Maybe her beauty and charm somehow would have opened those doors if she hadn't met the man who helped give me life. The fact is, she ran off to become a star and fell in love with a very married man. A man who didn't acknowledge me or help her for fear of tarnishing his social standing in the big city of Nashville, Tennessee.

A one-room shack in the hills of Tennessee is where my mother and I spent the first part of my life. Until the day she up and decided life would be easier in Alabama. On the southern coast, my mother—who I now call Jessica—could find work. And the sunshine would be good for us, or so she said. I knew she needed an escape, or maybe just a place to start over. If anyone could be a magnet for losers, Jessica fit the profile. Unfortunately, she was about to bring another child into the unstable life she managed to lead, where she greatly relied on someone else—me—to handle things. If only she had let me make her decisions for her in the dating world, like she did with the rest of her life. But, alas, we were headed to southern Alabama, where the sun is supposed to shine bright and wash away all our worries. . . . Yeah, right.

# Chapter One

**JAX**

This was it. Finally. The last stop on my tour. I shoved open the door to my private suite, and Kane, my bodyguard, closed it firmly behind me. The screaming on the other side of the door had only made my head hurt. This had been fun once. Now all I could think about was getting away from it. The girls. The relentless schedule. The lack of sleep and the pressure. I wanted to be someone else. Anywhere else.

The door opened and quickly closed behind me. I sank down onto the black leather sectional sofa and watched my younger brother, Jason, as he grinned at me with two beers in his hands.

"It's over," he announced. Only Jason understood my feelings lately. He'd been with me through this crazy ride. He saw my parents' need to push me and my need to push back. He was my best friend. My only friend, really. I gave up trying to figure out who liked me for my money and fame a long time ago. It was pointless.

Jason handed me a beer and sat down on the sofa. "You killed it out there. The place was insane. No one would ever guess you were looking forward to running off to Alabama in the morning to hide away all summer."

My agent, Marco, had told my parents about the private island on the Alabama coast. They were so ready to have somewhere other than our house in LA that they'd jumped at the idea.

Going back to my hometown—Austin, Texas—hadn't been something they wanted to do. Too many people knew who we were.

The security Sea Breeze offered had always allowed me the freedom I'd lost when the world had embraced me. For a few weeks every summer we were a family again. I was just another guy, and I could walk out to the water and enjoy it without cameras and fans. No autographs. Just peace. Tomorrow we were headed back there. It was our summer break. But this year I was staying the whole damn summer. I didn't care what my mother or my agent thought I should do. I was hiding out for three months, and they could all kiss Marco's ass. What had started as my mother's insistence that we spend the summers together in Alabama had become mine. I needed time with just them. I rarely saw them the rest of the year. It was the only house we had to call ours. I had my house in LA, and my parents and Jason had theirs.

"You're coming down, right?" I asked him.

Jason nodded. "Yeah. I'll be there, but not tomorrow. I need a few days. Mom and I had an argument about college. I want to give it a few days before I face her again. She's driving me crazy."

Our mother was a micromanager when it came to our lives. "Good idea. I'll talk to her. Maybe I can get her to back off."

Jason laid his head back on the leather. "Good luck. She's on a mission to make me miserable."

Lately I felt like she was doing the same to me. I no longer lived with her. I lived independently. I was the one who paid her bills. Why she thought she could still tell me what to do was beyond me. But she did. She always thought she knew what was best. I was done with that, and so was Jason. I'd talk to her, all right. She needed to remember who was actually in control here and back off.

"Take a few days. Enjoy yourself. Let me prep Mom for the fact that I'm not going to allow her to control your life. Then come south," I told him before taking a long drink of my beer.

## SADIE

"Mom, are you going to work today?" I rolled my eyes at my very pregnant mother, who lay sprawled out on her bed in her panties and bra. Pregnancy made Jessica an even bigger drama queen than before having unsafe sex with another loser.

She moaned and covered her head with a pillow. "I feel awful, Sadie. You just go on without me."

I'd seen this coming a mile away before school even let out. The last day of school landed yesterday, but instead of being able to go out and be a normal teenager, I was expected to make the money for us. It was almost as if Jessica had planned on me working in her place all along.

"I can't just go to your workplace and take your position. Haven't you explained the situation to them? They won't be okay with your seventeen-year-old daughter doing your job."

She pulled the pillow from her face and tossed me a sulk she'd perfected years ago. "Sadie, I can't continue cleaning house with my stomach the size of a beach ball. I'm so hot and tired. I need you to help me. You can do it. You always figure stuff out."

I walked over to the air conditioner and turned it off. "If you'd stop running it at a continuous sixty-eight degrees, we might be able to get by on less money. Do you have any idea how much it costs to run a window unit all day long?" I knew she didn't know, nor did she care, but I still asked.

She grimaced and sat up. "Do you have any idea how hot I am with all this extra weight?" she shot back at me.

It took all my restraint to keep from reminding her that she got this way because she hadn't used a condom. I bought them for her and made sure her purse always contained several. I even reminded her before she went out on dates.

Remembering who the adult was in our relationship could be difficult at times. Most of the time it seemed to me our roles were reversed. Being the adult, however, did not mean she made smart decisions, because Jessica simply did not know how to be responsible.

"I know you're hot, but we can't spend every dime we make on the air conditioner," I reminded her.

She sighed and flopped back down on the bed. "Whatever," she grumbled.

I walked over to her purse and opened it up. "All right, I'm going to go to your job today, by myself, and I hope they allow me inside the gate. If this doesn't work, don't say I didn't warn you. All I am qualified for is minimum-wage jobs, which won't pay our bills. If you would come with me, I would have a better chance of landing this position." I knew as I spoke the words that I'd already been tuned out. At least she had managed to keep the job for two months.

"Sadie, you and I both know you can handle it by yourself."

I sighed in defeat and left her there. She would go back to sleep as soon as I left. I wanted to be mad at her, but seeing her so big made me pity her instead. She wasn't the best mom in the world, but she did belong to me. After I got my clothes on, I walked past her room and peeked through the door. She softly snored with the window unit once again cranked to sixty-eight degrees. I thought about turning it off, but changed my mind. The apartment already felt warm, and the day would only get hotter.

I stepped outside and got on my bike. It took me thirty minutes to get to the bridge. The bridge would take me from Sea Breeze, Alabama, onto the exclusive island that was connected to it. The island wasn't where the locals lived, but where the wealthy came for the summer. Jessica had managed to snag a job as a domestic servant at one of the houses that employed full staffs. The pay was twelve dollars an hour. I prayed I would be able to take over her position without a hitch.

I found the address on her employee card I'd retrieved from her purse. My chances of getting this job were slim. The farther I pedaled onto the island, the larger and more extravagant the houses became. The address of my mother's place of employment was coming up. She, of course, had to work at the most extravagant house on the block, not to mention the very last one before the beach. I pulled up to a large ornate iron gate and handed Jessica's ID card to the guy working admittance. He frowned and gazed down at me. I handed him my driver's license.

"I'm Jessica's White's daughter. She's sick, and I'm supposed to work for her today."

He continued to frown while he picked up a phone and

called someone. That wasn't a good thing, considering no one here knew I was coming in her place. For good. Two large men appeared and walked up to me. Both sported dark sunglasses and looked like they should be wearing football uniforms and playing on NFL teams instead of black suits.

"Miss White, can we see your bag, please," one of them said, rather than asked, while the other one took it off my shoulder.

I swallowed and fought the urge to shudder. They were big and intimidating and didn't appear to trust me. I wondered if I seemed dangerous to them, all five feet six inches of me. I glanced down at my skimpy white shorts and purple tank top and wondered if they'd considered the fact that it would be impossible to hide weapons in this outfit. I thought it somewhat strange that the two big guys were reluctant to let me in. Even if I happened to be a threat, I do believe either one of them could have taken me blindfolded with his hands tied behind his back. The image popped into my mind and made me want to laugh. I bit my bottom lip and waited to see if dangerous little me would be allowed entrance through the bigger-than-life iron gates.

"You're free to enter, Miss White. Please take the servants' entrance to the left of the stone wall and report to the kitchen, where you will be instructed how to proceed."

Who were these people who needed two men the size of Goliath to guard their entrance? I got back on my bike and rode through the now open gates. Once I made it around the corner, past lush palm trees and tropical gardens, I saw the house. It reminded me of houses on *MTV Cribs*. I never would've guessed houses like this even existed in Alabama. I'd been to Nashville once and seen houses similar in size, but nothing quite this spectacular.

I composed myself and pushed my bike around the corner, trying to not stop and stare at the massive size of everything. I leaned my bike against a wall, out of sight. The entrance for the servants was designed to impress. At least twelve feet tall, the door was adorned with a beautifully engraved letter *S*. Not just tall, the door was really heavy, causing me to use all my strength to pull it open. I peeked inside the large entry hall and stepped into a small area with three different arched doorways ahead of me to choose from. Since I'd never been here before, I didn't know where the kitchen might be located. I walked up to the first door on the right and looked through the opening. It appeared to be a large gathering room, but nothing fancy and no kitchen appliances, so I moved on to door number two, peeked inside, and found a large round table with people sitting around it. A large older lady stood in front of a stove unlike any I'd ever seen in a house. It was something you'd find in a restaurant.

This had to be the place. I stepped through the arched opening.

The lady standing noticed me and frowned. "Can I help you?" she asked in a sharp, authoritative tone, though she kind of reminded me of Aunt Bee from *The Andy Griffith Show.*

I smiled, and the heat rose, threatening to spike out the top of my head as I watched all the people in the room turn to face me. I hated attention and did whatever I could to draw little to myself. Even though it seemed to be getting harder the older I got. As much as possible, I tried to avoid situations that encouraged other people to speak to me. It's not that I'm a recluse; it's just the fact that I have a lot of responsibility. I figured out early in life that friendships would never work for me. I'm too busy taking care of my mom. So I've perfected the art of being uninteresting.

"Um, uh, yes, I was told to report to the kitchen for further instructions." I quietly cleared my voice and waited.

I didn't like the once-over the lady gave me, but since I was here, I had no choice but to stay.

"I know *I* sure didn't hire you. Who told you to come here?"

I hated all those eyes on me and wished Jessica hadn't been so stubborn. I needed her here, at least for today. Why did she always do these things to me?

"I'm Sadie White, Jessica White's daughter. She . . . uh . . . wasn't well today, so I am here to work for her. I'm . . . uh . . . supposed to be working with her this summer."

I wished I didn't sound so nervous, but the people stared. The lady up front frowned much like the way Aunt Bee looked when someone made her angry. It was tempting to turn and run.

"Jessica didn't ask about you helping her this summer, and I don't hire kids. It ain't a good idea with the family comin' down for the whole summer. Maybe during the fall when they leave we can give you a try."

My nervousness from being the center of attention immediately disappeared, and I panicked at the thought of our losing this income we so desperately needed. If my mom found out I couldn't work for her, she would quit. I pulled my grown-up voice out of the closet and decided I needed to show this lady I could do the job better than anyone else.

"I can understand your concern. However, if you would give me a chance, I can and will show you I'm an asset. I'll never be late to work and will always complete the jobs assigned to me. Please, just a chance."

The lady glanced down at someone at the table as if to get an opinion. She moved her eyes back up to me, and I could see I'd broken through her resolve. "I'm Ms. Mary, and I'm in charge of the household staff and I run the kitchen. You impress me and you have the job. Okay, Sadie White, your chance starts now. I'm gonna team you up with Fran here, who has been working in this home as long as I have. She'll instruct you and report back to me. I will have you an answer at the end of the day. Here is your trial, Miss White. I suggest you don't blow it."

I nodded and smiled over at Fran, who was now standing.

"Follow me," the tall, skinny redhead who appeared to be

at least sixty-five years old said before she turned and left the room.

I did as instructed without making eye contact with any of the others. I had a job to save.

Fran walked me down a hallway and past several doors. We stopped, opened one, and stepped inside. The room contained shelves of books from the floor to the ceiling. Large dark-brown leather chairs were scattered around the room. None faced any of the others or looked to be used for any type of visiting or socializing. The room was clearly set up to be a library. A place where people could come, find a book, and lose themselves in one of the large cushy chairs.

Fran swung her arm out in front of her, gesturing to the room with a bit of flair. It surprised me coming from an older lady. "This is Mrs. Stone's favorite spot. It's been closed off all year. You will dust the books and shelves, clean the leather with the special cleaner, and clean the windows. Vacuum the drapes; clean and wax the floors. This room must shine. Mrs. Stone likes things perfect in her sanctuary. I will come get you at lunchtime, and we will dine in the kitchen."

She walked to the door, and I heard her thank someone. She stepped back inside, pulling a cart full of cleaning supplies. "This will have everything you need. Be careful with all framed artwork and sculptures. I warn you, everything in this house is very valuable and must be treated with the utmost care. Now, I expect you to work hard and not waste any time with foolishness." The tight-faced Fran left the room.

I circled around, taking in the extravagance of my surroundings. The room wasn't really big; it just seemed full. I could clean this. I hadn't been asked to do anything impossible. I went for the dusting supplies and headed to the ladder connected to the bookshelves. I might as well start at the top, since dust falls.

I managed to get everything dusted and the windows cleaned before Fran returned to get me for lunch. I needed a break and some food. Her frowning face was a welcome sight. She moved her gaze around the room and nodded before leading me in silence back down the same path I'd taken this morning. The smell of fresh-baked bread hit me as we rounded the corner and stepped into the large, bright kitchen. Ms. Mary stood over the stove, pointing to a younger lady, who wore her hair in a bun covered with a hairnet just like Ms. Mary's.

"Smells good, Henrietta. I believe you've got it. We will test this batch out on the help today, and if everyone likes it, you can take over the bread baking for the family's meals." Ms. Mary turned, wiping her hands on her apron. "Ah, here is our new employee now. How are things going?"

Ms. Fran nodded and said, "Fine."

Either this lady didn't smile much or she just didn't like me.

"Sit, sit. We have much to get done before the family arrives."

I sat down after Fran did, and Ms. Mary set trays of food in front of us. I must have been doing something right since Fran directed her words in my direction. "All the help eat at this table. We all come at different shifts for lunch. You may choose what you want to eat."

I nodded and reached for the tray of sandwiches and took one. I took some fresh fruit from a platter.

"The drinks are over there on the bar. You may go choose from what's there or fix something yourself."

I went over and poured some lemonade. I ate in silence while I listened to Ms. Mary direct Henrietta as they baked bread. Neither Fran nor I made any attempt at conversation.

After we were done, I followed Fran to the sink, where we rinsed our plates and loaded them into the large dishwasher ourselves. Just as silent, we returned to the library. I was a little less nervous now and more interested in my surroundings. I noticed the portraits as we walked down the hallway. There were portraits of two very cute little boys. The farther I walked, the older they seemed to get. Toward the arched entrance that led to the hallway where the library was located, an oddly familiar face smiled down at me from a life-size painting. A face I'd seen many times on television and in magazines. Just last night during dinner he had been on television. Jessica watched *Entertainment Daily* during our meal. Teen rocker and heartthrob Jax Stone was one of their favorite topics. Last night he'd had on his arm a girl rumored to be in his new music video. Fran stopped behind me. I turned to her, and she seemed focused on the portrait.

"This is his summer home. He will be arriving with his parents and brother tomorrow. Can you handle this?"

I simply nodded, unable to form words from the shock of seeing Jax Stone's face on the wall.

Fran moved again, and I followed her into the library. "He's the reason teenagers are not hired. This is a private escape for him. When he was younger, his parents insisted he take a break each summer and spend time with them away from the bright lights of Hollywood. Now he's older and still comes here for the summer. He leaves now and then to go to different events, but for the most part, this is his getaway. He brings his family with him since they don't see each other much during the year." Fran paused dramatically and then continued. "If you can't handle it, you will be fired immediately. His privacy is of the utmost importance. It's why this is such a high-paying job."

I straightened and grabbed the bucket I'd been using. "I can handle anything. This job is more important to me than a teenage rock star."

Fran nodded, but from her frown, I could see she didn't believe me.

I focused more energy into my work. At the end of a long day, I listened while the quiet, frowning Fran reported to Ms. Mary. She believed I would be a good worker and I should be given a chance. I thanked her and Ms. Mary. I figured I should be able to save enough money for the fall, when my mom would have the baby and not work, and I would be back in school. I could do this.

Yes, Jax Stone was famous, had incredible steel-blue eyes, and happened to be one of the most beautiful creations known to man. I made myself admit that much. However, everyone knows beauty is only skin deep. I assumed the shallowness radiating off of him would be so revolting I wouldn't care that I cleaned his house and passed him in the halls.

Besides, guys were a species I knew nothing about. I never took the time to talk to one even when they did their best to talk to me. I've always had bigger problems in life, like making sure we ate and my mom remembered to pay our bills.

When I thought of all the money I'd wasted on the condoms I'd shoved into Jessica's hands and purse before she went out with the countless men who flocked to her, I really had a hard time not getting angry with her. Even in thrift-store clothing, she looked gorgeous. One of her many disgusting men told me I'd inherited the cursed looks. From her curly blond hair to her clear blue eyes and heavy black lashes, I somehow managed to get it all. However, I had the one thing I knew would save me from certain disaster: My personality came across as rather dull. It was something my mother loved to remind me of, yet instead of being upset by it, I held on to it for dear life. What she thought of as a character defect, I liked to think of as my lifeline. I didn't want to be like her. If having a dull personality kept me from following in her footsteps, then I would embrace it.

The apartment we lived in for almost five hundred a month sat underneath a huge old house. I walked in after my first day of work to find that Jessica wasn't inside. With only four rooms, she couldn't have gotten far.

"Mom?" I got no answer.

The sun was setting, so I stepped out onto what Jessica referred to as a patio. If you ask me, it was really more like a small piece of slab. She loved coming out here to look out over the water. She stood out in the yard with her increasing stomach on view for all to see, in a bikini I'd bought at a thrift store a few weeks ago. She turned and smiled. The facade of sickness from this morning no longer appeared on her face. Instead, she seemed to be glowing.

"Sadie, how did it go? Did ol' Ms. Mary give you a hard time? If she did, I sure hope you were nice. We need this job, and you can be so rude and unsociable."

I listened to her blabber on about my lack of social skills and waited until she finished before I spoke. "I got the job for the summer if I want it."

Jessica sighed dramatically in relief. "Wonderful. I really need to rest these next few months. The baby is taking so much out of me. You just don't understand how hard it is to be pregnant."

I wanted to remind her I'd tried to keep her from getting pregnant by sacrificing food money to buy her some stupid condoms, which didn't help at all! However, I nodded and walked inside with her.

"I'm starving, Sadie. Is there anything you can fix up real fast? I'm eating for two these days."

I'd already planned what we would eat for dinner before I got home. I knew Mom was helpless in the kitchen. I'd somehow survived the early years of my life on peanut butter and jelly sandwiches. Somewhere around the time I turned eight, I realized my mother needed help, and I began growing up quicker than normal children. The more I offered to take on, the more she gave me. By the time I turned eleven, I did it all.

With the noodles boiling and the meat sauce simmering, I went to my room. I slipped out of my work clothes and into a pair of thrift-store cutoff jean shorts, which happen to be the core of my wardrobe, and a T-shirt. My wardrobe was simple.

The timer for the noodles went off, letting me know the food needed to be checked. Jessica wasn't going to get up and help out anytime soon. I hurried back into the small kitchen, took out a spaghetti noodle on a fork, and slung it at the wall behind the stove. It stuck. It was ready.

"Really, Sadie, why you toss noodles on the wall is beyond

me. Where did you get such an insane idea?"

I flipped my gaze up and over at Jessica. She was kicked back on the faded pastel couch, which had come with the apartment, in my bikini.

"I saw it on the television once when I was younger. It has stuck with me ever since. Besides, it works."

"It's disgusting, is what it is," Jessica mumbled from her spot on the couch.

She couldn't boil water if she wanted to, but I decided to bite my tongue and finish with dinner.

"It's ready, Mom," I said as I scooped a pile of spaghetti onto a plate, knowing she would ask me to bring her one.

"Bring me a plate, will ya, honey?"

I smirked. I was a step ahead of her. She rarely got up these days unless she absolutely had to. I slipped a fork and spoon onto the plate and took it to her. She didn't even sit up. Instead, she placed it on the shelf of a belly she'd developed, and ate. I placed a glass of sweet iced tea down beside her and went back to fix my own plate. I'd worked up an appetite today. I needed food.

# Chapter Two

**JAX**

Ms. Mary had the staff waiting when the limo pulled up in front of the house. I didn't wait for the driver to open my door. I was free to not worry about impressions here. I could do what I damn well pleased. I stepped out of the limo and stretched, smiling up at the house that represented freedom to me.

There was no threat of girls gone crazy beating down my door. I didn't have any places I needed to be. No interviews. Nothing. I could go lay out on that beach all damn day and no one would bother me. Life was good in south Alabama. My mom wasn't here yet, so I had time to go in and see Ms. Mary. Get some sweet iced tea and a buttered biscuit before dealing with her.

Ms. Mary came bustling out the door before I made it up

the steps. "Master Jax, you look like you've lost ten pounds since I seen you last. Come on in here and get yourself some good food. Growing boys don't need to be so skinny."

I'd actually put on ten pounds since she'd last seen me, thanks to my new trainer. But I wasn't going to argue with her. You didn't argue with Ms. Mary. Even my mom knew that. "Hello, Ms. Mary. You're looking more beautiful than the last time I saw you." It was something I'd been telling her every year for the past five years. Her wrinkled cheeks would turn a bright pink from the compliment.

"Hush now, boy. We both know that ain't true. But my biscuits, them's something you can gush over." She was proud of her culinary abilities, and I was pretty damn addicted to them myself. It was why I paid her well to stay on all year even when I wasn't in residence. I liked knowing I could come here whenever I wanted. Having it kept up during the year gave not only Ms. Mary a job, but some of the staff as well. Ms. Mary only had to hire on extra help for the summers.

**SADIE**

Things went much smoother the next day. I didn't have to be searched, and I was even given a card to show at the gate when I arrived from here on out. Fran even smiled at me once. After lunch Ms. Mary sent me to the third floor, which housed most of the bedrooms. It was easy to forget whose house I cleaned. I had no friends to tell about the job. And the fact that I stood in the rooms where the hottest teen star in the world would be sleeping all summer wasn't really so big of a deal.

I stepped into Jax's bedroom and spun around. This wasn't a typical celebrity's room. It seemed so old-fashioned, and it struck me as odd. I had to take a closer look.

One wall displayed bats and balls autographed by different players while some just looked well used. Jerseys he must have worn during childhood hung on the walls proudly. I could easily picture the little boy I'd seen in the portraits wearing these and playing Little League just like an ordinary kid. I went in for a closer inspection of the team pictures hanging under each of the jerseys. In the earliest ones, I struggled to figure out which little boy was the now famous rock star. After he appeared to be ten or eleven, I identified him easily. The jerseys and pictures were in year order from about kindergarten until age thirteen, and then they stopped. A year or so later was when I remembered first hearing his name on the radio. He seemed to have led a normal life up until the time a record label discovered him.

The wall space above his bed set the room apart from an ordinary teenage boy's room. Guitars of every shape, size, and color hung on the walls. Many were autographed; some sparkled with newness. One appeared to have real gold on it, which wouldn't be surprising at all. I got on my toes and examined it more closely. It said FENDER on it. I continued examining the signatures on the more expensive guitars. I ran my finger over the name Jon Bon Jovi and smiled. Apparently, even rock stars have idols. In the center of them all hung a small worn guitar. The fact that it hung in the center of this collection made it obvious this must have been the first and most loved.

I peeked back at the open door to make sure no one was outside, then went to stand under the small guitar I imagined had started it all. I wasn't a crazy fan, but seeing something responsible for spurring a dream seemed almost holy in a way.

My cleaning cart sat untouched in the doorway, and I knew I needed to get busy. I didn't want to learn new, personal things about him. I wanted him to stay shallow and untouchable in my eyes. Knowing he once was a cute little boy with dark brown curls and a smile that would one day cause a frenzy made him seem more real and not so godlike. I needed to keep my interest in him to a minimum. I quickly went about the room dusting and sweeping, and then I mopped the expensive hardwood floors. I decided I'd better get through with this room quickly before I came across anything else too personal. I focused my thoughts on my future and blocked out all thoughts of Jax Stone.

"Sadie, are you finished yet? The family has arrived, and we need to exit to the servants' quarters," Fran said from the doorway.

I walked out into the hallway, where a very nervous Fran stood, and placed my cleaning supplies back on the cart. "Sure, just finished up."

Fran nodded and headed toward the back elevator, in which house staff traveled from floor to floor without being seen by the family. Fran hurried inside as it opened, and I started to follow when a bottle of glass cleaner fell off the cart and spilled a little. I reached for a small rag and picked the bottle up from the floor. I wiped up the spill the best I could.

"Hurry, please," Fran called in an anxious tone from inside the elevator. The family must have been headed upstairs.

As I started pushing my cart toward the elevator, a tingling sensation raised the hairs on my neck. Startled, I turned and saw him standing there watching me. It wasn't the cute little curly headed boy, but instead the famous rock star. I froze, unsure of what to do since my presence here becoming known this soon wasn't something Ms. Mary wanted. A smile broke across his ridiculously sexy face, and heat burned through my cheeks as I glanced away and entered the elevator.

He didn't appear to be angry that a teenage girl worked in his home. His smile seemed more amused. Fran frowned when I glanced at her, but she said nothing. I put my cart away and went to report to the kitchen. Ms. Mary stood with her hands on her hips, waiting on our arrival. A silent conversation seemed to take place between Fran and Ms. Mary. After Ms. Mary nodded, she reached for something on the table and handed me folded black clothing.

"Everyone wears uniforms while the family is in residence. Also, you won't be cleaning the house anymore, but you will help me in the kitchen and help Mr. Greg in the gardens. And tonight I need you to serve supper. Mrs. Stone has requested that all servers seen by family and guests are attractive in appearance. William, the young man I hired to assist Marcus in serving the family, called in sick about ten minutes ago, and you are all I got. You've proved to be a hard worker, and you seem to be serious about this job. Your age concerns me since the master of the house is around your age and is an idol in most girls' eyes. My gut tells me that is not an issue for you. I hope you continue to show such maturity."

I didn't really know what to say after that mouthful from her, so I only nodded.

"Good. Now, you're to wear this every day when you work in the house. I'll have two more made in your size, and they are to be left here each night to be washed and pressed. Make sure you continue to enter at the same location and immediately change in the laundry room. When you're working outside you'll need to change into the shorts that match this. They will also be kept in the laundry room. Now I need you to help me begin preparing for the evenin' meal before you put these on. You gotta be tidy and clean when you serve."

For the next two hours, I chopped, sliced, stirred, and stuffed all types of meats and vegetables. By the time Ms. Mary told me to get changed and tidy up my hair, exhaustion already filled my body. I changed into the black skirt, which hit right above my knees, and the white buttoned shirt with a round collar. I put a black apron on over my shirt and skirt. Pulling my hair loose, I piled the curls up high on my head. I washed my face and hands and sighed at the face mirrored back at me. My mother's face had landed me a job as server tonight, but my reserved personality had gained me Ms. Mary's trust. Where my mother's eyes sparkled with mischief, mine stayed serious and guarded.

Jax Stone's smile had dazzled me in person as much as it did in the millions of pictures I'd seen in magazines and on posters. However, it didn't mean I would be silly enough to be attracted to him like the rest of the world. With a deep breath, I opened the door and went back to the kitchen where Ms. Mary stood waiting.

"Okay, now remember, you set this in front of Master Jax at the exact moment Marcus here"—she waved to a tall young guy with sandy blond hair I'd not met yet—"places Mrs. Stone's in front of her. They will be the only two at the table tonight. Mr. Stone and their son Jason will be arriving in a few days. So tonight you two will be the only two serving.

"Make sure you stand back quietly behind Master Jax while

he eats, and follow Marcus's lead. He'll help you with anythin' you aren't sure about."

I turned my full gaze on Marcus, who seemed to be only a few years older than I was, probably college age. His smiling green eyes immediately relaxed me.

He held out his tanned hand and grinned. "Marcus Hardy."

I slipped my hand into his, and he shook it. "Sadie White."

He nodded, still grinning, and reached for his tray. "I saw your brave performance yesterday as you secured your job here. It amazed me how your eyes went from nervous to determined in less than a second." He picked up the tray in front of him, and I smiled and lifted the tray set before me.

"You'll follow me . . . since I'll be serving Mrs. Stone's food." He gave me a wink before turning and heading down the hall toward the entrance to the dining room.

The large room wasn't new to me. I'd scrubbed the floors in there that morning. Marcus took his place behind Mrs. Stone, who sat with her back to the entrance. I walked around to stand behind Jax, who sat at the head of the table. I looked to Marcus to guide me. He nodded, and we set the salads down at the exact same time. I stepped back. Marcus nodded for me to stand beside him, so I did.

"I still don't see why Dad is making Jason go to the interview at Yale if he doesn't want to go there." Jax's voice sounded so smooth it seemed almost unreal.

I felt as if I'd walked into a movie, and I stood watching the scene before me.

"Your brother doesn't know what is best for him. He has the brains to be more than just Jax Stone's younger brother. He can make a name for himself if he will just focus on it instead of spending so much time fiddling with the stock market. His head for numbers is being wasted. He needs to decide what he wants to do with his future and do it. Stop messing around with things. If he wants to be successful in the stock market, fine. But don't play at it like it's a game."

Jax's eyes gazed up at me and seemed to smile before he directed them back down at his mother. "You both are going to push him away. You're right; he is smart. And he doesn't need you to think for him."

Mrs. Stone let out a short, hard laugh. "And you wouldn't be where you are today if I hadn't pushed you so hard. All you wanted to do was play baseball with your buddies and play in a silly garage band that had absolutely no talent other than you."

Jax sighed, took a drink of his ice water, and turned to his mother. "Enough, Mom. Don't start talking bad about the only real friends I've ever had."

Mrs. Stone leaned back, and Marcus touched my hand to draw my attention back to him and the reason we were in here. We stepped forward and, at the same time, removed the salad plates from in front of the Stones.

"May we get you something other than water to drink with your meal?" Marcus asked with a charming southern drawl.

I felt eyes once again watching me. I fought the urge to allow my eyes to shift back in Jax's direction and to those eyes.

Mrs. Stone sighed. "I suppose one glass of wine won't hurt me." She glanced over at her son and straightened her napkin in her lap as if trying to decide. "Bring me a glass of the best merlot we have in the cellar."

Jax leaned back, and I could see he still watched me. So I took a calming breath and looked at him.

"If I could have some of Ms. Mary's sweet iced tea, please."

I nodded and kept myself from returning his smile.

"Yes, sir," Marcus replied. He stepped back and waved his hand so I would lead the way back to the kitchen.

I exited the large dining room and immediately took a deep breath. I hadn't realized how nerve-racking this would be. As soon as we entered the kitchen, Marcus smiled at me.

"What? Did I screw up?"

Marcus shook his head, and a blond lock of hair fell into his eyes. "No, you were great. Now let's get the crab bisque out there before Ms. Mary has a fit." He turned toward the housekeeper. "Ms. Mary, we need merlot from the cellar."

Ms. Mary handed him the already opened bottle along with a glass. "I figured as much, and here's Jax's sweet tea."

"I'll deal with the drinks," Marcus said.

I was too grateful to ask why. I just nodded and followed him back down the hall toward the dining room. Right before we reentered, Marcus glanced back at me. "Ignore his watching you. You're a treat to the eyes. I can't blame him, but if you want to keep this job, try to become invisible." He winked, then opened the door.

My goal in life was to become invisible. I thought I'd been attempting to do just that. Apparently, I needed to try harder.

"I intend to get in a lot of time just relaxing on the beach. I like the private beach access we have here, and the thought of being able to chill on the beach with no one wanting to speak to me, meet me, or get me to sign an autograph is what I've been craving all year. I need a break. I know Marco hates the idea of me being unavailable for three months, but I need this for my sanity." Jax glanced up at me as I set the bowl of bisque in front of him. "Thank you," he whispered.

"I want you to have a break too. Gregory thinks a little time in front of your fans this summer would be great PR. Maybe you could do a beach concert, or just do a few movie premieres."

Jax shook his head. "Mom, I refuse to make my presence here known. I chose Alabama because it's not a highly populated area. Better yet, this little island here is private. I'll consider a few movie premieres, but nothing else. No concerts."

Mrs. Stone shrugged. "Well, I told Gregory I would try, and

I did. He can deal with you. You're an adult. I'm not going to pressure you anymore."

Jax continued to eat, and I stood beside Marcus, staring out the window and back at Jax's bowl, waiting for the moment when I would need to remove it. I glanced up at Marcus, and he met my eyes with a smile. He was all business, and I could tell he wanted me to do well here. I'd made a friend. Marcus lightly touched my arm and stepped forward. I immediately followed, and we removed their bowls.

"More sweet tea, sir?"

Jax glanced at me and flicked his gaze toward Marcus. "Yes, please."

Mrs. Stone's glass of wine was only missing a sip at most. Marcus once again stepped back and allowed me to lead the way out. We did the same routine as before, with Marcus carrying the tray of dirty dishes.

Once in the kitchen, Marcus picked up the tray already pre-pared with the most rich, exotic foods I had ever seen.

"Wow, they sure eat a bunch."

"Mrs. Stone has only tasted her food so far, and my guess is she will barely touch this as well."

"He eats all of his."

"Yep, but then, he's a growing boy."

I laughed at Marcus's imitation of Ms. Mary and followed him back down the now familiar hall. Once inside, I placed the food in front of Jax again, and Marcus handled the sweet tea for me.

Jax and his mother ate in silence this time. Occasionally I sensed him watching me and felt a brief touch from Marcus's hand, no doubt reminding me I needed to become invisible. I never acknowledged the curious steel-blue eyes. Mother and son exchanged a few casual words, but for the most part, they continued to eat in silence. Finally, after what seemed like an eternity, I inspected Jax to see if he'd finished, and our eyes met.

I tried to tear my gaze away, but his eyes held a hint of laughter. I stared down at my feet, and Marcus squeezed my arm. It startled me. I looked up at him, and he nodded for us to take their plates. We cleared the places in front of them at the same time. Then I walked toward the door, already in the routine.

"I won't be having dessert," Mrs. Stone said to Marcus. "I hate to leave you to eat alone, Jax, but I'm exhausted. I'll be in my room if you need me."

Jax stood as his mother left the table. Once she had exited, he sat back down. "I would love dessert," he assured us . . . or he assured me.

Marcus nodded. "Yes, sir," he said in his businesslike tone, and we left.

Once back in the kitchen, Marcus set down his tray. "Okay, this is sticky. You're supposed to take him his plate, and since his mother has left, I have no reason to return. I could go in your place, which would be the best idea, but I am afraid it could anger him. He may think I don't trust him with you alone. He has obviously noticed you, which I knew would be pretty unavoidable. But I'd hoped since he is famous, he wouldn't pay attention to another pretty face." Marcus sighed, leaned his hip against the table, and crossed his long legs. "I'm leaving this up to you."

"Me?"

"What do you want to do, Sadie? It isn't about your job; it is about mine. If you don't go back, I could lose mine for taking your spot. I think he has already picked up on my protecting you. If you go or not, your job is secure . . . for now."

I sighed and reached for the tray holding the dessert. I wouldn't jeopardize someone else's job to help myself out. "I'll do it."

Without another word, I headed back down the hall all by myself.

Once I entered, his steel-blue eyes met mine, and he smiled. "Ah, so he did let you come alone. I wondered if I would be seeing him instead."

I didn't want to smile at his comment, but I did. I set his dessert down in front of him and took my place.

"Do you speak?" he asked.

"Yes." Marcus had spoken for me all night.

"We don't normally have young female employees. How did you get through Mary?"

"I'm mature for my age."

He only nodded and took a bite of some sort of chocolate cake with more chocolate oozing out of the inside. After he chewed and swallowed, he looked back at me. I turned to stare out the window at the waves crashing against the shore.

"How old are you?"

"Seventeen." I hoped my simple reply would end his interrogation.

"How did you know I lived here?"

His question caught me off guard, and I met his gaze. "It's hard to miss the photos of you as I dust and mop."

He frowned. "You applied for this job not knowing I lived here?"

I realized he assumed a fan had squeezed through the cracks of his security, and he wanted to know how I did it.

"My mother has been cleaning here for two months. However, her pregnancy has progressed and she sent me in her place. I proved my worth, and Ms. Mary kept me. My being here has nothing to do with you, sir, but has everything to do with the fact that I want to eat and pay the rent." I knew I sounded annoyed, but I was annoyed, and I couldn't help it.

He nodded and stood up. "I'm sorry. When I saw you, and you are young and, well . . . attractive, I thought the only reason someone like you would be working here would be to get close to me. I deal with girls quite a bit, and my assuming you were working here to get near me wasn't fair. Forgive me."

I swallowed the lump in my throat. I felt this job slipping out of my hands, but I would not cry. "I understand," I managed to get out.

A boyish smile tugged at his lips, and he nodded toward the door. "I guess I should have figured you were taken, from the possessiveness of the other server tonight. I stared at you more than I should've, but I kept waiting for you to ask for my autograph or slip your number to me on a napkin."

I raised my eyebrows in surprise.

He shrugged. "Those things are a way of life for me. I just expect it."

I smiled back at him this time. He wasn't as bad as I'd anticipated. He wasn't about to fire me. "I'm here to do my job, sir, and nothing more."

"Do me a favor and don't call me 'sir.' I am just two years older than you."

I took the plate, careful not to touch his hands, and stepped back.

"Okay," I replied, hoping I could leave.

"So, is he your boyfriend?"

He caught me off guard with his question, and I halted in my tracks. "Who? Marcus?"

A crooked grin appeared on his face. He was hard not to stare at. "If Marcus is the guy who seemed quite determined to make sure you made no mistakes tonight, then yes."

"No, he is . . . he is a friend." It was strange saying those words. I'd never called anyone a friend in my life.

Jax smiled and leaned down to whisper close to my ear. "I hope someday soon you will consider me a friend as well. I don't have very many of those."

My face grew hot, and my skin tingled at his nearness. His warm breath on my skin made it hard to form words. I swallowed hard, trying to focus on his comment and not swoon at his feet like some crazy lunatic. "I only have one," I blurted out like an idiot.

Jax frowned. "I find that hard to believe."

I shrugged. "I don't have time for friends."

Jax stepped forward, opened the door for me, and smiled.

"Well, I hope we can find some time in your busy schedule, because I happen to be in need of a friend myself. . . . Someone who doesn't care who I am. . . . Someone who doesn't laugh at my jokes when they're not funny. If I'm not mistaken, you couldn't care less about the fact that I'm on the cover of *Rolling Stone* magazine this month and on the bedroom walls of every teenage girl in America."

His comment seemed to ease my momentary lapse of common sense from his nearness, and I shook my head. "Not every teenage girl in America. You've never been on my walls. So I guess you're right—I don't care." I walked away, leaving him standing behind me.

# Chapter Three

**JAX**

I forgot to get her name. Damn. I'd been so fascinated with her and her responses I hadn't gotten her name. I knew the guy's name was Mark or Matt or Marcus. Hell, I couldn't remember. I was just glad she wasn't with him. Not that it mattered. It wasn't like I was going to make a move on her.

When I'd seen her earlier outside my room, I'd thought she was going to have to go. I'd hated the idea of it even then because she was gorgeous, but I'd been with enough gorgeous girls to know that they could also be crazy as hell. This one didn't want me. I was pretty sure she didn't even like me. That was a . . . strange, yet refreshing, change.

For the first time in years I wanted a girl to like me. My brother would tell me I was losing my mind when he got here.

The sexy slant to those blue eyes of hers and the body that the outfit she was wearing hadn't been able to conceal wouldn't get to Jason. When it came to girls, he didn't trust many. He was cautious with who he chose to date. It wasn't just a pretty face that got his attention. He needed reassurance they weren't after him just to get to me.

When I walked into my bedroom, I made my way over to the window overlooking the front yard. I didn't want to think I was looking to see if she was leaving . . . but I was. Admitting it or not, I was looking for the girl.

## SADIE

Marcus was standing in the kitchen, drinking sweet tea and talking to Ms. Mary. He stood when he saw me. "Well, how did it go?"

"He thought I was a fan who slid in through the cracks, and he wanted to know how I did it. I informed him that I had replaced my mother because of her pregnancy, I wasn't a fan, and I didn't realize this house belonged to him when I took the job."

Marcus frowned. "How did he take your explanation?"

"I don't think there will be any problem now that he knows I'm not a crazy fan about to slip him my number on a dinner napkin. I doubt he notices my existence from now on."

Marcus raised his eyebrows as if he didn't believe me.

Ms. Mary walked forward and took the tray from my hands.

"Good. I knew you were gonna work out just fine. Now go change out of your uniform and head on home. You won't be expected in until seven in the morning."

I hurried to the laundry room. Once I'd changed back into my own clothing, I headed for the door. Ms. Mary hummed while she cleaned, and Marcus stood leaning against the door, waiting.

"It's late. Did you drive or walk?" he asked when I got to the door.

"I rode my bike."

He opened the door, and we walked out into the night together. "Let me put it in the bed of my truck and take you home." He genuinely seemed worried about me.

"Okay, thank you."

Once we were both in the truck, I relaxed and leaned back on the worn leather seat. "So, how long have you worked at the Stone mansion?"

He looked over at me. "I just started last summer. I only work summers here. I'm a local, but I'm currently attending the University of Alabama. This is a summer job for me."

"It's obviously just a summer job for me, too. I will begin my senior year this fall. We just moved here from Tennessee."

We sat in silence for a few minutes, and I watched out the window as families walked down the sidewalks, still in their beach clothing. I'd never seen the beach before we moved here. I couldn't help but be fascinated, catching glimpses of the waves crashing on the sandy shore.

"You seem so much older than a senior in high school. In fact, you're more mature than most girls I go to school with."

I smiled to myself. *If he only knew.* But tonight wasn't the night to unload my life story on someone who just might turn out to be a real friend. "I know. I have always been an old woman in a kid's body. It drives my mother crazy."

"I wouldn't call you an old woman, just more mature than the average seventeen-year-old girl."

The normal teenage girls laughed and flirted on the side of the street. Summer romance wasn't something I understood, but apparently it was a very big thing around here. The girls here referred to the tourists as the summer boys. I didn't really get it or understand it, but then again, I wasn't normal.

Marcus turned to me. "Did I hurt your feelings? I didn't mean to if I did. It was a compliment, really. I get tired of the silliness and shallowness of girls. You're like a breath of fresh air."

I turned my head back in his direction and smiled. He really was a nice guy. I wished my insides got all warm and tingly when he stared at me, but apparently my body reserved that response for teen rock stars, and the thought that I might be shallow made me feel sick inside.

"Thank you. I've never been complimented on my strange personality before."

He frowned and shook his head. "I wouldn't call you strange . . . more refreshingly unique."

I laughed at his attempt to make it sound better. "Thanks. 'Refreshingly unique' sounds much more appealing. Turn right at the next light, and it's two houses down on the left."

We remained silent the rest of the way to the apartment.

"Pull over to the side. We're not allowed to use the owner's drive. They own the house. We rent the small apartment below."

Marcus pulled up in front of the house.

"Thank you again for bringing me home."

He opened his door, jumped out, and got my bike from the bed of his truck. I watched as he lifted it down. "Anytime. If you leave the same time I do, I can always give you a lift." I thanked him again. He shuffled his feet and glanced up at me. "Since you're new here, and we are working together this summer, why don't I take you out one night after work, or on Sunday during the day when we are both off? I can show you what's fun around here and introduce you to some people. You know, just as friends."

"It sounds like fun," I said. "I would love to go enjoy this area with someone who knows where to go."

He grinned and ran his hand through his blond hair. "Great. I'll make plans this week and let you know what we are doing."

We said our good-byes, and I watched him get back into his truck. I waved and turned to go face Jessica and her doubtless twenty questions as to what took me so long.

The apartment was silent and dark. I peeked into Jessica's room and found her asleep on top of the covers with the window unit cranking nonstop. I grabbed a quilt and covered her up before going back to my room and getting ready for my shower. She'd gone to sleep early. No twenty questions, and no having to cook dinner. I smiled and headed toward the bathroom. I needed to be clean and needed sleep. Today I managed to get past my biggest hurdle. Tomorrow should be easier. No more encounters with Jax. Having a friend would make things even more enjoyable.

The next week I fell into a routine. I arrived at work and went straight to the kitchen. Ms. Mary talked much more than Fran, and her stories were entertaining. She told me all about her two daughters and seven grandchildren. One daughter lived in Michigan and had five daughters of her own. The other daughter lived in Georgia, and she had a nine-year-old girl and one little boy, who was loved immensely by a family full of girls. Hearing about her life raising her daughters made me realize just how dysfunctional my life with Jessica would sound. I imagined my life being as full and normal as Ms. Mary's. I knew I could one day make a life just as full of family and love as she seemed to have. I often daydreamed of a life like the one she told me about.

My first afternoons with Mr. Greg began a little tense since he wasn't real fond of having a teenage girl helping him, but after a day of not having to get on his arthritic knees, he seemed to appreciate my being there. After my fourth day working with him, Mr. Greg and I would sit and play chess out in the gazebo when our workday ended. He beat me each time, but I was learning the game and promised him that my skills would improve and one day I would beat him.

I saw Marcus in the evenings when we all sat around the table and enjoyed a bowl of soup and salad. Ms. Mary always sent a plate of food home for Jessica, and I suspected she sent it for my sake. Somehow, without my telling her, she seemed to understand how my life at home functioned. After Marcus got off work, he always drove me and my bike home. William was back at work to help Marcus serve, and things seemed to run smoothly with the staff and family.

Sunday morning arrived before I knew it. I lay in bed, covering my face from the bright sunlight streaming in the windows. It was good not to have to jump up and get ready. I enjoyed my job, but I also enjoyed sleeping late. I yawned and stretched. Today I would be going out with a friend. I was more excited than the normal person would be, but I couldn't help it. I sat up and rubbed my face, trying to wake up enough to go eat breakfast. It was still really quiet in the house, but Jessica normally slept till eleven every day. I went to the kitchen and fixed myself a bowl of Peanut Butter Crunch, then went to sit on the piece of slab outside our back door. The sun glistened off the water, and it warmed me as I enjoyed my bowl of cereal. Today felt like my first real day of summer. Today I would be able to go do something a seventeen-year-old would do.

"What are you eating?" Jessica asked as she walked out the door—or more like waddled out the door.

"Peanut Butter Crunch cereal," I replied, and took another bite.

She sank down in the lawn chair beside me and sighed. "Do you love me?"

I rolled my eyes, knowing what words would be next. "Yes," I replied, and took another bite.

"Then will you have pity on me and my enormous stomach and go fix me a bowl when you're done?"

This was an old game. She thought it cute to ask if I loved her before she asked me to go get her something. I ate the rest of my cereal and drank all my milk before I stood up.

"Going to get your cereal," I said as I walked back in the door.

"Thanks, honey," she replied, not opening her eyes.

I fixed her a large bowl so I wouldn't have to fix her a second one, and took it to her. I needed to tell her about Marcus before he got here. I gave her the bowl, and she sat back up from her reclined position in a chair that did not recline and took the bowl from me.

"Thanks a bunch," she said, smiling.

I sat back down. "I have made a friend at work, and he is coming to get me today to show me around and hang out."

Jessica put the spoon full of cereal back down. "A boy! You?"

"He isn't a boy I am dating. He is just a friend. He is from around here and wants to hang out today."

She smiled and took a bite of cereal. She'd barely swallowed when she said, "I can't believe you talked to someone enough to make a friend. Or is he a recluse too?"

I stood up, not in the mood for my mom's teasing. She loved to remind me how I lacked social skills.

I started back inside, and she laughed. "I'm just teasing, Sadie. Don't get so upset. I'm glad you've got a friend. Just don't forget about me and stay gone all day. It gets lonely around here."

I hated it when she laid on a guilt trip. "You have a car. Go somewhere and do something."

She gave a melodramatic sigh. "I do need to go get a pedicure since I can't see my toes anymore.

I shook my head. "No, something where no money is required. Like go for a walk down the beach."

She rolled her eyes this time, and I went inside. I made a beeline for the stashed money I'd saved for bills and hid it somewhere else. I didn't need to come home and find she'd spent all our money. After the cash was secured, I went to get ready for my day with Marcus. I needed to wash my hair and coat myself with sunblock. The sun here could be brutal. But first I needed to find a swimsuit and something to wear. I checked the time. I had thirty minutes until he would arrive to pick me up. I needed to be ready so Jessica wouldn't answer the door and find some way to embarrass me.

"Good morning," Marcus said when I opened the door.

"Good morning to you, too! Hold on just a sec and I'll grab my purse." I turned, went back into the living room, and picked up the purse I'd left on the coffee table.

"I'm gone. Get out and go do something," I said to my mom before I walked back to the door.

"What, you're not bringing him in?" She was still dressed in her black nightgown, which stretched over her stomach.

"No, Mom, not with you dressed in your nightgown."

She laughed, and I rushed back to the door.

"You ready to see this place through a local's eyes?" he asked, grinning.

I nodded, excited. "Yes, I am."

He opened the truck door for me, and I climbed in. He ran around, jumped in, and slid on a pair of dark sunglasses. "Do you eat raw oysters?"

"No way!"

He grinned. "I should have guessed—you're a Tennessee girl. But it's all right, they are also grilling burgers, corn on the cob, and ribs."

"I love burgers, corn, and ribs."

"Ah, good. Well, we're going to a friend's house. They're grilling out today, with raw oysters on the half shell as the appetizers."

I grimaced at the thought of raw, squishy, slimy blobs on a shell people were actually going to put in their mouths.

He laughed at my face. "I guess when you grow up around here, it doesn't seem so bad."

I didn't respond, because I wasn't sure how anyone could get used to eating slime.

"Rock has been my best friend since elementary school. You'll like the bunch over at his house. We're going to grill out and then go waterskiing. Rock has a boat, and we're going to go launch it at the marina. Ever been waterskiing?"

"I'm afraid not, but I would love to try." It seemed to be the thing to say, because a huge grin broke across his face.

"I can teach you. You'll be skiing before the day's over."

We pulled up to a single-story house on stilts, like most of the houses around here. It wasn't fancy, and it appeared to have survived a few hurricanes. The siding had been patched up quite a few times.

Marcus met me as I got out of the truck and slid a pair of sunglasses on my face. "You're gonna need these. Without them, the sun will give you a headache."

"Do you carry around women's sunglasses on a regular basis?" I asked teasingly.

He laughed. "No, I have a sister."

I didn't know anything about his family. I liked knowing something about him other than the obvious.

"Please tell me you put on sunblock. Even the best tanners get burned in this sun."

"Yes, I'm slathered up."

"Come this way," he said, pulling me behind him through some really tall grass, which grew in the sand. A simple rectangular in-ground pool stood in the center of the yard, surrounded by guys in swim trunks and girls in bikinis. They were slinging back slime from a shell, and I reminded myself not to grimace when they talked to me and ate those things. Marcus squeezed my hand and pulled me into the party.

"Marcus, it's about time you got here. All the shells are almost empty," called a guy with long brown dreadlocks.

Marcus smiled down at me and whispered, "I won't eat any in front of you, I promise."

I shook my head. "No, really, it's fine."

He laughed and pulled me over to the group of guys standing with the dreadlock guy. Several people called out to Marcus, and

ABBI GLINES

he waved and nodded. My stomach churned with nervousness when I realized the majority of the people here were staring at me.

"Hey, guys, this is Sadie. Sadie, this is Rock," he said, indicating a rather large muscular guy with a shaved head, "Preston," who was what I considered a beach bum, with long blond hair and dark tanned skin, "and Dewayne," the dreadlock guy, who also happened to have several tattoos and piercings. "We've all been friends since second grade."

Dwayne flicked the dreadlocks out of his eyes and grinned. "Ever since Rock beat the shit out of Preston and ol' Marcus here jumped in to take up for him, and then started getting pummeled by Rock until I jumped in, and about that time we all got suspended from school." The four of them laughed at the memory, and I tried to picture them all as little boys fighting.

"Our parents were all so proud. They had elementary school delinquents." Dewayne grinned and tipped back an oyster.

"Dewayne will reminisce all day if you let him. Don't act like you enjoy his stories. He won't stop," Marcus said, smiling.

The friendship among these four made me feel warm inside. It wasn't something I could relate to.

"So, Sadie, how did ugly-butt Marcus here find a beautiful blind girl?" Rock asked as he flipped a burger.

I glanced at Marcus to see him smiling at me. "We work together," I said. "He came to my rescue on my second day there, and my eyesight is twenty/twenty."

One of them let out a low whistle, and another laughed wickedly.

"Marcus is a regular ol' knight in shining armor, I tell ya," Dewayne said with a flick of his dreadlocks. Marcus shoved him playfully, and Dewayne burst into laughter.

"I'm going to take her to meet other people if you three can't behave."

"What did I do?"

Marcus sent him a mock glare before turning to me. "Are you thirsty?"

Dewayne reached into a cooler behind him and held out a soda. I took it, thanked him, and listened to the four of them talk about a beach volleyball game going on next weekend between them and a rival team. They would ask me questions or bring me into the conversation occasionally, but mostly they just planned and strategized. I had no idea beach volleyball was such a serious sport.

A platinum blonde in a hot-pink bikini that barely covered the important stuff, walked up behind Rock, wrapped her arms around his waist, and kissed his neck.

"Sadie, this is Trisha, Rock's fiancée, and Trisha, this is Sadie, a friend of mine."

Trisha smiled at me and ran her hand over Rock's head. "If you get bored with this bunch's conversation, you are welcome to come lay out with me and the girls."

"Okay. Thanks."

"Are you bored? Want to go in for a swim and cool off?" Marcus asked.

I wasn't really sure I wanted to take off my sundress in front of all these people. My hand-me-down red bikini wasn't nearly as skimpy as the ones the other girls were wearing, and I didn't fill one out like they did either. I thought of my long skinny legs and compared myself to the curvy, large-chested girls lying out, and I wanted to keep my clothes on. However, I also wanted to make friends and not let Marcus down, so I needed to lay out or swim. Since swimming kept me covered most of the time, I decided it would be the best option. "Swimming sounds good."

He grinned and pulled his T-shirt off to reveal a very tanned and muscular chest. I swallowed hard and wished I didn't have to do this, but I knew I would have to sooner or later. So I slipped the sundress off and laid it beside Marcus's shirt. I didn't want to make eye contact with anyone and wished I could just go jump into the water without having to actually walk calmly over to it and get in.

A low whistle from behind startled me, and I heard an "Ouch." I turned to see Marcus glaring at Dewayne and Preston.

"Sorry, Sadie, these two have no manners." He took my hand again. As before, he held my hand casually. It hadn't bothered me before, but being half naked made it uncomfortable.

"Come on. Let's go swim." He grinned at me and didn't even pay attention to my body.

It relieved and embarrassed me at the same time. I didn't want Marcus to like me as anything more than a friend, but I also didn't want to be so boyish in my bathing suit that he didn't notice me at all. I decided to stop thinking about everything so much, and I followed him into the water via the stairs. We joined in on a game of basketball with a floating hoop in the middle of the pool. I stank at it, but no one other than Marcus and a guy name Rick seemed to be any good, so I didn't worry too much.

After I raced Marcus the length of the pool and won one out of three times, we got out to get something to eat. I walked over to my sundress at the same time Marcus came up behind me and wrapped a towel around me.

"Thank you," I told him.

He smiled. Our friendship was working out nicely, and it made me smile a little brighter. Maybe my personality wasn't as bad as Jessica said.

Marcus leaned down and whispered into my ear, "Burger, ribs, or both?"

I thought of the mess ribs make and all the people in the small backyard. "Burger," I whispered back.

He nodded and made his way to the grill. He got me a burger and took a slab of ribs for himself.

We walked over to a table set up with stuff to put on the burger, and I added a little ketchup and cheese. Marcus grabbed us both a drink, and we headed over to an unoccupied shaded area. We sat down and ate in silence for a few minutes. I watched him go through at least fifteen napkins and laughed when he reached for more and all the clean ones were gone.

"You think my mess is funny, huh?"

I shrugged and let out another laugh I couldn't hold back. I reached under my plate and handed him my napkin.

"Thanks." He took the napkin and cleaned himself up. "Are you having fun?" he asked after he cleaned the barbecue off his face.

"Yes, I am. I feel like the youngest one here, but I am having fun."

Marcus nodded. "You are the youngest one here. I forget my old crowd has all aged just like me."

"No, I have really enjoyed myself."

Preston, whose attention seemed to be focused our way, shook his head.

"I'm afraid my friend over there likes you. You're going to have to just ignore him. He's a bit of a ladies' man."

I frowned. "He likes me! With all these older, more attractive women around?"

Marcus cut his eyes back at me and studied my face a minute, and he smiled. "You really believe that, don't you?"

"Believe what?"

"You believe the other girls here are better looking than you."

I laughed and shrugged. "I'm not blind, Marcus."

Marcus raised his eyebrows. "Either you are blind, or you don't have a mirror at home. Keep doing stuff as sweet as blushing, and you're going to have Preston singing love ballads outside your window."

I laughed and shook my head. "I seriously hope not."

Marcus looked at Preston. "He really likes legs, and you happen to be attached to the best pair I've seen in a really long time. But I think you hooked him when you batted your baby-blue eyes at him and smiled."

I frowned. "I don't recall batting my eyes at anyone, and my legs are just long and skinny."

Marcus smiled. "I hope you always stay this way. Sweet and innocent. But I want to be the one to enlighten you. Your legs are sexy as hell, and your eyelashes are so thick and long that when you blink it looks like you're batting them, and it is very attractive."

I wasn't sure I believed him, but I smiled anyway. "You're a nice guy. Thanks for trying to make me feel better."

"Is that what I'm doing?" he asked with a teasing grin.

I smiled. "I think so."

He laughed and shook his head. "Sure, whatever you say, Sadie."

# Chapter Four

**JAX**

I'd been watching her for days now. It was getting to be a habit. She intrigued me, and I wasn't able to ignore her even if it would be in both our best interests. It wasn't like I was going to be able to pursue her. But she sure made that hard to remember.

No one had noticed me bring my notebook and hide out in the gazebo earlier. That was part of the reason I loved this place. Even the staff left me alone. Hearing the blonde talk to Mr. Greg and not appear as if she was helping him out but rather following his instructions just to save his pride was even more eye-opening. When was the last time I'd met a girl who looked like her who was so damn thoughtful of an old man? I'd even heard Mr. Greg call her Sadie. Knowing her name made me smile. I'd wanted to ask Ms. Mary her name all week, but I hadn't. I was trying to keep my distance.

I heard footsteps and tore my gaze off her and toward the guy who served my meals at night. He was watching her too. He was always watching her. It was starting to piss me off. I wasn't sure why, but it was. It wasn't like I was jealous of him. That would be ridiculous.

## SADIE

Marcus came to find me in the garden. "Hey, Sadie, the Stone family is dining at a friend's house tonight, so I'm heading out early. How much longer until you get off?"

I glanced over at Mr. Greg, who seemed to be really suffering from his arthritis today, and I knew I couldn't leave early. It wouldn't hurt me to ride my bike home this evening. "You go on ahead. I have some work left here. Besides, I want to stop off at the grocery store and pick up a few things on my way home."

Marcus frowned at me as if he were trying to decide something. Finally he said, "I really don't like the idea of you riding home after dark, and then trying to ride a bike with bags of groceries."

I started to argue with him and assure him that everything would be just fine, but his gaze left mine and landed on something behind me.

I turned and saw Jax Stone coming toward us from inside the gazebo. I hadn't even seen him go inside it.

"I agree with you on her riding home in the dark with groceries. I'll supply her with a ride home. You may leave now. She'll be safe."

Marcus stared at me with concern. I smiled at him as if to reassure him that I liked this arrangement.

"Uh, um, yeah, sure, Mr. Stone, thanks. I'll see you tomorrow, Sadie," he said, a wrinkle between his eyebrows. I could tell he was unsure about this.

"See you tomorrow," I replied, and watched him reluctantly turn and walk away. Not because I wanted to stare at him longer, but because I needed to compose myself before I faced Jax. Somehow I'd become as pathetic as the rest of the teenage world. I'd caught glimpses of Jax outside, and every time he glanced my way, he smiled at me. My traitorous heart did a little flip. Before I knew it, I would have a stupid poster of Jax on my wall.

"Thank you," I managed to say without tripping over my tongue.

He gave me one of those grins meant to melt girls' hearts everywhere. "If I'd known you were riding a bike to get to and from work, I would have done something about it sooner. I'm glad I have such thoughtful employees. But then again, he is your friend, isn't he?"

I smiled at him. "Marcus is a nice guy."

Jax leaned in and said quietly, "And what about me? Am I a nice guy?"

I wasn't sure what to say to this, so I decided to just be honest. "I don't know you, really, but I do know you sign my paycheck, so I'm not exactly sure how to answer this."

Jax threw back his head and laughed. I caught myself smiling. He seemed almost touchable when he laughed. He offered his arm for me to hook my hand through.

"Well then, Sadie White, why don't you do me the honor of a stroll down by the beach so we can talk? Then maybe you can decide for yourself if I'm a nice guy or not."

The fact he knew my name surprised me. He'd asked someone because he had never asked me the night we spoke in the dining room. I didn't want the fact he had taken time to find out my name to affect me, but it did. Much more than it should. I glanced over at Mr. Greg. "I don't know if I can. You see, Mr. Greg has arthritis, and he needs me for the weeding, whether he wants to admit it or not. Getting down on his knees is not easy for him, and very painful."

"Really?" he asked with concern on his face, and he turned and went over to where Mr. Greg stood pretending to work, though I knew he'd been watching Jax and me.

I couldn't hear what Jax said, but Mr. Greg seemed to like what he heard, and nodded, shook Jax's hand, and appeared to be putting away his things.

Jax walked back over to where I stood. "Mr. Greg has decided to take the afternoon off and rest up his bad knees. He also wanted me to tell you he could wait until tomorrow for your chess game."

I grinned at the older man, whom I'd come to care about. He winked, and I shook my head at him. Jax once again offered his arm, and I hesitated before I slipped my hand inside his bent elbow.

"Okay." I wasn't sure what to say, and I wondered if he could hear my heart racing in my chest.

"Let's see, you not only worry over old men's knees, but you also play chess with them in the evenings."

I stiffened and stopped walking. Being teased about my relationship with Mr. Greg bothered me.

"Easy there, tiger." He patted my hand. "I wasn't making fun of you. I'm actually impressed. I haven't met a girl with compassion before, and I'm intrigued."

I relaxed. "I would imagine in your world, girls are much different from here in the real world. I'm sure if you spent some time with the everyday girl, you would find I am not unique."

He grinned at me. "The everyday girls are who write me fan mail and buy out my concerts. They are the girls who yell my name and run after me like crazed animals. You've not even tried to sneak into my room and squirt your perfume on my pillow."

I hesitated, my jaw dropping in shock. "Please tell me those last two haven't happened before and you made them up."

Jax shrugged and shook his head. "I'm afraid they have. They're only a few examples. I left out the ones not suitable for a young girl's ears. You don't even want to know the extent girls go to in order to get my attention. It's one of the reasons I need this summer getaway. If I didn't have this, I would have gotten out of the business a long time ago."

We reached the shoreline and stopped.

He waved a hand over the white sand at our feet. "Want to sit down?"

I sank down cross-legged. He sat down in such a smooth way it made me feel clumsy. Why did I care? I've never thought about the way I sat down before. I didn't need to start thinking of him as more than just a guy. A guy who signed my paycheck.

"So, tell me about yourself." He leaned back on his hands and stretched his long legs out in front of him.

I shrugged, not sure what to say. "What do you want to know? I'm not very interesting."

He chuckled. "I disagree, but we won't argue. Tell me about your family."

Blood rushed to my cheeks at his request, but I forced myself to talk instead of blushing like an idiot. "Well, I live with my mom, and it has always been just me and her. However, she is pregnant right now, so our two will soon be three. We just moved here two months ago from Tennessee. I love the ocean much more than the mountains, so the move has been a good one."

Jax watched me as I spoke, and I focused on staring at my hands.

"I don't want to be getting into your personal space, so tell me if I ask something you feel is none of my business. Where's the baby's dad?"

I laughed at his question because, yes, it was personal, and the answer was sordid, but something about him made me relax and tell him things I didn't normally talk about. "My mother is beautiful, but unfortunately she has no common sense. She likes the attention she gets from men and picks the worst ones." I gave a small smile I knew wouldn't reach my eyes. "When I say the worst ones, I mean *the worst*! They are married or engaged, or so worthless they would never consider settling down. The man who donated to my conception was married, and I even know who he is and where he lives, but I never intend to go introduce myself. This baby's father is also a loser. He isn't married, but he doesn't have any intention of helping out or contributing to the raising of this child."

I was airing too much dirty laundry, so I stopped talking and stared out over the ocean waves. He sat up, and his arm brushed against mine. Warmth rushed through my body.

"So, you're the grown-up at home, aren't you?"

I tensed at his correct description. I nodded since I could feel his breath close to my neck.

"No wonder you're so different. You've got too much on your shoulders to even consider hanging posters of some shallow teenage rock star on your walls."

I smiled at his humor. "You're not shallow. Granted, I thought you would be in the beginning, but you surprised me."

Long fingers slid across my thigh and took my hand. "Is this job what pays the bills, then? When you mentioned it paid for your food the first night we met, I thought maybe you were joking or being melodramatic, but now . . ." He stopped.

I picked up where he left off. "She's too far into her pregnancy, and it's too difficult for her to work. She doesn't hold down jobs well. During the school year, she struggles from job to job. She worked here until my first day out of school."

He didn't say anything, and neither did I. We just sat there holding hands and watching the sun set over the water. Just before it sank, Jax stood up.

He held out his hand for me to take. "We'd better head back before the sun sets completely."

His fingers never left mine as we walked back to the house. The only way to explain it is to say it was very close to an out-of-body experience. Holding hands with Jax Stone and feeling like we connected. He didn't seem like a rock star anymore. He wasn't the guy I saw on posters and in magazines. He wasn't the hottie I'd seen on MTV. He was just Jax. I thought about the times Marcus had held my hand, and how casual it had seemed. But the warmth from Jax's hand sent a tingling sensation up my arms. He was a rock star and I was his maid, for crying out loud. I cleaned his vegetables!

We stopped outside the servants' entrance.

"Thanks for the walk today." He smiled down at me again, and my insides went to mush.

I was in trouble. I liked this guy, and that was bad.

"You're welcome." I know it sounded stupid, but I really didn't know what else to say.

"When do you need a ride home?"

I shook my head. I'd almost forgotten about his promise to supply me with a ride home. "I will be fine, honestly. I have been to the store a million times on my bike. Marcus just doesn't realize it is very manageable."

"Out of the question. I'll have a car waiting for you at the front entrance. Whenever you're ready to leave, it's there. The driver will take you wherever you need to go." I started to argue, and he placed one of his very talented fingers over my lips. "Don't argue. I don't like the idea any more than Marcus. He's right. It isn't safe."

I knew it would be fine, but I didn't want to stand out here arguing over his doing exactly what he'd promised Marcus he would do. "Okay. I'll go see if Ms. Mary needs any help before I leave."

Jax smiled, apparently pleased that I wasn't going to argue. "Thanks for the walk," he said again, and turned to leave.

I wanted to watch him walk away, but I knew it wouldn't do me any good. No matter how insane the idea of a friendship with Jax Stone seemed, I really believed we were in the beginning of one.

I helped Ms. Mary finish up the dishes, then went back to the laundry room to change. I wanted to get home, lie in bed, and think about my time down by the water with Jax. I wanted to memorize each word and glance. I wanted to slap myself because my reaction bordered on ridiculous. I needed to be hoping he would keep his distance and not pursue a friendship with me, because I feared I just might become one of those crazed girls with a crush.

I said good-bye to Ms. Mary and exited through the servants' door. I walked around to the front of the house and stopped short at the very expensive silver Hummer limo waiting on me. I should have expected extravagance since I doubted Jax owned anything normal. I walked toward the car. A man dressed in black stood beside the machine. He stepped forward with a serious expression on his face and opened the door. I remembered him as one of the large men who'd been here the first day I arrived. "Marcus took your bike when he left. It should be at your home when you arrive."

I hadn't realized Marcus was taking my bike for me. I had actually forgotten all about needing to get my bike home. Jax had me completely flustered. "Thanks," I said, and stepped inside. I hadn't been expecting anyone else.

"My intention was to let you go home alone, but I didn't like that idea. I hope you don't mind the company." Jax sat in the seat directly across from me, drinking an expensive bottle of water and watching a baseball game. He held a remote in his hands and clicked off the baseball game showing on the television above my head.

I sat down on the black leather seat and smiled. My heart thumped in my chest, and I wanted to appear unaffected by his appearance. "Um, no, I don't mind."

He grinned and handed me a fancy water. "Thirsty?"

I took the water in the hope it would ease my suddenly dry throat. "Yes, thank you."

"You're welcome. Which grocery store do you want to go to?"

I smiled at the thought of Jax Stone asking where I wanted to go buy food. "Sea Breeze Foods will be fine. It's closer to my apartment."

He picked up his remote again, and with a click of a button the tinted glass between us and the driver came down. "Sea Breeze Foods, please, Kane." The giant in the front seat nodded, and Jax slid the glass back up.

"Do you mind if I go inside with you? I'm craving a Reese's Cup."

I frowned, remembering his wish to remain hidden. "No, I

don't mind, but won't it blow your cover if you're seen walking around Sea Breeze Foods?"

He smirked. "Yeah, it would, but I'm prepared."

He reached over the seat and opened a compartment. It took all my will power not to lean over and sniff him, he smelled so good. I'd noticed it earlier, but not as much as I did now in such close quarters. He sat back in his seat, and I composed my expression into a curious smile. He slipped a black baseball hat on with the letter *A* on the front, which I recognized immediately as the University of Alabama's logo.

"Nice touch," I said, grinning at his attempt to go incognito.

He then slipped on tinted glasses.

"Isn't it a little dark for those?"

He grinned. "Actually, these brighten up the nighttime. They're glasses used for seeing, not to shade the sun. I shouldn't stick out too much."

His designer jeans and the black T-shirt clung to his muscular chest and arms, and I frowned. "No, you're going to attract attention in that shirt."

He glanced down at himself. "You think so?"

I tried not to stammer from the shock my system took from his grin. "I know so. Any girl in a ten-mile radius is going to stare you down if you wear it. It's impossible not to."

A huge grin broke across his face. "So does this mean you like me in this shirt?"

I sighed and sat up a little straighter. "I'm mature for my age, Jax, not blind."

He laughed and reached back into the compartment over the seat. "As much as I like the idea of you being unable to take your eyes off me, I don't want to draw attention, so how's this?" He slipped into an old faded blue jean jacket. It covered up his impressive body.

"Better," I assured him as the Hummer came to a stop.

Jax slid the glass wall back down. "Kane, go park in the parking lot, and don't open our doors. I want to appear normal, so just hang out at the car."

Kane frowned and nodded.

"Let's go shop." Jax jumped out and took my hand, and I stepped out behind him. We walked in silence to the grocery store entrance. Suddenly my nerves assaulted me. What if people recognized him and bombarded him? I didn't want his attempt at being nice to be ruined by crazy teenage fans. We entered the store, and I looked back to see Kane following behind us. He stopped and stood outside the large glass window. Apparently, he would be standing guard in case of a mad rush of fans. I should have figured the large giant doubled as a bodyguard.

"Where to first?" Jax asked, grinning as he pulled out a shopping cart when we walked in.

"You seem really excited about shopping for food," I whispered, not wanting anyone around us to hear me.

"I haven't been in a grocery store since I was a kid hanging on my mom's cart, begging for Big League Chew."

I pitied the little boy inside who missed things as simple as grocery stores. "Well then, let's make this memorable. If you're good, I'll buy you some Big League Chew."

"They still make it?"

I shrugged. "Sure, this is the South, Jax. Things don't change here often. Time kind of stands still."

He nodded in agreement. "I know, it's part of the reason I love it here. No one is in a hurry."

I walked ahead of him, and he followed behind me with the cart. I was a little embarrassed when I realized he would witness my bargain shopping. I hadn't thought of the fact that he would see me worrying over the cost of bread. I couldn't get out of this now. I might as well swallow my pride and get what I needed. I reached for the store-brand loaf of bread. I didn't want to face him, but I knew he was watching me. I walked over to the cold meats and grabbed the deli shredded roast beef Jessica adored. I hated wasting money on such expensive meat, but if I didn't, I would be forced to hear Jessica whine for a week.

A loud whisper came from behind us. "No, Mama, I know it's *him*!" I turned to see a little girl about the age of nine studying Jax.

He smiled at her, and her face lit up. She left her mother's side, and her mother reached out to grab her arm but missed. "I'm sorry; she's convinced you're Jax Stone."

Jax only smiled and shrugged, and then he squatted down to her level. "Hello," he said in a voice I swear could melt butter.

"You're Jax Stone, aren't you?"

He glanced up at the mom and back down at the girl and put his finger over his mouth. "Yes, I am, but can you keep it our secret?"

Her little face lit up, and she grinned from ear to ear. The mother appeared stunned. Jax reached into his jeans pocket and pulled out a card. "Here, this has my contact number and e-mail address on it. Do you have a pen on you, Sadie?"

I was as mesmerized as the little girl. It took me a second to register what he asked. I grabbed my backpack, pulled out a pen, and handed it to him. He signed the card and asked her name.

"Megan Jones," she replied.

He pulled out another card and wrote her name on it. "Now, Megan, get your mom to call my agent. He'll be expecting a call from a Megan Jones. I'm going to be stopping in Pensacola, Florida, on my tour this fall, and this will get you a backstage pass and front-row seats."

The little girl began to squeal, and Jax put his finger over his lips again. She nodded vigorously and covered her mouth.

"Just keep my secret about me being here, all right?"

She nodded, and he kissed her forehead before standing up. The mother's eyes glistened with tears. I realized tears were filling my eyes too.

The mother smiled through her tears. "Thank you . . . I don't . . . I mean, I can't . . ." She took a deep breath and smiled. "Thank you. She loves you. You're all over her bedroom walls." More tears started spilling down her face, and she wiped them away. "I'm sorry I am being so silly, but this year hasn't been easy on her. Her dad was killed overseas, and things have been tough." A small sob escaped her, and she shook her head, smiling. "Thank you so much."

The little girl ran over to her mother and handed her the card. She turned back to Jax and put her little finger over her mouth and grinned. He bowed and blew her a kiss. Her small little hand reached out, grabbed the invisible kiss, and placed it on her lips. My heart melted as I watched them walk away, the little girl gazing back and smiling at him until they were out of sight.

I wiped the tears off my face.

"Yeah, that one got to me too." He wiped a tear off my cheek and tucked a strand of hair behind my ear. "However, I didn't mean to make you cry. I just have a soft spot for my younger fans."

"No, I loved getting to see you with her. It was precious. You were so sweet to her, and I got to see the highlight of her life."

Jax grinned. "I doubt it's the highlight."

I raised my eyebrows and countered, "Well, you're wrong. When she is thirty years old, she will be telling about the night when she met Jax Stone in a grocery store."

Jax smirked wickedly. "If I give you backstage passes and blow you a kiss, will it be the highlight of your life?"

I managed to keep from getting hypnotized by his incredible eyes focused on me so intently. "No, only works on fans."

He frowned and placed his hand over his heart. "Ouch."

I laughed and turned toward the cereal aisle, leaving him to follow along behind me.

We managed to get the rest of the things I needed without another spotting. Jax kept his eyes down. To the casual observer he appeared to be really interested in the things in the grocery cart. However, I knew he didn't want to make eye contact with anyone. He grabbed a large package of Reese's Peanut Butter Cups, and I found his Big League Chew at the checkout lane and added it to my cart while he wasn't paying attention.

Once the groceries were bought, he loaded the bags into the cart and we went outside. Kane stood waiting on us and again walked slowly behind us. The Hummer beeped and the lights came on as we got near it. Jax started to load the groceries into the back of the Hummer, either not noticing or ignoring Kane hovering behind us.

"I'll do it," Kane said in a deep, rough voice.

Jax looked back at the giant and smiled. "I can handle it. You just drive."

Kane nodded, stepped back, and let Jax finish, but he didn't move until he went to open the door for us. Jax sighed and motioned for me to go in first. He slid in behind me, this time sitting beside me instead of across from me.

"He's determined not to let me impress you with my chivalry and is taking all the glory." He smiled.

I no longer saw him as shallow and self-centered. Not after the scene I'd witnessed in the grocery store. For as long as I lived I would never forget the little girl's face when Jax kissed her head.

"Are you going to share those deep thoughts with me?"

I shrugged. "I'm just remembering the little girl's face. What you did was really nice. I didn't picture you like that."

He frowned. "Like what?"

"Well, I guess I didn't think you would have acknowledged a little girl, and not only did you speak to her, you made a dream come true for her. I mean, you could have just blown her off and acted like you were not Jax Stone." I stopped talking and gazed up at him because his mouth had formed a crooked smile. "What?" I asked.

He lightly ran his finger from my ear to my chin. "I think you're the first girl I have ever met who is impressed by my kindness to kids."

My heart thudded in my chest from his touch. Drawing breath into my lungs became difficult. "Well, you really need to be pickier about who you spend time with," I managed to say without sounding breathless.

He threw back his head and laughed, and I couldn't help but smile. "You're right, Sadie. I do, and I think I've found someone who I want to spend time with who happens to cry for little girls she doesn't know who have lost their fathers in the war."

I didn't want to think about the sweet little girl being fatherless. If I teared up again, I would seem ridiculous. "You'll get tired of me quickly. I'm boring," I admitted out loud before I realized it.

He slipped a finger under my chin and tilted my face up. "Nothing about you is boring. Just watching you think is entertaining."

I frowned, and he kissed my head much like he did the little girl's and laughed softly.

"Don't frown, beautiful. You fascinate me."

My face grew hot, and my heart pounded so hard in my chest I feared it might burst its way out. It wasn't fair that he could affect me with so little effort.

The Hummer stopped, and I realized we were sitting outside my apartment. I frowned at him. "I never told you how to get here."

He grinned and got out to open my door. "You work for me, Sadie. I made it my business to get your address from your file and give it to Kane before we left."

"I hadn't thought about that," I muttered.

He exited the vehicle and held his hand out to me. I slipped my hand in his and stepped out.

"Can I take your bags inside for you?" he asked.

"No!" The thought of Jessica seeing him, or even worse, the thought of what she might be wearing, terrified me. "Um, I . . . It's just, my mom is not real big on people coming in these days."

He opened the back. "Well, at least let me carry them to the door."

"Okay." I walked with him to the doorway. My bike was propped against the tree closest to the apartment. I needed to thank Marcus for bringing it home for me. That was sweet of him to think about it. I turned back to Jax and took the bags from him, and then I reached in and took out the gum. I didn't know what to say, so I just handed it to him, and his face lit up. A smile I remembered from the photos of him as a little boy appeared on his face. It wasn't a smile the world ever got a glimpse of in magazines.

"I take it I was good."

I nodded. "Thanks again for the ride and the company."

He bowed teasingly. "Anytime." I looked at him one more time and went inside. I closed the door and leaned up against it. Jax Stone had just rocked my world, and I wasn't sure what to do about it.

# Chapter Five

**JAX**

I had to stay away from her. That had been much too close. I wasn't someone who could do relationships, and Sadie wasn't the kind of girl who could do a summer fling. Even if I wanted to get a taste of her so damn bad it was driving me crazy.

I stood at the window in my bedroom and looked down into the backyard. I could pretend I was staring out at the ocean, but I wasn't. I was watching her. I was always watching her. But this time I would keep my distance. I couldn't spend any more time with her. That would only lead to problems. Maybe I'd be leaving Sea Breeze a few times this summer after all. Even if it was just to take a break from being near something I wanted and couldn't have.

The door to my room opened, and in stepped Jason without

knocking. I glanced back at him, then stepped away from the window. He had called me several times over the past couple of weeks with a different excuse as to why he wasn't here yet. I knew the real reason was our parents, but I let it slide. When he'd called yesterday he had told me he was flying out this morning. It was good to see him again.

"You made it."

He nodded and let out a weary sigh. "Yeah. Almost waited a few more days, but I decided you needed to get out of this house and live a little, and if I wasn't here you'd stay hidden away. All alone."

He knew me well. I liked being alone. I didn't get that enough. "I spoke with Mom. Let me know if she starts bothering you."

Jason smirked and sank down onto the large leather chair that sat in the corner of my room. "You might be a rock star with the world bowing at your feet, but our mother doesn't care. She won't shut up for you."

He was right. But I could throw out enough threats to keep her quiet for short spans of time. "Never underestimate my power," I replied, grinning. I was glad he was here. Jason was the only friend I had. If it hadn't been for him keeping me levelheaded, I'd probably be one of those teen rock stars strung out on crack. Jason never let me forget who I was.

"Getting to your head, big brother. Tone it down, would

ya? Me and that big ego of yours can't fit in this room at the same time."

I laughed and glanced back out the window just in time to see Marcus approach Sadie. He made her laugh. It bugged me. Jerking my gaze back toward my brother, I pushed all thoughts of Sadie away. I needed something else to focus on. "Hey, you want to have a party?" I asked Jason.

"Always," he replied.

## SADIE

Three days had passed since my trip to the grocery store with Jax. I hated that I caught myself searching for glimpses of him. Somewhere, deep down, I really thought he would seek me out again. However, after three days of not laying eyes on him, I knew our night at the grocery store apparently meant much more to me than him. Yes, he'd taken me shopping and then home, but only because of his promise to Marcus. Sure, he'd held my hand for a few minutes, but who was I kidding? Jax Stone probably held hands with a different girl every day. I needed to find the humor in my stupidity for assuming it meant more to him, or I would curl up in a ball and cry. He had said I fascinated him, but he really should have clarified to me that I was just the fascination of the day. I hated to think badly of him for not seeking me out again, because I couldn't forget the way he'd treated the little girl, and I knew he wasn't a shallow teen idol. After all, to Jax Stone I was just another girl.

He hadn't promised his undying love to me, or even told me he would see me again. We'd said our good-byes at my house with no promises. Nothing he'd said told me he would seek me out again. Sure, he'd said he liked spending time with me, but it didn't appear as if he was going to make good on his words. Thinking about it made me crazy. I needed to focus on other things. I'd turned down Marcus's invitation to go boating with him and his friends on Sunday. I was skipping out on time with my friend because I chose to sulk over Jax. I needed to move on and let it go. My night with Jax would be a really good memory I'd never forget, just like it was for the little girl.

When I arrived at the Stone mansion, Ms. Mary met me at the door. "Sadie, we're entertaining tonight. Master Jax is having some friends over, and there is gonna be dancing and an open bar as well as lots of food! Now, I need all my younger employees to serve all night. We got some special uniforms for this. Marcus will be here shortly with William, and they are bringing a few friends who will also be helpin' out. Don't worry about changing just yet."

She turned and grabbed a large bucket of something very unappetizing. "Have you ever peeled and deveined shrimp before?" Words failed me, and apparently my face showed my horror because she laughed out loud. "Of course not. You're a Tennessee gal. Come here and I'll teach you how. We have ourselves twenty pounds of fresh shrimp we need to peel and devein for different appetizers."

I nodded and prayed I would have the stomach of steel I knew I would need for this horrible task. Ms. Mary directed me to a wash sink, pulled out an empty bucket, and placed it inside. She brought over a large stainless steel bowl and put it on the other side of the sink.

"Here." She handed me a shrimp, which I did not like to see or touch battered and fried, much less uncooked. "First you peel 'em, just like this, and then you take this here deveiner, you slip it into the top right here, and use it to pull out this black string. Throw all the garbage in here, and then put the clean shrimp in the bowl."

I gave her a small nod, then swallowed the bile in my throat. "What is that black string?" I asked.

She smiled at me. "Girl, from the color of your face, you do not want to know. Now, you just ought to be glad Mr. Greg got here early and beheaded these fellas for you, because if you're thinking this is gross, you would've a fit pinching the heads off."

I held up my hand in protest. "Please, no more, stop," I said, my stomach churning.

She patted me on the back. "When you're done with these, you'll be a true south Alabama girl."

I studied the gross creatures in front of me and decided

right then and there that if this was what it took to be a true south Alabama girl, I'd much rather stay a true Tennessee mountain chick. Four hours later, after some help from Marcus and even a little help from Mr. Greg, there were twenty pounds of clean shrimp. Now, I will never put one in my mouth, but I sure can peel and devein one "like nobody's business" . . . or at least, Mr. Greg said I could. Ms. Mary walked over and handed me a bowl of lemon juice and water.

"Here, girl, soak those hands in this. The smell will be gone in about ten minutes."

I stared in horror at my hands and realized that the smell I'd managed to get used to after hours of working with the nasty little things now clung to my hands. I sank them down into the cleansing concoction as quickly as I could. My face must have expressed my thoughts because Ms. Mary threw back her head and laughed one of her deep belly laughs that always made me smile.

"Girl, you sure keep this place interesting. I don't know what I did before you came here to make me smile."

Marcus walked into the kitchen and saw my hands in the lemon juice mixture, then sat down beside me and slipped his in it too.

"I just got a whiff of these fingers outside and realized I needed some help."

I slid my hands over and gave him plenty of room. "What

I don't understand is why people eat these things willingly. I would think their appearance is all it would take to turn them off. And if the nasty look of them isn't enough, they should sit and try to peel and devein the little things."

Marcus grinned and shrugged. "I happen to like them."

I rolled my eyes. "It is because all you beach people think they are the food of the gods, when they are really just nasty old ocean-floor feeders."

Marcus wiggled his eyebrows. "Maybe so, but they sure taste good."

I made a gagging noise, and he laughed.

"Okay, you two, I need you cleaned up and dressed within the hour." Ms. Mary stood with her hands on her hips. She said to Marcus, "When will William and the others get here?"

Marcus glanced over at the digital clock on the large industrial-size stainless steel refrigerator and then back at Ms. Mary. "In twenty-three-point-four minutes, ma'am."

She rolled her eyes and turned back toward the stove. "Once they get here, I expect you and William to give them their orders. Sadie, just do as Marcus directs you. He has done this thing before for Master Jax, and he knows the ropes."

Marcus slipped his hands out and dried them on the towel beside me. I considered taking mine out too but decided I'd touched more shrimp than the rest of them and needed more soaking, so I stayed put.

"It's not like when you're feeding the family," Marcus said. "You'll be expected to smile and mingle among the guests with food on a tray, and not bump into anyone or drop it."

His gaze darted to Ms. Mary, whose back was still turned, and then back at me. "One thing I want to warn you about is the fact that there will be guys here tonight. They are not going to find you invisible." He reached up and tugged at one of the curls falling down out of my ponytail. "This hair and those eyes are hard to miss, and although I have to give it to Jax—he's a nice guy and not like most guys in his position—some of the guys here tonight will not be so nice."

I nodded, not sure what he meant by this. "Okay," I said, hoping he would elaborate.

He leaned down toward my ear. "They will flirt with you heavily, and some may touch you in areas they have no business touching. Tell me if they do. I don't care who they are or how much money they have, it isn't all right for them to do those things."

"Okay," I said again. I feared my voice would betray my nervousness if I said more.

Marcus stood. "You won't be alone, so don't worry. Preston and Rock are coming. Which is another reason you should tell me if someone messes with you. If Preston were to see, I think he might get us all fired." With a wink, he left the room.

I sat there with my hands in the lemon juice and thought of

what flirting heavily might entail, and how I might get out of tonight's event.

"Girl, the smell left your hands an hour ago. Now you're just turnin' them into lemon-scented prunes."

I took them out of the lemon mixture and dried them off on the same hand towel Marcus used. I sniffed them to ensure their fresh scent and smiled at their lemon aroma. "Ah, much better."

Ms. Mary laughed and shook her head. I stood and took the bowl to the sink, poured it out, and placed it in the dishwasher. I didn't have a whole lot of time to get changed before the party started, so I forced myself to get focused and not dwell on what might happen. Besides, I'm pretty tough. Heck, I'd just peeled and deveined twenty pounds of shrimp. I could do this. I couldn't expect Marcus to sacrifice his job to stand up for my honor. It wouldn't be the first time a guy made unwanted advances at me. Preston might be a concern, but I wasn't convinced Marcus was right about Preston's interest in me. How long could this last, anyway? I could handle anything for a few hours . . . right?

The outfit the girl servers had to wear reminded me of a French maid's costume with a little more fabric. Marcus seemed so worried about making me comfortable about tonight that I couldn't let anyone know how nervous I really was. First off, I knew I would see Jax tonight. The fact that he'd made no effort to see or speak to me after our trip to the grocery store stung, but honestly, I shouldn't have expected more. He was famous, rich, and beautiful, and I worked in his kitchen. It irritated me when I thought of all the things I'd told him. Something about his eyes made me want to spill my soul. I was too mature to stoop to mooning over a teenage rock star. I pulled my hair up into a loose bun on top of my head, which I always thought made me appear older. Right then I needed all the confidence I could muster. If I dwelled on my actual age, I tended to freak out in stressful moments. I would be serving the oysters, nasty little things, and the shrimp cocktail, which I seemed to have formed a weird bond with, so I didn't mind those as much. Marcus stood in the kitchen talking to Preston and Rock. Trisha and a girl I remembered from the pool were standing over to the side, giggling.

"Hey, guys," I said, forcing a smile. Despite the butterflies in my stomach, I acted casual.

"Sadie, you can work with me," Preston offered with a wink, and Marcus elbowed him.

"Stop it, or I'll send you home without the money."

Preston sighed and shrugged. "Can't a guy be nice?"

Marcus rolled his eyes. "Now, everyone, remember what I said. Girls ignore and discourage any advances." We all nodded.

Ms. Mary cut in. "It's showtime! I want you all lined up so I can inspect you." Seeing Ms. Mary get all serious caused me to smile. In the beginning she had seemed intimidating, but now

I knew better. Ms. Mary was just the sweet-hearted lady who kept things under control.

"Your trays will always be on the receiving table, lined up and in the same place. You will go to your assigned pickup and get whatever tray I have set out for you. There is no time for breaks, and if you must go to the bathroom, I have to approve it. I hope none of you smoke, 'cause I won't tolerate you taking a break for a puff." She wiped her hands on her apron and nodded. "Let's get moving."

Everyone stepped forward and took their tray. Marcus led us down the hall and into the dining room. "We will enter through here. When I send you out, I am going to instruct you which way to go first. Do as I've instructed and this will be the most interesting cash you've ever made." He grinned at us, and the other girl giggled.

I wanted to roll my eyes at her giddy expression over the fact that she was about to meet Jax, who was at least two years younger than her. I wanted to tell her to grow up, but I remembered the butterflies in my stomach, and as much as I hated to admit it, I knew they were there because of Jax. I really couldn't cast stones.

My turn arrived, and I stepped up to the door.

Marcus smiled at me and winked. "I'm here. You will be great. Now, head left and work your way around the room in a big circle."

I took a deep breath, stepped out of the dining room, and made my way directly into the ballroom. A familiar band warmed up on a stage, obviously brought in for the occasion. The guests all reminded me of walking Abercrombie ads. They mingled together, dancing and talking. I tuned out the overload of sight and sound, focused on the oysters on the half shell on my platter, and began my circle. Things were going smoothly. I smiled as I walked up to each group of gorgeous people, some of whom I recognized from television or magazines.

They took the oysters as if I were serving something that actually tasted good, and they slung those nasty things down their throats before placing the shell back on the tray. It ranked high on my chart of one of the grossest things I'd ever seen. I kept my smile in place and watched Marcus and the others out of the corner of my eye. I wanted to make sure I didn't forget anything. I found Marcus, whom a guest was flirting with openly, and bit back a smile. Warm breath tickled my ear. I froze but didn't turn to find the source.

"It appears my guest likes your friend," Jax whispered in my ear.

I turned my head toward him. "He's an interesting person."

Jax studied me as if he were trying to gauge my attitude. I offered him the tray and he grinned. "Your feelings won't be hurt if I choose not to take what you're offering, will they? I just can't bring myself to try one of those things."

I stifled a laugh and shook my head. "I don't blame you," I whispered.

Jax raised his eyebrows. "We have something in common."

I gave him my best carefree smile. "Apparently."

I knew standing there and chatting with Jax would start talk, and I didn't want attention, so I nodded as I left him. Without a backward glance, I walked up to the next group. It took all my concentration to forget the warmth still clinging to my ear and focus on my job.

"I'll only eat one if you let me feed you one first." A tall "all-American blond" winked at me, and I woke up from my Jax daze. I gave him a forced smile and shook my head.

"Sorry," I managed to get out without my voice betraying my nerves.

"You won't let me feed you oysters, huh? Well, what about a little stroll down to the beach?"

I started to say no, when the guy next to him stepped beside me, and I recognized him instantly as Jason Stone. "Trey, leave the help alone. Jax will send you packing."

Trey frowned and turned his attention back to me. "I would think if she is all right with a walk, then after she gets off tonight Jax would have no say in the matter. Besides, what did he expect when he let a gorgeous blond southern belle serve food? He is flaunting her in front of people. He should expect this."

Jason glanced over to where Jax stood, but I didn't dare do

the same. I noticed Jason seemed a little nervous. "Listen, Jax doesn't hire people. We have someone else to handle the hiring of employees. He didn't purposely put her here as if on the menu, so leave her alone."

Jason nudged me, and I took it as my cue to leave. I took a step toward the next group, my hands shaking and my heart racing.

"Wait, I never got my oysters." Strong fingers clamped around my arm, and I fought the urge to jerk free and run. I let him pull me back since my other option would involve dropping oysters all over the floor. I quickly searched the crowd for Marcus, worried he would come flying to the rescue and lose his job. I needed to remain calm to keep him from knowing about my predicament. Keeping the pained expression off my face from his tight grip was starting to prove difficult. Suddenly another set of warm fingers gently but firmly took my other arm.

"Let her arm go and pray she hasn't got a bruise," a familiar voice said in a low, angry tone.

I shuddered from relief at the sound of Jax's voice.

Trey released my arm and shrugged, grinning. "I just wanted an oyster, and she wouldn't serve me."

I opened my mouth to protest, when the warm fingers holding my arm softly squeezed me in reassurance. So I stayed quiet.

"Jason, please escort your friend to the door. I have no other reason to speak with him—unless Sadie has a bruise, or any lasting mark from his hand, and then he will see me again."

Jax took the tray from me and handed it to Marcus. I hadn't realized he was standing there. Marcus took it with a concerned frown on his face. I gave him a small smile, hoping to ease his worry.

"Come with me," Jax said in a voice only loud enough for me to hear.

I let him lead me down the hall and into the library. He closed the door, then turned me around to face him.

"Are you all right?" he asked in a concerned voice. Chill bumps covered my arms.

I nodded. "I'm fine, really. Marcus warned me something like this might happen. I was mentally prepared."

Jax muttered what seemed to be a curse and pulled me over to a large leather chair. "You shouldn't have been serving tonight. I don't know what Mary was thinking."

His words stung. I immediately felt the need to defend Ms. Mary as well as myself. "I am a very hard worker, and I believe she entrusted me to serve and follow instructions well. I don't see how it's her fault some jerk thought I was on the menu."

Jax gazed down at me, confused, and then grinned. He stepped over and sat down beside me. "I didn't mean I thought you're not capable of serving. I meant you're too young and too beautiful to be flaunted in front of guys who think they have enough money and power to take what they want."

My throat went dry at his words.

He smiled, leaned over, and asked in a soft voice, "Do you know you're beautiful?"

I swallowed, hoping my dry throat would allow the words through without making me sound all choked up. "I wouldn't say 'beautiful.' I realize I have nice hair and eyes. I got those from my mother. But I don't have a good personality. So it really takes away from the others." My words sounded stupid said aloud, but I realized I had managed to bare my soul to this boy yet again. The power Jax held over me disturbed me.

Jax smiled. He took one of my loose curls and played with it absently. "So your personality is bad, is it?" He laughed then, and I stiffened. He traced my cheekbones and the bridge of my nose. "I hate to be the first to break the news to you, but your personality happens to be your most charming quality."

I searched for any sign in his perfect face telling me he didn't mean what he said. "I can't believe you said that," I finally heard myself say.

He touched his finger to my lips. "I think these rank right up there with your personality."

A warm, tingly sensation worked its way through my veins, and I shivered.

"Ah, and you go and do something as enchanting as shivering and almost break my resolve."

He dropped his hands from my face and stopped doing

those incredibly wonderful things to me. He stood, walked over to a bookshelf, and leaned up against it as if he were posing for a camera. "I can be good over here. This is safer territory." I frowned, and he gave me a guilty smile. "You tempt me. You're sweet, honest, caring, and perfectly unique, and because of all those reasons, I'm keeping my distance from you."

I frowned, unsure why all those things meant he needed to keep me at a distance.

"Sadie, I have always gotten what I wanted. Even before I became rich and famous, I had a gift for getting what I want. Now I have the fame and fortune to get what I want when I want it, and for the first time in my life, I want something I can't have." He gave me a sad smile. "For the first time, the well-being of the person I want is more important than fulfilling my desires." Before I could form words to reply, he opened a drawer and pulled out several magazines, then laid them in front of me. "These are from my mother's collection," he explained.

They were pictures of him with movie stars, rock legends, and even the president. His name was linked with several famous females, and his personal life was laid bare for everyone to see. I had seen articles like these before, but after actually meeting Jax and finding a real person, it was hard to think of him as the rock star the media portrayed.

"See these?" he said with a grimace. "My life isn't normal. There is no room for me to have a friendship, or any relationship, with someone like you. I want to spend more time with you, and to be honest, friendship isn't really what I want anymore. I find myself wanting much more, but any girl who enters into a relationship with me has to be cold to put up with the life I live." He smiled. "You're everything I write about in my songs but can never have."

I studied the pictures in my lap. It was easier than watching him say things I didn't want to hear. Even if he was right. If I spent more time with him, I would want more too, and I didn't know the guy in those photos. He was someone completely foreign to me. I just knew Jax. The sweet guy who wanted to go into a grocery store and buy himself a Reese's Peanut Butter Cup and took the time to be kind to little girls. I'd never be able to fit into his world. I wanted to disagree, but I couldn't. I couldn't make myself protest.

"There'll be transportation for you out front within moments if you want to leave," he said. "Ms. Mary will be given directions to let you leave for the evening. Wipe the frown from your pretty face because by now she knows what happened, and she'll be worried about you."

He stepped around me and went to the door. "Stay here as long as you need. I have a room full of guests wondering what I'm doing with the gorgeous blonde I abducted." He grinned wickedly at me, but immediately it faded to a sad frown before he left the room.

# Chapter Six

**JAX**

She was getting closer to Marcus every day. I was standing by and watching it happen. Telling myself it was for the best. Marcus could be a part of her world. They were similar. They worked together. They lived in this town.

But it was the hardest thing I'd ever done.

I didn't want her with Marcus. I didn't want her laughing up at him or climbing into his truck every evening. Did he kiss her when he took her home each night? Did he get to touch her? Had he felt her body pressed up against his? Did he know just how soft her skin actually was? *Fuck!* I slammed my hand against the window frame and growled in frustration. This summer was supposed to be relaxing. I was supposed to be free of all stress. I couldn't leave now, and I wasn't going to make her leave. This was all one big train wreck waiting to happen. I was either going to cave and go after her or she was going to end up with Marcus.

## SADIE

Everything stayed the same. Ms. Mary still gave me a smile and a hot breakfast every morning. Mr. Greg told me stories of his time in World War II and beat me at chess. Marcus and I still talked on our way home at night. I even went waterskiing and kneeboarding with Marcus, Preston, Rock, Trisha, and Dewayne on Sunday. But even with new friends and a job with people I really cared about, my life seemed to be missing something. There was a void, and I knew why. The frustrating part was that I missed him. I'd forced myself to come to grips with the fact that I'd lost my heart to Jax Stone that night in the grocery store. The night in the library when he'd admitted to having an interest in me put another nail in my coffin. He starred in my dreams both day and night. My heart raced at the chance of a glimpse of him. His words haunted me. I thought of those times when I couldn't believe Jax would ever notice me enough to want me. I remembered the sadness in his eyes when he walked out the door, and I really believed he meant it.

Nothing changed the fact that I worked in his home. He signed my paychecks. If nothing else, for those two reasons anything between Jax and me would be impossible. Yet those weren't the only two. I would never fit into his world.

I sat out on the beach, waiting for Marcus to finish his shift so he could take me home. Mr. Greg had left early due to his not feeling well. It left me with nothing to do. I pulled my knees up under my chin and enjoyed the view. The waves were smooth tonight. I let myself think about Jax and his face when he smiled. It helped to remember him smiling and happy, instead of the expression he'd had on his face when he left me in the library. It was depressing enough to be a Shakespearean tragedy. The girl who never thought she would fall for a guy falls for the one she can never have. Somehow my sitting here comparing my life to Shakespeare proved just how badly I'd fallen.

Footsteps drew my attention out of my Jax-centered thoughts, and I realized Marcus must be finished. I didn't turn around. I stayed put and waited until he stopped behind me.

"Beautiful view, isn't it?" he said.

"Yeah, it is. Are you in a hurry to get home, or can we enjoy it together?"

He shrugged and sank down beside me. I smiled to myself when I realized he wasn't very graceful either. I was more on common ground with Marcus than with Jax. Even if he didn't make me get goose bumps and go all warm and tingly. Those feelings were addictive, and they couldn't be healthy.

We watched in silence for a few minutes before Marcus turned to me. I met his gaze and smiled. My friend. That thought made me smile even bigger. He sighed and shook his head.

"What?" I asked, confused.

He gave me a sheepish grin. "Sadie, when you smile at me, it makes my heart do crazy things." He blushed and flicked his gaze back toward the water. "I know I'm three years older than you, but you seem so much older than your age." He took a deep breath. "Okay, here goes. I'm trying to prepare myself for the letdown, so bear with me."

This could not be happening to me. I didn't know what I would say. Would this mess up our friendship? If I said no, would he still be my friend? I stared at him, waiting for the words I feared would change our relationship forever, while a sick knot formed in my stomach. I didn't want this to happen. It seemed so unfair. First I'd lost Jax, whom I never really had to begin with, and now I was going to lose my friend, the guy who always made me laugh when I needed it the most.

"Sadie."

A voice I only heard in my dreams these days broke the silence, and I turned around. Jax was walking toward us. I wanted to cry tears of joy. I wasn't sure if they would be from seeing the object of my obsession or from hearing him say my name again.

"Jax," I said, a little too breathless as I stood up and faced him.

His gaze brushed past Marcus. "You can go. I've arranged transportation for Sadie." He dismissed Marcus as if he were angry at him.

I glanced at Marcus. A challenge flashed in his eyes, and I realized I would have to deny myself what I wanted most, time alone with Jax, in order to save my friend his job.

"Thank you, Jax, but I would really rather Marcus took me home."

Jax's eyes left mine, and he frowned at Marcus before turning back to me. "Please, Sadie, I know I don't deserve it, but I want to talk to you. I need to talk to you."

My resolve cracked at hearing him say please. I didn't think I could tell him no again. I looked back at Marcus, his face angrier than I'd ever seen him, and it brought me back to the reason I'd said no to begin with.

"Jax, this really isn't necessary. Marcus takes me home every night, and we were in the middle of a conversation we need to finish. You have better things to do than take your kitchen help home." I hadn't meant for my words to come out sounding so harsh, and when Jax winced, I hated myself.

He stepped aside so Marcus and I could pass. "Of course," he said, his eyes on the water instead of on me.

If hearts could shatter, mine just did.

Marcus took my hand and gently pulled me away from Jax and toward his truck. I knew I should look away, but I couldn't. As if he heard my thoughts, Jax turned toward me, a haunted expression in his eyes. I stopped walking, and Marcus dropped his hand from mine.

I heard Marcus's frustrated sigh before he said, "I hope you know what you're doing, Sadie. He's only gonna hurt you."

I nodded because I knew he was right. "I'm sorry," I whispered.

Marcus deserved an explanation, but I wouldn't give him one. This was between Jax and me. I turned and left Marcus there and walked back to Jax. A relieved smile spread over Jax's face. I almost laughed when he took a deep breath as if he had been holding it, waiting to see if I would come back.

Jax squinted against the glare of the setting sun. "You were right. You should've left with him."

I shook my head. "I tried, but I couldn't do it."

He reached out and took my hand in his. A warm, tingly sensation coursed up my arm and through every other limb of my body.

"Come on, Sadie. Let's go for a walk."

We held hands as we walked along the edge of the water. Neither of us spoke. I'd returned to him because I couldn't walk away. I needed to know why he had come for me, but I didn't ask. I just waited. Finally he stopped and stared down at me.

"Do you know why I didn't want Marcus to take you home?"

Allowing myself to believe he missed me wasn't a safe path for my thoughts. I shook my head.

Jax let out a small laugh. "I'm jealous, Sadie."

I stood there trying to let his admission sink in. If he said he missed me, I could believe him. Jealousy, however, seemed too hard to comprehend. "I've stood in my room watching the two of you drive away for the past week, and it killed me each time I watched you leave with him. I would sit in my room and contemplate how I would handle it if you fell for him. How could I stay here and watch you look at him with those breathtaking eyes the way I wanted to see you looking at me?"

He ran his hand through his long dark hair and sighed. "Tonight I couldn't stay in my room. I watched you out here all by yourself and fought the urge to come to you. Then he came walking out, and I watched the two of you together for longer than I should have. My resolve to stay away from you broke, and I made my way out here before I could stop myself."

A frown creased his forehead, and he turned away. "He seems like a man who knows what he wants, and the problem is, he wants what I want. If it were anything or anyone else, I could stand back and let him take it." His blue eyes gazed back at me. "But I can't let him have you."

If he only knew how my every thought wrapped around him. "Marcus will always be just my friend. My feelings for him will never run any deeper than that."

Jax reached out and twirled one of my loose curls around his finger. I held my breath and watched him. Finally, after a moment, he tucked it behind my ear. "I'm afraid I won't be able to sit back and watch you from a distance anymore. Trust me when I tell you I have tried hard to push you from my thoughts." He stepped toward the water, focusing on something far off. "My life hasn't been normal for years. This is the only time I get to be just me. The rest of the time, I'm on the road, and sometimes I am in the air on my way to Tokyo, Paris, or Rome. I travel constantly. My name is all over the magazines with pictures of girls I am supposed to be in relationships with, but the fact is, I have no time for a relationship. If another famous female teen is in the vicinity, our pictures are taken together. It is just what is done and expected."

He spoke of a guy I didn't know. I hated being reminded that he was this untouchable idol. He turned back to me and smiled sadly.

"It's selfish of me, but I don't think I can stand it anymore. What little time I have for an average life, I want to spend with you. Well, as average as my life can get. . . ." He spread his hands out at the house and beachfront property around him and gave me a smile that didn't quite reach his eyes. "When I'm on the road this year, traveling from city to city, I want to have the memories of my time with you to keep me warm."

He held out his hands as if offering himself. "I don't want to beg or promise you things I can't give you. There isn't much of me to give, but what I have is yours. This is all up to you, Sadie. If you want me, I'm yours. If you can't do this, then I'll walk away and leave you alone. I swear."

I stood and stared at the guy standing in front of me, and I knew I should tell him no and walk away. My heart reminded me with a loud thump in my chest that I would always regret not saying yes. I doubted I'd ever feel the same way about anyone ever again. I stepped forward, and he immediately reached for me and pulled me against him. We stood there, me wrapped in his arms for a while, before moving or speaking. I knew it wasn't the smartest decision, because when September rolled around and summer was gone, I would just become the summer girl. But right now that didn't matter.

Loud enough for him to hear me, I whispered against his chest, "I want whatever part of you I can have."

His arms tightened around me. This might eventually shatter me. His lips touched my head, and I closed my eyes and enjoyed the sweetness of the moment. No one else's arms could ever feel this right.

"I want to spend as much time with you as I can. I don't want to waste a minute," he said, and I nodded against his chest, then leaned back and smiled up at him. "Tomorrow will you go deep-sea fishing with me?"

I faltered at his question. I worked every day but Sunday. He knew my hours.

"I still have a job," I reminded him.

Jax frowned and shook his head. "You're not still going to work for me."

I stiffened. "Jax, I've got to work. If you don't want me here, I have to go find another job."

He placed a finger over my lips and shook his head. "No, I'll take care of your bills and needs."

I stepped back, away from his arms. My stomach clenched. I would not be like my mother. I didn't need a man to take care of me. He wasn't going to pay me to spend time with him. I took a deep breath, hoping I could explain this so he understood.

"Jax, listen. It's important to me that I earn my own money. I can't be paid to spend time with you, because that would make it cheap somehow. I want to be with you. There should be no money involved. I need to be an equal, and as crazy as it sounds, the only way I can hope to achieve that in any way is to work for the money I earn. Please. I enjoy working with Ms. Mary and Mr. Greg, and Marcus, too. I could go somewhere else if you don't want me working for you, but I really like it here."

Jax sighed and reached out to take my hand. "I'm sorry. I'm used to people taking my money with no reservation. You're not like anyone I've ever known, so I should've realized you wouldn't be comfortable with that kind of setup. You can remain here as long as you want. It'll give me a reason to visit the kitchen more." He winked, causing me to blush.

"Thank you," I said through the tightness in my throat from fighting back tears of relief and joy.

Jax smiled. "I should be the one saying thank you. I don't deserve you, but I'm damn lucky you don't realize it."

I laughed at him.

"Come on inside with me while Kane gets our ride ready."

We walked up to his house. I realized he was taking me through the family's entrance, and I stopped.

"What's wrong?" he asked.

"I, um . . . I need to go in through the side entrance."

He shook his head. "I am agreeing to your working for me, but you are not going to be confined to using the servants' entrance. You're with me, Sadie. When you're off the clock, you're not my employee. You're my . . . air."

I frowned at him. "Your air?"

He grinned. "Well, 'girlfriend' seems too shallow a word for what I feel for you. These past two weeks it's been as if you control my breathing. When I watched you with Marcus, my chest would tighten, and it became hard to breathe. But then I would see you smile or laugh, and I could take a deep breath again."

No wonder this guy wrote songs. My eyes stung, and I hated that I always seemed to get all weepy with him.

"Wow," I whispered, for lack of better words. I wasn't gifted with his talent for weaving words so beautifully.

"So does this mean I win? Will you do me the honor of accompanying me into my house as a guest instead of the hired help?"

I grinned. "As long as I'm off the clock." He sighed in defeat. "I'll take what I can get." He took my hand and led me into the house. I wasn't sure how I would handle facing his mother or father. How were they going to react when they found out he was dating the help? But then again, I doubted they even knew I worked here. Except for the one time I'd served Jax and his mother, I'd never been around either of his parents.

Jax squeezed my hand. "Wait here. Let me grab my cell and have Kane bring our ride around front."

I nodded and watched him go to the coat closet and open it. He reached inside and took out the black leather jacket I remembered seeing him wear in a recent magazine photo.

He took a smart phone out of his pocket and tapped it a few times, then slipped it into his pocket. He turned his smile on me and crooked his finger. The expression on his face made my knees go a little weak.

"Let's take you home," he said, reaching out to clasp my hand in his.

# Chapter Seven

**SADIE**

I walked into the kitchen the next morning and hung my back-pack up on the hook before glancing at the stove, where I knew Ms. Mary would be working on the Stones' breakfast.

"Morning, Ms. Mary. I'll be back to help as soon as I get changed."

Ms. Mary cut her eyes toward me, then back at the table with a frown. I followed her gaze. Leaning back in a kitchen chair, looking ridiculously sexy for seven in the morning, sat Jax. He gave me a crooked grin and my heart went into a frenzy.

"Hey," I said without sounding affected by his presence. I knew he'd said he would be hanging out in the kitchen more often, but I hadn't realized he'd meant this early in the morning. "What? Why are you here?"

He raised his eyebrows and grinned at me. "I kinda thought that was obvious."

I knew I was blushing. I turned to Ms. Mary, then back to him. I knew she wasn't happy about his presence, and I realized this might cause a problem.

"It's okay, Sadie. She isn't mad at you. She's upset with me. You happen to be who she's protecting."

"I, um, need to go change. I'll be right back," I said, hoping Ms. Mary's scowl wasn't for me.

I walked to the laundry room. My heart was racing from the frustration of my mixed feelings. Knowing Jax wanted to see me made me extremely happy, but I also didn't want to upset Ms. Mary. I needed to hurry up. I didn't want to leave him by himself with Ms. Mary. Which seemed silly, since she worked for him.

I stepped into the hallway, and just before I reached the door that led into the kitchen I overheard Jax talking to Ms. Mary. I paused. They were talking about me.

"I'm not going to hurt her," Jax whispered. "I know she's special, and I tried to stay away, but when I'm with her I don't feel so cold and alone." Jax stood in front of the table with his attention on Ms. Mary. I froze outside the door.

Ms. Mary turned from the stove and pointed a wooden spoon at Jax. "I understand that. But that girl has a lot on her shoulders for a kid her age, and, well, you can't help it, but you'll break her heart when you leave." Her whisper wasn't very quiet. She went back to stirring the pot and shook her head. "I just don't want her hurt."

Jax didn't reply right away. Finally he said in a whisper, "I'm trying to figure out how I'm going to keep her from getting hurt. Hurting her is the very last thing I want to do."

I waited a minute more, then walked back into the kitchen. "Okay, Ms. Mary, where do I start?"

Ms. Mary handed two plates to me. "You go on ahead and enjoy your breakfast with Master Jax."

The staff didn't eat breakfast here. Sometimes we would sneak a biscuit or a piece of bacon but we didn't get to sit down and eat. That wasn't in our job description. I turned toward him as he walked up beside me. "Don't argue, please," he whispered, and then took the plates from my hands and went back to the table. I stared helplessly at Ms. Mary.

She grinned and handed me two tall glasses of orange juice. "Just eat with the boy before he starts begging and embarrasses himself," she said loudly enough for him to hear.

Grinning, he set the plates down.

"It's the truth and you know it," she said to him. I couldn't help but smile. I took the glasses and went to the table. Jax pulled out my chair, and I sat down. He sat down beside me and reached under the table and took my hand.

"Thank you for having breakfast with me."

I smiled at him and nodded. I didn't think saying *You're welcome* sounded right. I should be the one thanking him.

I was so hungry, and today's breakfast tasted much better than what I normally scarfed down after the Stones finished *their* breakfast. I picked up a piece of bacon and chewed, but the weight of Jax's gaze made me uncomfortable.

I swallowed and whispered, not wanting Ms. Mary to hear me, "I won't be able to eat if you're watching me."

He grinned. "Sorry, it's just something I've never seen before."

I frowned, not really sure what he meant. "You've never seen a girl eat?" I asked, confused.

He laughed. "Well, now that you mention it, no, I haven't seen many eat. They normally can't eat in front of me, or they just don't as a rule. But what I meant was I've never seen you eat, and it's cute. I didn't mean to stare. I'm sorry."

He reminded me of that little boy again, trying to get out of a punishment, and I couldn't help but smile. "It's okay, but now you have seen me, so stop watching and eat your breakfast before it gets cold."

He grinned and looked down at his own food.

The kitchen door swung open, and Marcus stepped inside, whistling. "Morning, Ms. Mary. Got me something good to eat?"

Ms. Mary shot him a silent warning that clearly said *Behave*, and Marcus frowned and turned toward us. Jax leaned back in his chair and took a drink of his juice.

"Ah, good morning, Sadie, Mr. Stone."

Jax nodded toward Marcus, and Marcus's gaze didn't linger. He just headed back to the laundry room to get into uniform. I sighed in relief that he hadn't said anything stupid. Jax leaned toward me.

"Nothing he can say will make me fire him, unless it's against you. Stop worrying. I realize he's angry with me, and part of me doesn't blame him, and the other part is just relieved you wanted me."

The place in my heart where Jax had taken up residence grew. I smiled at him. "Thank you."

He shrugged and leaned back again. "You have nothing to thank me for, but you're welcome."

The rest of breakfast went smoothly, and Jax pulled me aside before I went to help clean up from breakfast.

"I'll try to stay away from you, if I can, while you're working. But as soon as you're off, I'm coming to get you."

A silly grin plastered itself on my face, and I nodded. He took my hand and kissed it before turning to walk away.

I forced myself to push all thoughts of Jax aside in order to stay focused the rest of the day. Several times a warm, tingling sensation coursed through me, and knowing he watched me made my heart race. The end of my workday couldn't come soon enough. Just as I walked out of the laundry room after changing out of my uniform and into my clothes, a hand came out and grabbed me by the arm.

"Come with me," Jax whispered, and I let him lead me up steps I'd never used and through several doors and halls I hadn't known existed. Finally we were at his bedroom door. I remembered clearly the last time I'd been in there, but walking into it with my hand in his made everything different. This was the place where he slept and wrote songs. Something inside me knew that each time I got closer to him would make it so much harder when I let him go. I stepped inside, and he closed the door and turned to grin at me.

"I wanted you to see my room. Well, I guess I should say I wanted you to see my room with me."

He took my hand and pulled me over to the wall of guitars. He reached for the old worn guitar in the middle and took it down. The reverence he seemed to have for the instrument made me smile.

"That must've been your first one. It looks well loved."

He nodded and held it out to me. I took the cool, hard wood in my hands and studied the writing on it. I thought at first it was autographed by someone else, but holding it up close, I saw the childish signature: *Jax Stone*. I ran my fingers over the name, thinking how long ago it must seem to him now.

"When I was seven, I begged my parents for a guitar. They

wouldn't buy me one since I'd also begged for drums the year before and not stayed with my lessons. I promised them I'd learn to play without lessons if I could just have one. It took two years before I finally wore them down. I woke up one Christmas and it was standing in front of the Christmas tree. I'll never forget the thrill that ran through me. I grabbed the guitar and ran straight back to my bedroom. I played it until I figured out the chorus to 'Wanted Dead or Alive.' It was then I realized I could play by ear."

I'd read that tidbit once, but I had chalked it up to publicity fiction. "I bet your parents were surprised."

He laughed and nodded. "Yes. It isn't every day a nine-year-old boy picks up a guitar and strums out a Bon Jovi song without any formal training."

I grinned and handed him the guitar. "So, this is how it all began. No wonder you have this one in the center."

He nodded and turned to hang it back on the wall.

"No, wait." I reached out and touched his arm. He glanced back at me. "Play it for me."

He turned back to the wall of expensive guitars. "Well, I actually lured you in here to unleash my chick magnet gift on you." He gave me a crooked grin. "Considering my star persona doesn't impress you, I was going to cheat and pull down the Fender Stratocaster original over there and play you one of my number ones. See if I could get you to become putty in my hands, or at least throw your panties at me."

I laughed and shook my head. "I'm sorry to disappoint you, but your Fender Stratocaster original and a number one hit I have heard countless times on the radio will not make me putty. And as for the panties, nothing is getting me to throw those at you. However, if I can hear you play on that guitar, the first song you ever played, I'll see what I can do about turning into putty."

He sighed playfully and sat down on the edge of his bed. He patted the spot next to him, and I sat down. "I'm working with a handicap of an old worn-out guitar and a song I haven't played in years, but if this is what it takes to impress you, then here goes nothing."

He began to play, and soon his voice joined the guitar. If he had been aiming for putty, he succeeded, because the sound of his voice made me warm all over. I wanted to close my eyes and picture the little boy in his room on Christmas morning. I could see the boy before he had become a star. If only he was a normal guy and not a rock star then this thing between us would be so easy. But I'd chosen this when I had said yes to our spending the summer together. I knew walking into it exactly who Jax was, and I couldn't change it. I let myself look at him as he sang the words with a grin on his face. I pictured him singing to himself as a boy as he roamed the outdoors, pretending to be a cowboy.

The song came to a close, and he grinned at me. "Well, what did you think?"

I smiled back. "Perfect."

He laughed and shook his head. "Most girls want love sonnets, and you want a song I loved as a kid."

"You don't still love the song?" I asked.

Jax sighed and a sad smile touched his face. "Yeah, it means something different for me now than it did then. When I was a kid I wanted to be a cowboy. But that isn't really what the song is about. It's about this life I lead. The craziness of it all. I relate to it better now than I did then."

He hung the guitar back up on the wall.

A knock sounded on the door, and Jason entered. He noticed me and stopped. "Uh, sorry, I didn't realize you had company. I just walked by and heard you playing that old song and thought I would stop in and see what the reminiscing was about."

Jax turned and grinned at his brother. "It's okay. You can come in." Jason stepped into the room and closed the door behind him.

"I brought Sadie in here to play one of her favorite number ones I've done, and come to find out, she didn't have one. She doesn't like me at all."

I laughed at his expression, and Jason's shocked look instantly went to a smile when he realized his brother meant to tease me.

"Not true. I happen to really like the song you sang about fighting to find yourself."

Jax reached for another guitar and froze. He turned back to me. I didn't know what I'd said wrong, but he gazed straight into my eyes very seriously for what seemed an eternity. A smile slowly formed on his perfect lips right before he asked, "Really?"

I nodded, not sure why this surprised him.

"Me too," he finally said, before taking down the other guitar.

I glanced over at his brother, confused, and Jason smiled at me. "'Inside War' was the first song Jax ever wrote. He fought tooth and nail to get it released. Up until that point in his career, he'd recorded songs written by other people. He fought hard for 'Inside War,' and it never made it all the way to number one, but got into the top ten. From then on, he was given free rein to decide what he sang on his albums."

I nodded.

Jax stood by the bed with the other guitar, watching me. "Most girls like my love songs." He shrugged. "You keep surprising me."

I tried to remember a love song he'd recorded, but none came to mind. At home Jessica forced me to listen to eighties music. She listened to little else. Music wasn't something I knew a lot about.

"Okay, sing me one of those famous love songs."

He grinned and played a soft, smooth melody. Soon his voice joined in, and I found myself unable to take my eyes off of him.

*"Just to make your eyes sparkle, I'd do anything.*
*I could give it all up to know you were my girl.*
*Just being with you and listening to your laugh is what*

*makes up my other half.*

*I was lost and cold inside when your heart called out*
*to mine.*

*Now I know you're the only thing that keeps me*
*hanging on, when the rest of the world seems to come*
*crashing down.*

*"Don't leave me now! I'll never make it!*
*Don't leave me now. I'm not strong enough!*
*You're the reason I can take this guitar and make it sing.*
*Don't leave me now, or I'll fall apart.*

*"I know sometimes life with me is hard to handle.*
*I get caught up in the lights and the crowd.*
*But you're the reason I keep on playing.*
*Without you, girl, it would all die down.*
*Hold on to me through this ride, please,*
*because if you let go, I will too.*
*If the sparkle in your eyes starts to fade,*
*my heart won't beat and my song will disappear.*

*"Don't leave me now! I'll never make it!*
*Don't leave me now. I'm not strong enough!*
*You're the reason I can take this guitar and make it sing.*
*Don't leave me now, or I'll fall apart.*

*Don't leave me now, or I'll fall apart.*
*Girl, if you leave me, it will all fall apart."*

His smooth, husky voice stopped, and the guitar playing slowed. When the song ended, I stared at him, unable to say anything.

He smiled sheepishly. "The first number one I actually wrote. It's the song girls always want to hear."

I smiled, then sighed. "I wish I could make a wisecrack, but after that performance, I'm torn between standing up and clapping or swooning."

He threw back his head and laughed. "Ah, finally!"

"I wish I'd learned to play the guitar. I've never seen a girl *not* get reeled in when he breaks into a love song," Jason said.

I shrugged in defeat. "I wish I could argue, but I have to admit, watching him sing that song and play the guitar is incredibly hard to resist. I've heard it before, but never with the view he just gave me, and I'll never turn the station when it comes on again."

Jason burst into laughter, and Jax grinned at me. "You couldn't let it go without reminding me how unaffected you are by who I am, could you?"

"We wouldn't want you to get a big head."

Jason laughed again. "His head has been big since the first time he realized he was a prodigy."

"I'm just teasing. I've never turned your songs off. The truth is, I hardly ever listen to the radio. We have one radio at our house, and my mother loves the eighties. I know more songs from that time frame than I do current songs."

"I hate eighties music. That sucks for you," Jason said with sincerity.

I smiled and shrugged. "It's not so bad when it's all you've ever known."

Jason raised his eyebrows like he wasn't so sure. "Ah, yeah, sure," he said, and grimaced. He looked past me at Jax, then cleared his voice and stood up. "Um, well, I guess I'll be going. I got somewhere to be. See ya later, Sadie."

"Okay, bye."

"Yeah, see ya."

I turned my attention to Jax after his brother's hasty departure.

"Why did you run him off?"

Jax faked innocence. "I have no idea what you're talking about. You heard the man, he has somewhere to be."

I laughed. "Sure he did."

Jax grinned at me, walked over to a tall chest of drawers and opened one. "If I give you something of mine, will you accept it if I really want you to have it?"

I wasn't sure how to answer. "Um, I guess it depends on what it is you want to give me."

He pulled out an iPod and brought it over. "I want you to take this. It's mine and has some really great artists on there, but I want you to have it because every song I have ever recorded is on there too."

I took the iPod from his hands. "Thank you."

"If you don't want to listen to me, it's all right. If there are other artists you want on there, just bring it to me, and I'll put them on there for you." He reached back into the drawer. "Oh, and here are some earbuds. I'll get you a wireless pair, but I need to have them made to fit your ears. We can get those on Sunday."

I laughed at his eagerness. "These earbuds are fine."

He shook his head. "You say that now, but if you ever used wireless earbuds, you would know it's not true."

I sighed and agreed. "Okay."

He seemed so excited about being able to give me something, I didn't want to spoil it. I liked seeing him act like a little boy. My insides turned to mush during the times he opened up enough to show his vulnerable side.

"I'll listen to you as I go to sleep at night," I assured the little boy who seemed anxious about his gift.

He closed his eyes tightly. "You don't know how good thinking about it makes me feel, but now I'm going to have a harder time going to sleep at night knowing I'm singing in your ears."

He opened his eyes to look at me. I saw something there I'd only wished for, or my heart was lying to me.

# Chapter Eight

**JAX**

I'd missed three calls from my mother. Once Sadie was safely inside her apartment and Kane was headed back to the beach house, I called my mother back. The missed call from Marco earlier today probably had something to do with my mother's determination to get ahold of me.

"Where have you been? Marco has tried calling you, and I have tried several times. You can't just go on a vacation from everything, Jax. It doesn't work that way. The public, your fans, expect some of you. You need to remember why you are where you are. Now call Marco. You have a movie premiere to be at tomorrow night. He is setting up publicity photos, and you need to make an appearance. No arguing. Just do it."

And without allowing me to respond, she ended the call.

I dropped my phone into my lap and laid my head back on the leather seat. I didn't want to go to some damn movie premiere. I wanted to stay here with Sadie. Why couldn't they all give me a break? My phone started ringing again. I picked it up and Jason's face flashed on the screen.

"Hey."

"Dad was looking for you. He's back here from whatever meetings he's been at. He wants us to go golfing as soon as you get back from the movie premiere. And I need you as a buffer. Don't make me go play golf with him alone."

Jason already knew about the movie premiere. That meant Mom had been bitching about it all day.

"I'll find him when I get home. We can golf when I get back, but it needs to be an early morning tee time."

Jason chuckled. "Got it. We need to be back before Sadie gets off work."

"Exactly."

**SADIE**

A note greeted me when I arrived at work the next day. Ms. Mary sighed heavily and handed it to me as soon as I walked in. I glanced over at the table, and a wave of disappointment hit me at the sight of the empty seat where I had hoped Jax would be sitting.

"No need to be so upset. Read the note, then hurry along and get ready."

I walked back to the laundry room before opening the letter. I didn't want to read anything in front of Ms. Mary's prying eyes.

Sadie,

I am sorry I won't be at breakfast this morning. I have been so busy wallowing in my not being able to have you, and then being given the gift of . . . my air . . . that I forgot about a movie premiere I am expected at tonight. I am flying out to Hollywood early this morning, and I will be back as soon as this is over. I intend to get on a plane and head right back to you as soon as possible. Please forgive me. I will see you soon. Miss me.

Jax

I swallowed the lump in my throat, aggravated with myself more than anything. Jax was a famous rock star. He had a band and people who depended upon him. He had to go to things such as movie premieres. I knew the more time I spent with him, the more things like this would be hard on me, but I also needed to decide whether or not I wanted to be with him enough to get over this. I changed quickly and splashed my face with cold water. I needed to focus, not to think about Jax and his real life.

It was something I would never know or understand. I needed to get a grip. I dried my face on a towel and walked back into the kitchen.

"Where do I start?"

Ms. Mary turned to me. I gave her a smile, and she frowned, then reluctantly smiled back. "I got ten pounds of potatoes over there fresh out of my garden. Start scrubbing 'em, then get them all peeled for me."

I nodded and went right to work. Cleaning potatoes proved to be a great way to get my mind off other things. I wished I didn't miss him so much. Two days and I was so addicted to his presence I was lost without him. But then I remembered my iPod, and I jumped up and went to my bag and pulled it out. I'd sat in my room the previous night figuring it out. I found Jax's latest album and put the earbuds in my ears. Listening to him helped. I didn't see a star on the stage when I heard him sing. I saw the guy sitting on his bed with his old guitar, grinning at me. His voice helped the potatoes, and the morning, go faster. I got so lost in my thoughts and the music I jumped when someone tapped my shoulder. Marcus gazed down at me.

"Lost in the music, I see," he said, smiling.

I nodded and slipped the earbuds out of my ears. "Yes, I guess I was."

Marcus pulled up a stool and sat down beside me. "Let me

guess who you're listening to. Could it be the number one chart topper for the past three weeks, Jax Stone?"

I was glad Marcus seemed to be in a teasing mood. I nodded and grinned up at him. "I guess I'm pretty obvious."

Marcus sighed. "Unfortunately, yes, you are."

"I know I spend all my time with Jax. I only have this summer with him, and then he'll walk out of my life and I'll have to learn to keep living."

Marcus leaned back against the wall and frowned. "You know when he leaves this summer, it's over. I mean, he has told you this, right?"

I thought about how to answer. It was between Jax and me, but Marcus was my friend and he needed some answers. He deserved some answers. "We both know trying to have a relationship, while he rocks the world and I finish high school, is impossible. We knew this going into the relationship, and we both agreed being together now was what we wanted."

Marcus stared at the large bucket of potatoes. "And you're okay with this? I mean, you're fine with dating him now? Then he just walks away when the summer ends, and you won't be heartbroken?"

I let out a short laugh. "I didn't say my heart wouldn't be broken. I'm afraid it's inevitable."

Marcus leaned forward on his knees and studied me. "Then why're you doing this to yourself?" he asked, low enough so no one nearby could hear him.

I put the last potato in the bucket. "It's too late now, Marcus. I love him. I no longer have a choice."

He reacted like I'd slapped him, and I hated hurting him, but I knew he needed to know.

"He doesn't deserve it. He can have any girl in the world's love, and he took yours. Someone who deserves so much more than a summer fling." He stood and started to walk away, but stopped and glanced back at me. "If you were mine, I'd never let you go." He left the kitchen.

The rest of the day went slowly, and I was glad when it was over. I went to change clothes and was starting out the door when Ms. Mary called my name.

"I forgot to tell you, there'll be a car waiting out front to take you home when you're ready."

I sighed and thought about riding home alone in one of his cars and shook my head. "It's okay, I want to ride my bike home tonight. It's still early, and I want some fresh air."

Ms. Mary shook her head. "He ain't gonna like hearing that. You rest assured, Kane'll tell him you rode your bike home."

I smiled and opened the door. "He's my . . . friend, Ms. Mary, not my keeper," I replied.


Riding home on my bike while the sun set was really pleasant. I stopped at the public beach and sat for a few minutes while I watched families enjoying the last bit of daylight. Red-skinned tourists covered the beach, and I recognized several kids from school working at the chair, umbrella, and WaveRunner rentals. Everyone seemed to be closing down for the day. I took in a deep breath and let the wet ocean air fill my lungs. Something about the air here seemed healing to me. As if it made everything okay just by being clean and pure and full of something beautiful.

"Sadie White?"

I heard my name and turned to see a girl I recognized from biology class standing beside me in a red one-piece bathing suit. I couldn't remember her last name, but I remembered her first. "Yes. Amanda, right?"

She smiled a friendly smile and nodded. "Yep. I haven't seen you since school let out."

I nodded. "I've been working."

She grinned. "Don't you know the great thing about being a local is you can work at the beach?"

I thought the exact same thing at the beginning of summer. I'd wanted to have a job on the beach back then, but now things were much different. "I'm sure it is, but I make good money doing domestic work."

She frowned. "But where is the fun in that? . . . Unless there are cute boys around? You should come take the lifeguard test. Lifeguarding is so much fun. Hot guys are everywhere. . . . A lot of times you get to work with one!" She nodded toward a tall, tanned blond guy coming down the lifeguard ladder in a pair of red swim trunks. "Like Todd Mitchell! He'll be a senior this year and is going to Tuscaloosa next fall to the university. He is soooo cute! Can you swim?"

I nodded, trying to keep up with her quick-paced conversation. "Yes, but I'm happy with where I am right now. However, if I get too bored, I'll remember the lifeguard job."

She frowned prettily, and in a way that reminded me of Barbie's little sister.

"Okay, I guess. Hey, you should come to the July Fourth party at Dylan McCovey's. He has a house on the beach, and he throws a party every July Fourth. It's always a good time."

For some reason, this bubbly girl liked me. Me, with no personality. And I didn't want to let her down again. "Okay, well, sure. Um, I'll let you know. I have to check on my work schedule and everything." I thought about Jax and wondered if he would want to spend July Fourth with me.

Amanda nodded and reached into her bright-pink polka-dot bag and pulled out a cell phone. "What's your number?"

I thought about it a minute. I wasn't sure what to tell her. Jessica owned a cell phone, but the bill wasn't always paid on it. I figured I could give her the cell number and hope Jessica would tell me when Amanda called, if it worked this week.

"555-0100"

She punched it into her slim pink cell phone, and slipped

the phone back into her bag. "Cool. I'll call you later this week and see if you can make it."

I nodded, and we said our good-byes. She turned and bounced away. She seemed so happy and friendly. Everything I wished I could be. However, I didn't necessarily want to bounce when I walked. I went back to my bike and headed home. I would be home in time to make dinner for Jessica.

The moment I walked in the door, Jessica called from her room, "Sadie? Is that you?"

"Yes," I replied as I walked back to see her so we wouldn't have to yell at each other. I stopped when I got to her bedroom door and found her standing in her panties and bra in front of the window unit with a large cup of ice in her hand.

"The heat is killing me, Sadie! I swear, I can't wait until I've got my body back."

I sighed and bit my tongue to keep from reminding her this was her fault. "I bet," was all I allowed myself to say.

"So, you're home early today. You didn't get fired, did you?" she asked, all serious as the idea of me without a job began to take root in her thoughts.

I shook my head and leaned against the door frame. "No, the family is out tonight, so I got to come home early."

She still didn't know about Jax. I didn't want her to find out and get it in her head I could somehow get money out of

Jax. Mooching off men was her gig, not mine. I didn't want any man to take care of me. I wanted to be self-sufficient. I would never want my teenage daughter to have to pay the bills and cook the meals.

"Hmmm, well, that works out good for me and the baby. We're starving, and the thought of working in a hot kitchen is just too much."

I nodded and turned. The kitchen contained all I needed to make tacos, and Jessica loved tacos. I got the meat out of the freezer and put it in some warm water to thaw.

"I've got to go to the clinic tomorrow to have a checkup. Are you working?"

I wanted to laugh at her question. I'd worked every day since school had been out, except, of course, for Sundays. Not that I was complaining, because if I didn't work, I didn't make money . . . and I didn't see Jax.

"Yes," I called back.

"Oh, poo! I hate driving."

I didn't respond. Instead, I searched through the cabinet for the taco seasoning.

"You know, I'll be thirty-one weeks this Monday, and in two months' time, I'll have this baby. I haven't even picked out a name yet."

A nervous knot grew in my stomach at the thought of her bringing home a real baby. The baby hadn't seemed real as long as it remained unnamed, and the thought of naming it made me very nervous.

"I was thinking I liked the name Sasha if it's a girl. You know, stick with the *S* names. Sadie, Sasha."

I said nothing.

"Or if it is a boy, how about Sam?"

I tried to ignore her. I really did not want to give this baby a name. It made my insides do funny things. The thought of formula, baby food, diapers—and, well, a baby—scared me. I could see Jessica coming home and saying she couldn't take it and handing the baby to me. I had no idea what to do with a baby. I really needed her to be the mom. I needed her to be a grown-up with this baby. Because I wasn't ready.

"Okay . . . so you don't like that name?" she called out again.

"No, I like it. I just don't really have a preference."

She remained quiet for a moment, and I wondered if she picked up on my fear. And then she said, "Well, I think it's going to be a girl, so I'm going to name her Sasha Jewel White."

I swallowed the lump that formed in my throat and forced out a reply. "Sure, Mom. Sounds good."

Jessica ate in front of the window unit in her underwear, and I ate alone at the table. After we finished, I washed up the dishes and went to get a shower. I would be getting in bed earlier than usual, and sleep suddenly seemed very appealing.

"Sadie!"

I sat straight up in bed at the sound of my mother yelling my name. I slung my feet onto the hardwood floor, and before I could even get to the door she began yelling again.

"Sadie!"

I ran across the hall and into her room. She was sitting up on the edge of the bed, holding her stomach, with sweat on her face.

"Something's wrong," she panted. "It hurts like hell!"

I grabbed her housecoat and slipped her arms in. "Come on. We're going to the hospital."

She grunted and stood.

We made it halfway down the hall before she let out another bloodcurdling scream and bent over, holding her stomach.

"Help me, Sadie! This hurts so bad!" she said through tears.

It was hard to mask my panic. Seeing my mother screaming in pain terrified me. I got her into the car, then remembered her purse and ran back inside to grab it. On my way in the door she screamed again, and I hoped someone would hear her and offer to come help. Right now I didn't feel competent enough, and I really wanted help. I ran back out to the car, flung open the door, and jumped inside, and headed for the local hospital. Luckily, we were only a few miles away. I glanced over at Jessica as she rested her head back on the seat.

"You okay?" I asked, praying for a yes.

"For now," she said quietly.

I didn't ask her anything else. I didn't want to cause her any pain. We made it to the emergency room fast, since the roads were empty at four in the morning. I pulled up to the entrance and ran around to open her door. She hadn't experienced any more pain since we'd left the house, and I was grateful. Focusing on the road was hard enough with my heart beating out of my chest and my palms sweating.

"Wait here. I'm going to go get help. Don't walk."

She gave me a tight nod, and I ran inside.

The smell of sanitized hospital hit my nose, and for once the smell comforted me. A lady stood behind a desk, watching me.

"My mom is in the car. She's pregnant and in a lot of pain."

The lady went quickly into another room and came out with a wheelchair.

"The car is parked right out front," I said.

We walked out to the car quickly. The lady and I helped Jessica into the wheelchair. The lady immediately started asking her questions, and I bit my tongue to keep from asking her to stop for fear it would make the pain come back. Once inside, they got her information and then instructed me to stay in the waiting area while they checked her out. Which sounded good to me. I didn't want to go with them. Sitting down alone for a few minutes in order to calm my racing heart was greatly needed at that point. There were a lot of empty seats at that hour, so I found a chair facing a television hanging on the wall, and I watched the soundless news.

"Hello." A hand lightly shook my shoulder, and a woman's voice woke me up.

I sat up in my chair. "Um, yes, sorry. Is my mom okay?"

The nurse smiled. "Yes, she's fine. She had a bad case of Braxton Hicks brought on by not drinking enough liquids, but she is fine and so is the baby."

I sighed with relief.

"She's asleep, and we have moved her to a room. Once we have her hydrated and are sure her contractions have stopped, we will release her. You can come up to her room if you like."

I nodded and stood. The soundless television said 7:30 in the right-hand corner, and I froze and realized I should've been at work an hour ago. "I need to make a phone call before I go up. Do I need to go outside to use a cell phone?"

She smiled. "Yes, you do. I'll be at the desk when you're ready, and I'll take you up."

I thanked her and headed for the door I'd brought Jessica through a few hours before.

I reached into my mother's purse and pulled out her phone. I knew she'd stored Ms. Mary's number in there somewhere. Of course the phone was powered off. When I turned it on, I saw there were several missed calls. Ms. Mary. I called her back.

"Hello, Sadie." Ms. Mary's anxious voice answered on the first ring.

"Hey, Ms. Mary. I am so sorry! I had to bring my mother to the hospital at four this morning, and I fell asleep in the waiting room. They just came and got me. I'm so sorry I didn't call."

"Oh, my lordy, is she okay?"

"Yes, yes, she's fine. It was Braxton Hicks brought on by dehydration, and they're keeping her today until she's hydrated and stable. I have to stay and take her home when she's ready. I'm so sorry."

"Girl, you better stop apologizing to me. I'm just glad you're all right. Now, here is Master Jax's number. You need to call him. He has gone to your house looking for you. I ain't never seen that boy all worked up and worried as he was when you didn't show up. Don't you worry about a thing, and call him, please, before he gets the police searching for you."

I thanked her and said good-bye, then quickly called Jax's number.

"Hello?"

"Jax, it's Sadie."

"Are you all right? Where are you?"

"I'm fine. I brought my mother to the hospital around four this morning. She was in pain. But she's fine now, and they are pumping fluids into her. She should be able to leave soon."

"I'm on my way."

"No, Jax, wait. You can't come here."

He paused. "Why?"

I laughed. "Because you'll get mauled by adoring fans."

He sighed. "I can make a few calls and get in privately."

I laughed again. "No, there's no reason. We'll be leaving soon. And I haven't explained you to my mom yet, and today isn't really a good day for that."

"I guess you're right."

"I am."

"I miss you."

I got all warm and tingly at his words. "I miss you, too."

"You know, I could get you a few posters for your walls. . . ."

I laughed. "I'll pass. I happen to be interested in someone I don't really see as the guy in those posters."

He hesitated a moment, and then said, "Thank you."

"See you later," I said, and hung up. I squinted up at the morning sun and smiled before turning and heading back into the hospital to check on Jessica. She wouldn't get dehydrated again if I could help it. The whole experience was not something I wanted to repeat.

They released Jessica around lunchtime. She seemed tired and whiny. I couldn't wait to get her home and go to work. As soon as I deposited her in bed with a large pitcher of ice water and a glass beside her, I headed outside.

# Chapter Nine

**JAX**

"This is the kinda stuff that girl's life is made up of. See why I want you to stay away? She don't need no more problems than she already has." Ms. Mary had her hands on her hips, glaring at me.

"I want to make things easier for her. Not harder," I tried assuring her.

"You can't. Don't you get that, boy? What happens if'n the media gets ahold of this? Hmmm? Thought of that? They will hound her. They will flash her pretty, sweet face all over the news. You want that for her? I don't."

That wasn't going to happen. I wouldn't let it. I might not be able to promise Sadie anything more than a summer, but I could make sure I protected her. Someone needed to. "I will make sure she is safe from any of that. Calm down, Ms. Mary. I'm taking care of her. That's all I want to do. Make things easier for her. The media doesn't even know I'm here. I've been coming here for years and they've never found me."

Ms. Mary made a "hmph" noise and turned back to her stove. "Just make sure that girl don't suffer because of you. She don't deserve it."

That wouldn't happen. I'd never let it.

"Dad wants to know if you're coming with us," Jason said as he walked into the kitchen. He made his way to the stove and took a biscuit from Ms. Mary's iron skillet.

"I can't, Jason. You know that." I hated letting him down but Sadie needed me now.

"Yeah. I get it. I'll survive Dad alone." He bit into the biscuit and smiled. "I like her. She's good for you."

"Boy, don't you talk with your mouth full," Ms. Mary scolded.

Jason chuckled and kissed her cheek before heading for the door.

I'd make it up to him later.

## SADIE

When I opened the door, a black Jaguar sat in the drive. Jax stepped out and walked over to meet me.

He smiled sheepishly. "I had the hospital call as soon as they released your mom."

I smiled. His eyes were hidden behind black sunglasses. He wore a New York Giants baseball cap pulled down low on his forehead.

"I see you're in disguise?" I asked.

He grinned and nodded.

I looked over at the Jaguar and laughed. "You should drive a vehicle that doesn't draw attention if you're trying to go around undetected."

He frowned. "What? That's the cheapest thing in my garage."

I laughed. "So, you're taking me to work?"

He shook his head. "Nope, we're going to the movies. You're off for the rest of the day."

"You can't go to the movies."

He raised his eyebrows. "Wanna bet?" He opened my car door, took me by the waist, and lifted me into the tank he called cheap. He slid into the driver's side and headed toward the largest movie theater in town.

"Jax, you do realize people are going to recognize you in your disguise if they pay close attention."

He smiled at me. "I know, but they won't get a chance."

I waited for an explanation.

"I've been doing this for a while now, so I know how to hide from fans. Trust me."

I hoped he was right. I would hate for us to get bombarded

by crazy teenage fans. He might be used to it, but it wasn't something I wanted to experience. We pulled around to the back of the theater, and a door swung open. An older man dressed in a black suit stepped outside.

Jax grinned. "I'll get your door."

I started to say I could get it, but he put his finger over my mouth and winked.

"I want to get you out."

I melted in my seat. My door opened, and he picked me up by the waist and set me on the ground.

"Mr. Stone, if you will come this way, we have a theater closed off just as you requested."

Jax took my hand. I realized we were walking in through the emergency exit of a theater, and no one but this man knew we were here. I hadn't thought of this. We walked inside, and Jax waved his hands out toward the stadium seating.

"Take your pick." He grinned.

I pointed to the middle, and he sighed with relief. "Perfect! My favorite spot."

He turned to the man at the door. "All the doors have been secured?" Jax asked.

The man nodded. "Yes, sir. No one can enter."

Jax handed the man what I assumed must be money. Jax turned and took my hand, and we went to our seats.

"What're we watching?" I asked as the man who let us in

wheeled in a cart with two popcorns, two drinks, two nachos and cheese, and one of every candy available from the concession stand. I frowned at Jax. "Did you invite an army?"

He laughed and put the drinks in our cup holders. "No, but movies make me hungry, and I didn't know what you wanted."

"Popcorn."

He reached for a box, handed it to me, and grabbed the other one. "You asked what we were seeing."

I nodded and put a handful of popcorn in my mouth.

*"Night Horse,"* he replied.

I'd wanted to see this after seeing the previews on television the other night. And then it hit me. "But *Night Horse* isn't playing yet. It won't be in theaters until next Friday."

He grinned at me and winked. "For everyone else. But for you and me, it's about to play right now."

As if on cue, the lights faded, the big screen widened, and the movie began. When I realized we were not going to have to sit through previews, I started to say something but thought better of it. Today was the first day I'd really felt like I was dating someone from another world. Before, Jax had been a guy, a regular guy, whom I could talk to. Today he became the rock star. It bothered me. I glanced over at his face and saw the boy who had sung 'Wanted Dead or Alive' on a guitar he had begged for and worn out. A small smile touched his lips.

I blushed, and he leaned down to whisper in my ear. "If you

keep looking at me like that, I'm going to have a harder time staying focused on this movie than I am already."

I frowned. "Why're you having a hard time?"

He grinned wickedly and set his popcorn down before taking my hands. "Because I'm with a beautiful girl who completely fascinates me, and we're in a dark room all alone, and all I want to do is sit and stare at her, but I know if I do, I won't be able to keep myself from kissing her very perfect, very tempting lips."

I swallowed hard, and my heart pounded in my chest. Suddenly the dark around us seemed to close in, and a force neither of us seemed to be able to control kept our eyes locked on each other's. Jax's hand slipped out of mine and slid behind my neck, and he leaned in. The lips of the only boy I would ever love touched mine, and I forgot where we were and everything else around us. His other hand slipped behind my head, and he cradled it as he softly kissed me. His tongue touched my bottom lip, and I opened cautiously, knowing it was what he wanted. The moment his tongue slid into my mouth, a low moan escaped my throat, and his hands pulled my head closer. Soon my hands wound their way behind his neck and tangled in his hair. It seemed like I was falling, but I didn't care. I held on to him and let my tongue explore. He groaned, released me, and sat back, putting distance between us. I worried I had done something wrong, and I froze, watching him, not sure what to say.

He rubbed his face with one hand and gave me the crooked grin I loved. "I'm sorry, but, wow, I, uh, wasn't . . . I mean, I knew it would be good, but, wow, Sadie, you taste amazing."

I kept my eyes cast downward, still not sure what had happened. I could have kissed him all day. The "wow" led me to believe he liked it as much as I did, but I wanted to know why he'd stopped. However, I wasn't about to ask. I studied my hands a moment. His finger slid under my chin, and I let him tilt my face up to meet his eyes.

"What are you thinking?"

I shook my head. I wasn't going to answer. "You do know why I stopped, don't you?" I wanted to seem mature and say yes, but I also didn't want to lie, so I reluctantly shook my head.

He sighed and smiled at me. "Now, I know what you're thinking." He turned in his seat to face me completely. "Sadie, that was the most incredible kiss I have ever experienced in my life. Never have I gotten completely lost in a kiss before. It made me want things I'm not about to try and get. It was perfect. You're perfect. But I don't have the strength to kiss you for a very long period of time and still keep my hands off you."

I let his explanation sink in and nodded. I focused my attention on the screen, and he groaned. Suddenly his hand slid into my hair, and he turned my face to his. His smile became a smoldering gaze right before my eyes, and he once again touched his lips to mine. I opened sooner this time, and he was inside my mouth, making my heart race and my hands tremble. I slipped my hands into his hair and once again allowed myself to touch his tongue. This time when he let out a low growl, he pulled me closer, and I heard a moan I realized came from me. I scooted over as far as my chair would let me and pressed close. I wanted to be even closer. He broke the kiss again, but before I could mourn the loss, he pulled me onto his lap. He seized my mouth again and let his hands run down my arms as he kissed me. Jax's breathing became fast and shallow, and I melted into him. When I ran my hands up his chest, his body shuddered under my touch. He groaned, and his kisses became more frantic. It became difficult to breathe, and my heart hammered wildly in my chest. I pressed up against him. Another growl tore from his chest as he pushed me back. We sat there looking at each other, gasping for air. I didn't need an explanation this time.

"I don't want to push you to do anything you're not ready for," he whispered.

I was more than ready for this. When I shifted on his lap he sucked in a sharp breath and his piercing blue eyes made me shiver as he held my gaze. They were intense. This wasn't a look I'd seen in a magazine or on a poster. This was a different kind of look. One I wanted to call mine. I leaned forward and pressed my lips to his jawline firmly, then kissed a trail back to his ear. His hands instantly tightened on my waist, but he held still.

"More, please," I said softly in his ear.

His tense body immediately responded, and his hands slid up from my waist and under my shirt. The warmth of his palms on my skin caused me to gasp, but before he could question himself I pressed my chest closer to his as an invitation.

"God, Sadie. You keep making those little noises and I'm going to lose it." His voice was husky. I liked the change in it.

I straddled him, so that the hardness between his legs pressed just the right spot between mine. It felt so good I couldn't keep from letting my head fall back as I sighed in pleasure.

"Fuck," Jax growled, and his hands were instantly on my breasts. The feel of his long, talented fingers tugging down the front of my bra until he had both my breasts bared and in his hands had me trembling. Maybe I shouldn't be doing this. Maybe I should put a stop to this, but it felt so good. "You feel incredible," he said with a fierceness in his tone that startled me. His eyes dropped from my eyes to my chest as he stared at the fabric hiding the fact that he was gently cupping my breasts as his thumb and forefinger teased my nipples.

I rocked against him, needing some friction between my legs. I wasn't used to this feeling, but I knew there was more and I wanted it. My shorts had ridden up my legs, so the tender skin of my inner thighs was rubbing against his jeans-clad legs. It was making me a little crazy. One of Jax's hands slipped out of my shirt, and I started to protest. But then I felt him touch my leg and slide up the overheated skin until his hand touched the edge of my shorts.

I forgot to breathe. Was he going to do something more? Was I ready for that? No. Probably not. My mother had made stupid decisions based on sex. I couldn't do that. I wasn't her.

Then his fingers slipped under the leg of my shorts and his forehead rested against my shoulder. I could hear his hard, heavy breathing as we both seemed frozen. I wanted to stop him, but I couldn't. The ache between my legs was throbbing so badly now that his fingers were moving closer to its heat. Even though I knew this was a bad idea, I wanted it. My body wanted it.

One long finger brushed the crotch of my panties, and I grabbed his shoulders and squeezed to keep from bolting off his lap.

"Sadie," he breathed out heavily, and swallowed loudly. "You're soaking wet . . . and so fucking hot."

I didn't know what that meant exactly, but I didn't have time to think about it because he ran that one lone finger back across my panties and groaned loudly. I was shaking. My entire body was ready to explode. Then his finger slipped under the fabric of my panties and touched me.

"Ohgod!" I cried out, and this time it was my head that fell against his shoulder. "Ohmygod," I repeated, unable to control my hips, which were moving closer to his touch. My body had decided my brain no longer mattered. It was taking over.

"Does that feel good?" he asked against my ear, then let his finger run back and forth across my swollen, very aroused flesh.

I managed a nod and bit my bottom lip to keep from crying out as the pad of his finger brushed a hot spot. One that had me wanting to rip his clothes off and force him to make this feeling go away. I wanted the fireworks.

"Do you know how much of a turn-on it is that you're so wet for me? Damn, baby, I don't know how I'm going to stop this. I wanna make you come. In my lap."

Oh, God. I liked dirty talk. I didn't know it until this moment, but I did. I liked it a lot. I made a pleading whimper and moved against his finger.

"I'll make it feel better," he promised, and started running his finger over the wetness he was so happy about. I was close to something, but I wasn't sure what just yet. Then I felt his hand shift and more fingers slipped inside my panties. I wasn't sure I could live through more of this.

The gentle nudging of his finger on my entrance made me freeze. What was he doing? His finger slid up inside me slowly, and instead of hurting, it felt amazing. I was breathing in short, fast gasps when his thumb ran over a spot that seemed to be holding all this intensity and he rubbed back and forth over it as his finger slid in and out of me.

I didn't have time to remember to breathe or to consider the fact that I was in a movie theater. I made a noise I didn't really recognize, and then the world went up in flames around me. I was pretty sure I'd just cried out Jax's name, and I was also pretty sure I was holding on to him for dear life as my body convulsed with pleasure.

As I slowly came down from what I knew was an orgasm—I'd heard about them and I knew I'd just had one—I buried my face in the crook of his neck. I couldn't look at him. I was pretty sure I'd just been very loud and screamed his name. His hand slipped out of my panties and I cringed from embarrassment. He slipped his arms around me and pulled me closer to his chest.

"Nothing . . ." He stopped and took a deep breath. "Nothing I have ever experienced has ever been that damn sexy. No, that doesn't even describe it. It was the hottest thing—no, it was the most amazing experience I've ever had. I'm gonna want more. You"—he let out a low chuckle—"you're gonna own me, Sadie White. Damn, baby, that was sweet."

Sweet? I had just screamed his name and acted like a crazy woman on his lap. I lifted my head to look at him. My face felt flushed, but I wasn't sure if it was because I was embarrassed or because of what had just happened. My body was still humming. "I was loud," I stated.

Jax grinned and reached up to run his thumb over my bottom lip. "Yeah, you were," he replied. "And it was really damn sexy."

I didn't understand this boy. But the way he was looking at me with such an adoring, worshipful gaze, I decided I didn't care. A giggle built up in my chest, and I pushed it down. "Um . . . that was . . . uh . . . really, really . . . good. I mean, it was more than good." I closed my eyes because unlike him, I was not good with words.

"It blew your mind and now you want to stay right here on my lap for the rest of the summer. I'm good with that. I like you straddling me." I could hear the teasing tone in his voice, and I laughed this time.

"I feel like I'm supposed to say thank you or something," I managed to say and sounded like an idiot.

Jax's grin only got bigger. "I can think of ways you can thank me. Let's start with you moving your cute little ass back into your seat so I can calm down a little. Because as perfect as you feel pressing up against me, I don't think I can take much more before I combust."

"Okay," I replied, and slid off his lap. His groan as I moved only made my heart rate pick back up again. I wanted to crawl right back up there and do that again, but I didn't. Because he was obviously still hard . . . and I wasn't sure how I could fix that. Was I supposed to?

"Your . . . um . . . you, uh . . . Can I do something to help that . . . er, I mean, you?" I asked, staring down at the erection outlined in his jeans.

"No. But please stop looking at it, because that's making it all kinds of painful."

I frowned up at him. "It hurts when I look at it?"

Jax closed his eyes tightly and laid his head back against the chair. "Yeah, it does. Think of it like this. It wants you. It wants parts of you it can't have. But he doesn't know that so he is very ready to take that part of you, and I have to convince him to calm the fuck down. But you looking at him confuses him and he ignores me and stays ready."

Had he really just referred to his penis as a person? I smiled and looked away from him and at the screen. It was very tempting to reach over and feel him because I was pretty sure he'd enjoy that, but then I was worried about him being in pain. But I wasn't ready for that. Especially in a movie theater. So I didn't look at him again, and I didn't touch him.

At some point, we finally caught up from what we missed in the movie. Jax managed to get himself calmed down enough to eat all his popcorn, a bag of M&M's, and some nachos and cheese. I only made it halfway through the popcorn, and I ate a few of his nachos and cheese, which he fed me. Well, he didn't have to try very hard. The minute he held one up to my mouth, I took it.

We exited the theater as easily as we'd entered. Jax slipped his disguise back on. "How about a walk on the beach?"

I liked that idea, especially at this time of day. I also liked the idea of kissing him again. I wanted to touch him this time. "Sounds good, but don't go to the public beach."

He pointed to his hat and glasses. "I'm in disguise, and no one will look close enough to realize it's me."

I thought about Amanda and her friends. If they noticed Jax, things would get out of hand, and quickly. "I know people on the public beach. Remember, I live here. I go to school with these kids. If any of them come up to speak to me, then they'll notice it's you."

Jax didn't say anything, but a frown set in on his perfect features.

"What did I say?" I asked when he didn't reply.

He glanced at me as if he didn't want to answer my question. "I guess I forget you have a life other than my house and me. I like having you all to myself, and I know it's selfish, but the fact that you're going to go back to school to live a normal teenage life with parties and football games and dances makes me jealous as hell."

I let out a shocked laugh. "My life is a lot easier to accept than yours. You leave to go to movie premieres, and you're on the covers of magazines, and the entertainment shows follow everything you do. I have to live with you going back to another world. When you're onstage, you belong to everyone."

He didn't respond for what seemed like forever. We pulled into a secluded part of the beach, and he turned off the engine.

"I know being with me isn't easy. But I want you to understand that no one has me, or has ever had me, except you."

I swallowed, emotion building inside me. I nodded, not sure my voice would work.

He slipped a curl behind my ear. "I've never met anyone who has seen past the star and found the real me inside. But even if you hadn't found the Jax the world doesn't know, I would be yours. When you smiled at me that first time, I was a goner. I just got lucky with the rest of you."

I wanted to lean in to him, but I didn't.

"Come on, let's go for a walk before I start kissing you again and am forced to use superhuman willpower to stop myself."

I laughed, and we climbed out of the Jaguar. As we walked toward the water's edge, Jax took my hand in his.

The night breeze and the sounds of the waves were soothing. It was easy to forget reality out here.

"When I came home last night, I wanted to call you right away and realized I couldn't. It proved really hard to go to sleep without hearing your voice and knowing you were okay," Jax admitted.

"I'm sorry you couldn't call me, but it makes me happy to know you missed me too."

He laughed. "I didn't just miss you. I obsessed over what you were doing and if you were okay and who you were talking to. I realized I'm going to have a really hard time when the summer is over. And now that I've touched you and had you come apart in my arms, I can't stand the thought of sharing you. I know that sounds selfish because of who I am. But I don't want anyone else to touch you."

He stopped, and I turned to him.

"I have a charity event I've got to be at next week. They're auctioning off some of my things, and I have to be there too. I want you to come with me."

My heart hammered in my chest. Going with him into his world wasn't something I'd ever expected to do. "I don't know. I have work and my mom."

"Please, for me. Don't make me go again without you."

I turned away from his pleading eyes. They made me want to promise him anything. "Jax, I won't fit into your world. I don't have any clothes to wear to something like that, and I have no idea what to say to people or how to act, and the cameras will make me a nervous wreck."

He stepped up behind me, pulled me up against him, and rested his chin on my head. "You'll be dressed by my personal stylist, and you won't have to speak to anyone but me. Yes, the cameras will be going, but all you have to do is smile. I'll never leave you alone, except when I have to sing, and then you can stand backstage and wait for me."

I wanted to make him happy. I wanted to know every part of his life, but it terrified me. "I don't know," I whispered.

We stood there for a long time without words.

Finally, he turned me around to face him. "Please. I need my air."

My resolve crumbled, and I nodded. "Okay, I'll talk to my mom."

His earnest face broke into a grin, and he kissed me again. He held back, and it made me want to press closer. He pulled back before I could press him.

"You taste so good," he whispered. He ran his fingers through my hair and curled a strand around his fingers. "I love your hair," he said softly, and continued playing with it.

# Chapter Ten

## JAX

The way Sadie's eyes had lit up with excitement when I touched her had me thinking all kinds of things I didn't need to be. From the way she'd come apart in my lap from such a simple touch, I had no doubt she was innocent. Then she'd also been so fucking tight, there was no way she wasn't still a virgin. That was something that I had a hard time imagining. Were guys in Alabama idiots? Blind? How was it that Sadie was so untouched, as gorgeous as she was? It made no sense, but I could already feel a possessiveness taking over me. I'd never been possessive over any girl. I hadn't had to be. Normally, I was pushing them away or hiding from them. With Sadie I wanted her beside me all the time. And after today I wanted her in my arms, or on my lap. Who was I kidding? I wanted her in my bed.

That wasn't something that was going to happen, though. My plans to leave hadn't changed. I had to leave when the summer was over. I had a tour scheduled, and my life had no room for relationships. At least, not the kind that I'd want with Sadie.

"Why are you frowning?" Sadie asked, and I pulled her closer to me. I hated the idea of walking away from her and leaving her here, available for some other guy to experience what I'd just experienced—or more. I felt my chest tightening, and the urge to grab her in my arms and run off with her somewhere no one could find us was overwhelming.

Sadie's hand cupped the side of my face. "Did I make you mad?" she asked softly.

I had to get this under control. She didn't understand the sudden rage pumping through my veins. I'd kill another guy if he touched her. That sounded unfair, and it also sounded impossible, but if I ever saw another guy touch her, I would lose my mind.

"You could never make me mad. I'm just thinking about things that upset me, and I shouldn't. I'm here with you. And all I want to think about is how I got so damn lucky."

Sadie grinned up at me. "That's silly. You're the untouchable rock star. I'm just a girl. The world would see it as me being the lucky one."

The world didn't have a clue. I was normally a selfish bastard when it came to girls and relationships. I didn't want them around unless I was in need of some relief. I didn't care about their feelings, and I didn't have time to cuddle them and make them feel needed. If a girl wanted me, then she got nothing more than me physically. I wasn't into anything more. Until now. Until Sadie.

I didn't have words for her. I couldn't explain to her what an absolute ass I'd become. The guy she knew was the guy I'd once been. The guy I'd been before the world knew my name. She had found me and reminded me of what it felt like to be real. To care. To need. I slipped my hands around her waist and lowered my mouth until it hovered over hers. "You saved me, Sadie. You may not realize it, but you did," I told her before claiming her mouth.

## SADIE

Ms. Mary started fussing over me the moment I walked in the door. Jax smiled and enjoyed it immensely as I assured her that Jessica and I were both fine.

"Girl your age havin' to run her mama to the doctor in the middle of the night ain't right, I tell ya. You're too young to be sleeping in a waiting room all by yourself." She turned and pointed her spoon at Jax. "You should have been there. What good are you if you ain't there when she needs you?"

"Ms. Mary, he didn't know about it either. I didn't call anyone. You can't blame Jax for anything."

Ms. Mary let out a loud "hmph" and started stirring her

pot of cheese grits again. "Well, you should've called him. He would've come. You're too young to be alone in hospitals. Crazy people out there."

Jax took my plate to the table, then crooked his finger for me to come sit down. I sat beside him.

"I didn't think about calling anyone. I've been taking care of my mother for a long time now. It's no big deal."

Ms. Mary spun around and pointed her spoon at me. "And that's not right. Who takes care of you?" She waited for my answer, and getting none, she nodded. "That's right, no one does. You don't know when to ask for help because you never had anyone to ask before. Well, now you do. You got a boy right there who looks like he would drink your bathwater if you asked him, and you got me and Mr. Greg and Marcus. Take your pick. Just stop trying to do it all alone." She let out a deep sigh and turned back to her stove.

Jax squeezed my hand. "She's right. Call me."

I smiled at him, and he grinned.

"And, yes, if you want me to, I'll drink your bathwater."

I laughed out loud and shook my head. "You're crazy."

"About you."

My heart skipped a beat, and I took a deep breath to calm down. "I'm sorry I didn't call you. She's right. I'm not used to asking for help. But it's nice to know I have people around me who care. This is all new to me."

Jax leaned over and whispered in my ear, "No matter where I am, I'll always be there when you need me."

I shivered from his warm breath against my skin and nodded, but I didn't meet his gaze. I needed to get my heart out of my eyes first.

Marcus walked in as we were finishing our breakfast. He stared at me when he stepped into the kitchen. "Is your mom all right?"

"Yes, thank you."

He gave me a forced smile. "Good," he said, and walked to the laundry room to get dressed.

I turned to Jax as he finished his juice. "I need to get to work too."

He frowned, then stood up and took both our plates to the sink and rinsed them. I went to get my apron, and Ms. Mary shook her head.

"No, Mr. Greg needs you outside more than I need you in here. He's battling his arthritis today. He won't admit it, but I can see it on his face. Go help him."

I nodded. I would need to go change into my shorts. I looked back at Jax to say good-bye before I left.

He smiled at me. "I have a song I'm working on, and sitting out at the gazebo today sounds like the perfect place to be creative. I'll see you in a few minutes."

Knowing Jax would be outside with me today made the day

seem much brighter. I walked over to Mr. Greg, who was kneeling in the herb garden, mumbling to himself.

"Morning, Mr. Greg. Why don't you get off those knees and let me do this?"

He frowned at me. "I have a bone to pick with you, young lady. Ain't no girl your age supposed to be gallivanting across town in the middle of the night. You should've called me."

My insides grew warm and toasty. I really had made a new family here. "I know, Mr. Greg, and I'm sorry. I'm just used to taking care of things on my own, and I didn't think about the fact that I have people who care enough to help me."

He stood up slowly, and I fought the urge to give him my arm. I knew his pride wouldn't take my offer very well.

"Just so you understand you've got people to help you now. Lord knows the Stone boy would've come running if you'd called him. I ain't never seen such a lovesick puppy in all my life."

I blushed. "I wouldn't call him lovesick."

Mr. Greg raised an eyebrow. "Is that so?" he said, and shook his head. "Well now, I guess we got work to talk about, now, don't we? Go ahead and weed this here garden, but be careful of the herbs. Once you're done, go ahead and pull some rosemary and dill weed for Ms. Mary. She needs some for the kitchen. I'm going to go rake the sand and get it smooth around the bridge."

I nodded, kneeled, and started weeding. Herb garden weeding was never easy, because so many herbs resembled weeds. It wasn't something I could do mindlessly, so I focused on my job.

The sound of a guitar broke my concentration, and I glanced up to see Jax sitting in the gazebo, strumming away and watching me. I grinned and waved, then turned back to my weeds. It proved hard to think about what I needed to be doing when his voice floated across the yard. I stopped several times to listen to his words, but I didn't dare look at him. His music soon became sporadic, and I turned to see him writing on a piece of paper and working diligently over his guitar. His frown and concentration made it hard not to stare. I knew if he caught me, it might mess up his process. Other times, I caught him watching me, and he would wink, and I, in turn, would blush. However, the heat of the day made my cheeks pink, which thankfully helped hide it.

After I'd finished weeding and had taken Ms. Mary the rosemary and dill weed, I was given the job of picking up any debris that might have blown in overnight. I'd just finished carrying a handful of twigs over to Mr. Greg's wheelbarrow when Jason came out. He went over to Jax, and I went back to picking up debris. Jax got up and followed Jason inside. I tried not to wonder about where the brothers were going, and I focused on my job.

Marcus came out to get me for lunch, and I went inside to eat with him, Ms. Mary, and Fran. Everyone seemed quiet, so I didn't talk much either. Fran mentioned she needed to write up a list of cleaning supplies to be picked up from the store, and

Marcus made us all laugh with stories about the new guy at the front gate. Ms. Mary seemed nervous about something, and Fran wouldn't meet my eyes. Only Marcus seemed his normal self. After we ate, I started cleaning and preparing the fresh fruit Ms. Mary had bought from the farmers' market.

I tried to stay focused on my job, and at dinnertime, when Jax still hadn't returned to the gazebo, I agreed to a chess match with Mr. Greg. I'd put him off several times the past week because Jax had always been waiting on me. Although I seemed to be getting better, and had even won a few matches recently, today Mr. Greg won because my mind stayed on Jax. I let the old man gloat, and I smiled at his teasing, then went inside to the kitchen.

Marcus stood over by the table with a tray of food. He smiled at me. "Hey, you. Who won the chess game? I saw you two hard at it when I came in."

I smiled and shrugged. "He did. I was off my game tonight."

Marcus frowned and sighed. "Yeah, I can understand. You two have been inseparable lately. I can see why her arrival would bother you."

His words startled me. "What do you mean? Her who?"

Marcus darted his eyes at Ms. Mary, who made a "tsk" sound but kept her back to both of us.

"Uh, sorry, I thought you knew. I, um . . ." He paused and shuffled his feet like he would rather leave the room.

Ms. Mary let out a sigh. "Go ahead and get it out, boy. You done let the cat out of the bag. Don't leave her to wonder."

Marcus nodded and said to me, "I don't know how much of the celebrity stuff you read, but Star Holloway, the pop princess, and Jax have been an item for a while now. Even before he came here this summer. She flew in on his private jet this afternoon and is staying the night before she heads back out to finish her tour."

My knees went weak.

"Now, don't go making it sound worse than it is, boy," Ms. Mary scolded. "I believe she is just a friend of Master Jax's. The way he has been following you around like a puppy dog, I can't fathom he has another girl."

I couldn't form words. I stared at Marcus, who shrugged. I didn't know what to say or what to think. I needed time alone, so I headed to the laundry room to change. The idea that Jax had a pop-star girlfriend didn't make sense to me. He'd never spoken of her before. But I didn't think Marcus would lie to me. Star Holloway was in this house, and she also happened to be the reason Jax had never came back out to the gazebo. It hurt that he'd never taken the time to explain. But then again, what could he tell his guest, "Excuse me, but I need to go tell the kitchen help you're here that and I won't be coming back to see her today"? I mean, really, this situation would be hard to grasp for someone in his world.

I took a deep breath and reminded myself I'd known all along a relationship with him was impossible. He was a rock star, and I worked in his kitchen and his garden. I'd walked right into a situation with no happy ending, and I'd known it but taken that road anyway, just because a pair of steel-blue eyes made my heart race and a boyish grin made me melt. "Stupid" might be too kind a word for me. I swallowed the lump in my throat and stepped out of the laundry room.

I walked past Ms. Mary, who stood wringing her hands, waiting for me. "I knew you was gonna get hurt," she said with worry in her voice.

I bit my bottom lip, still not trusting myself to speak. "You wait, now, on Marcus. He'll take you home." The thought of having to talk to Marcus, and waiting at the house any longer while Jax sat in the dining room with a pop princess, who for obvious reasons made a much better match for him than I did, panicked me. I needed to escape. I swallowed again and said to Ms. Mary, "I'm fine, but I want to go home now. I'll see you in the morning. A bike ride is just what I need."

I smiled, but it didn't reach my eyes. Ms. Mary frowned and reminded me to be careful. I headed home as quickly as I could. The farther away I got, the harder the idea of going back the next day seemed. The thought hurt so badly I wasn't sure I could do it. I'm only so strong; I have a breaking point. I'd asked for this when I'd agreed to this thing with Jax. I'd allowed myself to be dazzled by his good looks and charming personality. His intense eyes and boyish grin somehow made me stupid and careless. I needed protection from myself. The horrifying thought that I might be like my mother hit me, and tears burned my eyes. I'd let him touch me, and I'd even wanted to touch him. I hadn't even known he had a girlfriend. Maybe if I'd watched more television I'd have known this. How stupid could I be? I knew nothing about Jax but that he was a rock star. I hadn't thought to check into his personal life.

I stopped at the public beach. A walk would help calm me down before I went home to face Jessica.

Amanda started coming down from the lifeguard stand. When she saw me, she shot her carefree, bubbly grin at me. "Sadie! I called you just this morning, but I didn't get an answer. I left a message, though. So, are you coming?"

I'd forgotten about the party. "Um, sure, I'll come."

She appeared genuinely happy. I couldn't figure out why this nice, cheerful girl seemed so anxious to be my friend.

"About the lifeguarding job. How much does it pay?"

She beamed at me again, apparently thrilled at the idea of my being a lifeguard. "Twelve dollars an hour, and you get the benefits of being at the beach all day!"

That was what I made now. It was good money, but I wouldn't get nearly as many hours. But it might be enough. "All right. If I were interested, what would I need to do?"

She grabbed my hand and led me over to the building located off the boardwalk, with bathrooms, a beach bar, and some offices. "You need to go in there and see Jerry in the morning. He can give you all your info. There is endurance training and a few days of classes. How long it takes depends on how well you do. But Jess just quit last week, and we're short a lifeguard, so now is a good time to go see him."

I nodded and tucked the information away. "Thanks. I'll see you tomorrow night, then."

Amanda smiled brightly. "Cool. See ya."

I turned and walked down the beach. I'd worn shorts and a blue tank top, but the evening breeze still held the day's warmth, so it didn't matter. I walked to the edge of the public beach and sat down on one of the deserted wooden chair rentals. Without the cushions that came with them, they were a little painful, but if I sat on the beach I'd get all sandy.

I lay back and closed my eyes, letting the sound of the ocean waves soothe me. I'd let this happen. I'd known when I agreed to spend time with Jax I would end up caring way too much. He'd never said we were exclusive. He'd never said he loved me. Yes, he had said many other things, like about my being his air and his needing me, but now all those words seemed almost unreal. Frustrated with myself for doing exactly what every other girl in America would do, I knew I wasn't any different from the rest of them. His eyes and smile melted me and sent warm shivers down my spine. I needed to get a grip and get over it. Jax liked spending time with me because I happened to be a no-strings-attached deal. He liked being around me because I didn't think everything he did was wonderful. He had enough admirers. He hadn't asked for or required my love. I'd gone and fallen in love with him of my own free will. I rubbed my eyes with my fists and fought the stupid tears spilling out. Crying would not help this or make it better. Yet here I sat, alone on the beach, crying like a lovesick loser.

"Ugh!" I sat up and wiped my face with my shirt and decided I wouldn't cry another tear over Jax Stone.

My chest ached at the thought of leaving Ms. Mary and Mr. Greg and Marcus. . . . Heck, I would even miss Fran. But could I stay there and see him and be at his house, loving him the way I did? I let out a sigh, not sure what to do. At times like this, I really needed a mother with common sense and wise words.

"Sadie."

I turned. Marcus was walking toward me. I wiped the rest of my tears away and stood. He still wore his white dress shirt from work, but it was untucked and the collar was loosened.

When he got close enough to me to hear my voice over the wind and waves, I asked, "Marcus, what are you doing here?"

He grinned sheepishly and pointed with his thumb over his shoulder back at the lifeguard station. "I've got an inside source."

Confused, I frowned and looked to where I'd talked to Amanda.

He saw the frown on my face and gave a dramatic sigh. "Do you know Amanda's last name?"

I shook my head slowly, trying to remember if she'd told me her last name.

"Amanda Hardy, a.k.a. my little sister."

My mouth formed an O, and I turned back to him, studying his attractive features. Suddenly I realized he and his sister shared the same eyes and smile. "Does she know I work with you?" She'd never said anything to me before, and her friendliness made a lot more sense coming from the sister of my friend.

He nodded as if found guilty of a crime. "Yes. I mentioned you on your first night of work when I got home, and she remembered you from school."

I nodded, still shocked at the connection. I'd really never thought about the fact that Marcus had family around here and that I might know the people in it.

And then it hit me: She knew about Jax. "Does she know ... ?"

Marcus shook his head. "No. No, I can't tell her about Jax. She would freak out and start stalking my workplace."

I smiled sadly, but a wave of relief washed over me. "I don't see her as the stalking type."

Marcus laughed and raised his blond eyebrows. "Jax Stone happens to be all over her bedroom walls."

I smiled and sat back down. "Why did you come to find me?"

Marcus sat down in the chair beside me. "You're my friend, and I didn't like knowing you were hurt. I wish you would've waited on me to take you home, but I understand why you wanted to leave."

I didn't reply, because I wasn't really sure what to say. We stared out at the water for some time.

Finally, Marcus said to me, "You knew he would only be here for a little while. He's gonna leave, and you're gonna be left here. Your worlds are too different." He stopped and cleared his throat. "You're not like other girls, Sadie, and that's attractive to a guy. We get tired of the same stuff, and when someone as beautiful as you comes along, with all your sweet, naive, accepting ways—someone like you is what we're all searching for."

I started to argue, but he held up his hands to stop me.

"I'm not saying any of this right, so let me finish and see if I can explain this better. When I first saw you, I was immediately attracted to your outward appearance. However, after talking to you, getting to know you, and watching you at work, I realized I would've been attracted to you if you were plain and mousy. My guess is, Jax hasn't been around anyone with your traits in a long time, and mix it all in with the fact that you're a gorgeous blonde and *bam*, he got hooked. I can't blame him for wanting you." Marcus's hand fisted in his lap. He seemed angry now. "But I can fault him for acting on his interest in you. He unleashed all his charm on you, knowing it could only be for a short time. And for that, I'm going to make sure he pays."

A sudden knot of fear formed in my stomach. "Marcus, *no*! I chose this. You're right, I knew it wasn't as serious to him, or even long term. I let myself care too much, and it's my stupidity. Nothing he did was wrong."

Marcus shook his head. "He's older and more knowledgeable about the ways of the world than you. I blame him."

I laughed. Not sure how, but I did. "I need a friend, Marcus, not a white knight."

Marcus grinned. "I am your friend, Sadie, and that will never change. However, I wouldn't mind being your white knight, too."

I shook my head. "I didn't really choose him, Marcus. My heart did. I didn't want to love him. I knew he would end up breaking my heart, but I couldn't stop it. Every time I got around him, I fell harder. He isn't the guy everyone sees on television. He isn't some rich, shallow rocker. He has a kind heart, and there is this little boy inside him who still needs approval from those he cares about. He accepts others for who they are, and he never judges anyone."

Marcus's expression seemed so sad. "You got inside the star and found the heart. It'll only make this harder on you." He reached over and took my hand. "I'm here with a shoulder to cry on, whenever you need it."

I wanted to cry now, but I knew I couldn't do so in front of

Marcus. I didn't want him mad at Jax because I'd turned into a silly lovesick fool. Instead, I stood up. "I need to head home."

I slipped my hands into the pockets of my shorts. The evening wind had begun to cool.

"Can I take you home?"

I thought about it, then shook my head. "I'm close to home, and the ride will be good for me."

"Okay, if that is what you want."

"It is," I assured him.

"Will you be at work tomorrow, or are you going to be up here for the lifeguarding job?"

"I'll be at work." I hadn't realized I'd made my decision until I said it aloud.

# Chapter Eleven

**JAX**

Star had taken up more of my time than I'd expected. I wasn't good with females' tears, so I had sat there and let her cry and tell me over and over again how upset she was that Shawn hadn't trusted her enough. When she'd said that she wasn't sure she had made the right choice of career, I had for a moment understood her. The life we'd chosen to lead didn't make it easy for anyone to ever get close to us.

Once she'd finally stopped crying and gone up to the guest bedroom Ms. Mary had put her in, I'd gone to find Sadie and explain this mess. I had wanted to tell her when Jason had come to get me earlier, but he'd said Star had taken one look at him and crumpled to the floor and begun to sob. I'd needed to go then and help him calm her down.

I walked outside, and there was no sign of Sadie or Mr. Greg. Frustrated, I turned and headed to the kitchen. Maybe she'd gone in there to wait for me.

When I got inside, Ms. Mary didn't look up at me. She continued to wash the large pots in the sink. That was odd. She always stopped what she was doing and asked if I needed something. More important, though, was the fact Sadie wasn't in here, either.

"Ms. Mary? Do you know where Sadie is?"

Ms. Mary made a "hmph" sound, then let the pot clang in the sink before looking up at me. "Marcus called and said he found her at the beach. She was fine and headed home."

She was gone? *Shit!* "Why did she leave?" I asked, already fearing the answer.

Ms. Mary threw her dishcloth into the sink and put her hands on her hips before glaring at me. "You really asking me that, boy? 'Cause I don't know how things are done up there in Hollywood, but here in the South, girls don't know how to play your games. 'Specially sweet girls like Sadie. She don't got no time for this funny business. You said you wouldn't hurt her, and it took you no time to do just that. Now, Marcus is gonna be there to let her cry on his shoulder, and you go back to your girlfriend and leave poor little Sadie alone. God knows Marcus has a thing for the girl. He'd be good to her. He comes from a good family. He can take care of her too."

I was torn between wanting to beat the shit out of Marcus for going near her, and not being able to breathe because she was hurting. I didn't want Sadie hurting.

"Star isn't my girlfriend," I said defensively.

"Well, the rest of the world only knows what the media tells us, and last we all heard, she was. And Sadie knows you been locked up there with her all day. She ran outta here so fast I had to let Marcus go early so he could run after her and make sure she was safe."

Marcus was all in my business. I didn't like that guy. He was waiting. He wanted me to hurt her so he could move in. He lived here, and when I was gone he was planning on moving in on her. I could see it, and the red-hot jealousy from the idea of Marcus touching Sadie made me go a little mad.

"I'm going to her house. I need to see she's there."

Ms. Mary shook her head and turned back to her dishes. "Girl needs a man who can take care of her. Not a rock star."

She was right, but dammit, I loved her. I couldn't give her up. Not now.

**SADIE**

I lost count of the times I'd attempted to talk myself out of returning to the Stone mansion. I kept reminding myself that we needed the money, and that I would not act like Jessica. I did *not* run away from life. I faced my problems and dealt with them. I could be stronger than a broken heart. Foolishly, I'd given my heart away to someone who didn't need it or expect it. It was my fault, and my fault alone. Lesson learned. I'd learned a long time ago not to make the same mistake twice.

I opened the kitchen door, and Ms. Mary turned to look at me. Relief washed over her face. She must have worried I wouldn't come back. Her expression, and knowing that I would've been missed, made my returning worth it.

"Morning, Ms. Mary." I glanced over at the table, expecting it to be empty, and I froze in place at the sight of Jax sitting in his usual spot. A concerned frown wrinkled his forehead.

I nodded a silent hello and forced myself to face Ms. Mary. "If it's all the same to you, I would like to get an early start on the garden this morning. Can I come back later to help you with the food prep?"

Ms. Mary cleared her throat. She seemed a little unsure, and finally managed to nod. "Mr. Greg will be happy to see you so early."

I went straight to the laundry room and changed. I couldn't deal with Jax this morning. I needed time. Besides, I needed to work and didn't have time to talk. My uniform would be cleaned and pressed, hanging in the closet with all the others. I sifted through until I found mine. The last time I'd been doing this exact same thing, my heart had been racing wildly, knowing Jax would be waiting on me. So much could happen in a day. My heart broke a little more, and I shook my head to clear my thoughts. I could not keep going like this. I needed to get some form of control over my emotions.

Why was it when I finally fell in love, I had to choose a teen idol? Couldn't I be like normal girls and fall in love with a guy from school? Or a guy from work? Take Marcus, for example. Why did my heart have to do the tango for Jax, but not even skip a beat for Marcus? I growled in frustration at my own stupidity. I would find a way to get over this.

I buttoned up my shirt and took one more deep, calming breath, just in case Jax still sat in the kitchen.

When I opened the door to the laundry room and stepped out, Jax blocked my way. I should have expected him to follow me. Jax Stone didn't get blown off by a girl. This couldn't be something he knew how to handle. I sighed, knowing I couldn't get past without him letting me by, so I backed up to put some distance between us.

"Sadie, please, come talk to me."

"I need to get to work."

He reached out for my hand, and I immediately snatched it back and pocketed both of my hands. "Sadie, please." I hated that when I saw the insecure little boy I saw in his eyes, it got to me. Dang it.

"There is nothing to talk about, Jax. I work here; we're friends, I guess; and you spent some extra time with me. Your girlfriend is here. No big deal. Now, if you'll move."

He took my arms and gently but firmly pushed me back into the laundry room and closed the door behind him.

"What're you doing?" I asked when I realized he'd locked us in.

"We need to get a few things clear, and I can't let you go to work until I know you understand."

I hated the way he acted as if I needed to be reminded of reality. I stiffened and turned to glare out the window.

"Do you remember when I told you I have to get my picture taken with every female teen star in the vicinity for publicity?"

I didn't turn or acknowledge his words.

He sighed. "I know you do. Anyway, Star and I have been thrown together since we were fifteen. She's the female me in the teen world, and people like to dream up romances between us. Because we have both spent our teen years in front of the camera, we've become friends."

Nausea boiled inside me. I didn't need a reminder that Star would be a much better match for him.

"But friends is all we've ever really been. I'm not going to lie, because in the beginning we did try out a relationship. It seemed natural for us, but it failed miserably. We were able to call it quits and remain friends. I didn't know she was coming yesterday. She has been in love with a boy from her hometown for years. They've struggled to make things work, but with her lifestyle, they never had enough time together. She just found out he is getting married next week. He got a girl pregnant, and Star is torn up about it. So she came here to see me. She needed a friend."

He stopped talking, and I knew I needed to turn around and respond. I just wasn't sure how without acting like the hopelessly lovesick idiot I'd become. I took a deep breath and exhaled, hoping to calm my emotions, and turned around.

"You didn't have to explain anything to me. I've known all along you live in a world I know nothing about, nor will I ever know anything about. I'm just another girl you spent time with for a couple of weeks one summer." I forced a smile and nodded toward the door. "Now we have all this cleared up, I need to get to work."

I stepped toward the exit, and Jax's hand shot out and grabbed my arm. I closed my eyes and waited for him to speak.

"You think you're just someone I spent time with?"

I swallowed the lump in my throat. He looked at me incredulously, and I wasn't sure what to say. I returned his stare. He seemed angry and hurt. I hated knowing I'd hurt him.

"What am I, then, Jax?" I heard myself whisper. "How can I ever be more than that?"

He pulled me up close to him. "You have been more than that since the first night I took you home. You want to know what you are?" He took my hand and placed it over his heart. "You're the person who owns this."

Tears stung my eyes. "I don't want to love you," I forced out through the thickness in my throat.

"God, I hope you do, because you own me completely," he whispered, and then leaned down and kissed me with such emotion the tears escaped and slid down my face. He held my face as he kissed me, until my knees went weak and I held on to his arms to keep from falling. When he broke the kiss, he didn't let me go, thankfully, because without his support, I would not have had the strength to stand.

"I should've come and told you, but she kept crying and going on and on about everything they had been through. She needed an ear, and I gave her one. I knew when I came to get you last night and you were gone, I'd screwed up. Promise me you won't ever ride home by yourself again. I sat in your driveway last night after I'd made sure your bike was there and watched the windows for a long time, wondering which one was yours. If I'd known, I would've come to you then, but I didn't want to wake your mom." He tucked a curl behind my ear, and I shivered at his touch. "I'm trying to make myself let you go before Ms. Mary comes to get you, but you go and shiver at my touch and weaken my resolve to stop holding you."

He laid my head against his chest, and I smiled. He loved me. I knew heartache would be inevitable when he left, but I knew he loved me.

I waited on Jax out in the gazebo after work. I'd promised Amanda I'd come to the party with her tonight. She sent a message through

Marcus about where to meet her and what time. I'd forgotten until he reminded me. I needed to talk to Jax about it, because if he wanted to do something with me, I would cancel my prior plans. Now I wished I hadn't accepted Amanda's invitation, but she had seemed so excited about introducing me to people.

"Why the frown, gorgeous?" Jax stepped into the gazebo and came to sit by me.

"I didn't realize I was frowning. I'm just thinking."

"About?"

I sighed. "I've been invited to a party at a guy's house from school. Marcus's younger sister, Amanda, is in my grade, and she invited me to come with her. I told her yes, but it was last night when I was angry with you because of Star."

He leaned back and put his arm behind me. "Well, would you be against going to the party with a date?"

I stiffened. "A date?"

He smiled. "Yes, unless you're ashamed to be seen with me in public."

I didn't know what he meant. Surely he couldn't mean he would go himself. "You mean, you want to go to a party?"

He nodded. "Yes, I think I do."

I frowned and decided to point out the obvious. "You're aware these people are going to flip out over you, right?"

He shrugged. "Probably at first, but I figure they'll get over the initial shock and leave us alone."

"I can cancel."

He shook his head, sat up, and turned toward me. "I'm going for a selfish reason. I want them to know you're mine."

"Okay, but what purpose does this serve, except to make me the envy of every female in town?"

He grinned. "It'll let the male population know you're not available and to stay away."

I laughed. "All right, then, Mr. Hotshot Rock Star, let's go to the party so you can intimidate all the guys in a fifty-mile radius."

We stopped at my house so I could run inside and change clothes. Apparently, the dress code was swimsuits. I slipped a black see-through cover-up over my bikini and a pair of black heeled sandals on my feet, and let my hair down to its wild, natural, curly mess. For the first time in my life, I could be accused of being vain, and I knew it, but I wanted to look worthy of Jax tonight. I put on some red lipstick and mascara, and then stood back and appraised myself. My reflection surprised me. The black mascara really made my already dark lashes stand out. I went into the living room to tell Jessica bye. She stopped watching her reality television show and looked me up and down, then broke into a smile.

"You can thank me for those good genes you've decided to flaunt tonight."

I rolled my eyes. "I'll be late."

She waved me off. "Be careful and all that stuff." I sighed and headed for the door. She hadn't even asked me whom I'd dressed up for. Most girls my age wished their mothers would leave them alone, and I wished mine would just care. I grabbed my purse and headed back out to Jax and his Hummer. I'd left him outside for fear Jessica would be parading around in her underwear. He stepped away from the Hummer, and his gaze took me in. I was glad I had put the heels on because I knew it helped make my long legs seem less lanky.

He let out a low whistle. "Wow, you're incredible."

I smiled and blushed. "Thank you," I replied.

He frowned. "Now, could you go back inside and make yourself less sexy?"

"What?"

He sighed. "You were worried about me attracting attention, and you've gone in there and unleashed all your deadly weapons." His gaze skimmed my legs again. "Damn, Sadie, I'm going to have a hard time with self-control tonight, and I swear, if I catch one guy ogling you, he's going to be able to tell the world he got his ass kicked by Jax Stone."

I laughed out loud and rolled my eyes. "You're a little biased."

He raised his eyebrows. "Do you have mirrors in your apartment?"

I nodded.

"Did you use any of them, or did you manage to become every guy's fantasy without any visual help?"

I stepped around him. "You're overreacting. Now come on, let's go."

His arms slid around my waist from behind me as he pulled me up against his chest. He buried his face in my neck and groaned. "You smell heavenly."

I smiled and leaned back against him. "Thank you."

He kissed my neck and nibbled on my ear. My knees went weak, and goose bumps broke out on my body.

"Jax," I whispered, "if you keep this up, you're going to have to put me in the Hummer. I'm only so strong."

He chuckled against my neck, opened the door, and set me in my seat. He gave me one last smile, which sent shivers through my body, then closed the door. I'd never really felt sexy before, but tonight I did. I knew it was because of him. Just maybe our being together would be believable. But I doubted it seriously.

We pulled into the driveway, and I immediately spotted Amanda watching for me and my bike.

I turned to Jax. "When Amanda sees me step out of this vehicle with you, she's going to flip out. So get prepared."

He laughed. "You act like I'm not used to being treated like a celebrity." He squeezed my hand. "It's fine. Stop worrying. I'm used to this. I don't normally live in hiding like I do here. I know how to handle it."

I took a deep breath and exhaled. "Let's go."

Jax put his hand on my leg. "I'm getting you out, so stay put."

He held my hand as we made our way toward Amanda, who stood frozen in place with her mouth hanging open.

"Hey, I, um, brought a guest. I hope it's all right." It sounded stupid, but I didn't know what else to say.

She covered her gaping mouth with a trembling hand. "Yes, it's fine," she said through her hand, staring at Jax in disbelief, and I smiled because I completely understood her disbelief.

"Amanda, this is Jax. Jax, this is Amanda, a friend of mine from school."

Jax held out his hand and unleashed his lethal grin on her, and I was afraid she might faint. She shook his hand and gawked at him, but she didn't seem to be able to speak. "It's nice to meet you, Amanda."

Amanda whimpered.

Jax finally broke the handshake and stepped back.

She gathered herself back together. "Okay, great. Um, you guys come this way. Dylan is going to, uh, want to meet you."

I turned to Jax, and he smiled to reassure me. We followed Amanda, who kept glancing back at us every few seconds to make sure we hadn't vanished. The two-story yellow beach-style house seemed nice, but nothing like what Jax lived in. I saw people in every doorway and some windows. We went past the house and toward the sound of live music. In the center of the backyard stood a large stage. People were dancing in front of the stage and all down a bridge connecting the yard to the sandy white beach.

We followed Amanda into the large party area. A bonfire blazed down on the beach, and more people were out there. I began to notice people staring at us, trying to decide whether or not this was, in fact, Jax Stone. Amanda led us to a group of guys sitting around a hot tub, drinking with a few girls in tiny bikinis. She cleared her throat, and a tall, lanky guy with a shaved head turned toward her.

"Dylan, this is my friend Sadie I told you about."

He looked at me and gave me a slow smile. "Amanda said you were at school last year. How did I miss you?" he asked, his smile turning into a cocky grin.

Before I could think of anything to say, Amanda cleared her throat again and said, "And this is her date tonight, Jax Stone."

Dylan stopped leering at me and shifted his gaze toward Jax, who slipped his arm around my waist. Jax acted so calm and comfortable, almost as though he knew everyone here and wasn't about to get slammed with crazy fans.

"Jax Stone." Dylan stood and stared in disbelief.

Jax, once again, ever so politely, held out his hand. "I'm sorry about crashing your party."

Shaking his head, Dylan recovered a bit and took Jax's hand. "No way! Hell, you aren't crashing my party. You're Jax *fuckin'* Stone. You don't need an invite anywhere, man. Especially here!"

The girls in the hot tub stirred from their initial shock and got out of the water to come around to where we stood.

"Oh. My. God! I'm such a big fan! My name is Gabby Montess. I have your newest CD in my car. Will you please sign it for me?"

Jax smiled politely and nodded. "I'd be glad to, Gabby."

Gabby grabbed her still speechless friend's hand, and they squealed together as they ran for the CD and a pen. Others, realizing what was happening, had us surrounded within seconds. Girls calling Jax's name shoved paper and pens toward him, as well as shirts and shoes and bags and even a pair of panties. Jax had been forced to release me to sign autographs, so I decided to get out of the chaos. I stepped back, and a girl standing behind me pushed me aside. I sank farther back out of the crowd, getting elbowed, and I forced my way to freedom. Once one person lost control, it became a frenzy.

The band stopped playing. I listened to squeals and proclamations from girls in the crowd saying they must be dreaming. Girls pushed and shoved, and yelled his name. Guys even fought to get close to him. I overheard some guy say he had written a song he wanted Jax to listen to. This was crazy, and I had let him walk into it all. I sighed and turned when I heard a girl ask someone standing beside her, "I wonder if he'll auto-graph my boobs?"

I realized how much I didn't like other girls throwing them-selves at him. I'd had him to myself, and it was easy to think we were normal, but he would never be ordinary. He would always be someone I couldn't hold on to. I stared out at the water and decided to escape to the serenity of the now deserted beach.

"Excuse me! Excuse me! Listen up, please!" Dylan McCovey's voice came over the sound system. I turned to see him standing onstage. He appeared to be very pleased with himself. "I realize we have a special guest tonight, but if you want to stay at this party, I'm going to have to ask you to act like he's just one of us and give Jax some breathing room. If you can't do this, I'm going to have you escorted off the property."

I glanced back at the crowd around Jax, and several girls protested and complained following Dylan's speech, but they listened to him. Even through the thinning crowd, I didn't see Jax and figured he would still have to deal with several more fans before he managed to get free. I turned toward the shore and wondered if he would be able to find me if I went down to the beach.

Hands slipped around my waist. "Don't tell me you were going to leave me to the crowd and go down there all alone," Jax whispered in my ear.

I leaned against him and enjoyed the comfort of his arms.

I hated how lost I'd felt when he'd been everyone else's instead of mine.

"Dylan's not a bad host. All it took was my letting him know I wanted freedom tonight with you, and he took over."

I smiled. "Well, you're making his party the hottest event this town has ever seen."

Jax kissed my head. "Are you okay?" he asked quietly.

I nodded. "I'm fine."

He relaxed his hold and came to stand beside me, still holding me against his side. "Do you want to escape down there by ourselves, or do you want to attend this party we came to? Just so you know, I'm good with whatever you choose."

I wanted to escape and keep Jax to myself. But I'd also come here tonight because Amanda had invited me, and I wanted to hang out with her and meet some of the others. The crowd was slowly getting back into the party. Many still watched Jax. I couldn't blame them. I wanted to stare at him myself.

"I guess I should go find Amanda and mingle," I said reluctantly.

Jax took my hands and pulled me close. "When this is over, we can have some time alone." He grinned wickedly at me. "Maybe I can show you my room again."

My stomach did an excited little flip at the thought of being with him in his room. We turned back toward the heart of the party. As we passed people, they introduced themselves, and Jax never failed to be nice and polite. He shook hands, and some of the braver guests asked him to autograph their items.

Amanda came up beside me. "Hey, I'm sorry about earlier. I hope Dylan has made it easier."

"Yes, he did. We expected it, or something similar, so it wasn't a big surprise."

Amanda grinned. "Well, he *is* the hottest teen idol in America."

Jax smiled at her, and she looked like she might faint. I elbowed him in the ribs. He needed to work on not overwhelming girls with his smile.

Amanda got a grip on herself. "Okay, so, I want to introduce you to some friends," she said, "but they're probably going to be more interested in meeting your date."

"It's okay, I know."

She led us over to a group of girls who seemed familiar. I remembered a few of them from school.

"Hey, girls, I wanted to introduce you to Sadie. She was at school for the last few weeks. She'll be a senior next year too. Sadie, this is Jessie," she said, introducing a petite blonde with pixie hair, "Mary Ann," a petite redhead with wavy hair and surprisingly tanned skin, "and Peyton," a tall brunette. All the girls smiled at me, but their eyes strayed to Jax.

"I remember you from Spanish," Peyton said, looking from me to Jax.

When I glanced over at him, Jax's attention seemed to be solely focused on me. He smiled reassuringly.

"So, how do you two know each other?" Mary Ann asked, and all three pairs of eyes went to Jax. Only Amanda seemed to remember my presence.

Jax squeezed my hand. "I met her through a mutual friend. Then I fell under her enchantment, and I can't seem to get enough."

I blushed, and all four girls got sappy smiles on their faces. One of them even sighed. "Wow, I can't believe Jax Stone's girlfriend lives in Sea Breeze."

I started to correct her. I wasn't Jax's girlfriend, and he would be gone soon. "Well—"

"She worries about my privacy. But then, I like the fact that she wants to keep me all to herself." His hand squeezed mine, and I bit back a laugh.

Amanda sighed. "Does my brother know about Jax?"

I glanced up at Jax, and he nodded. "Yes, he does."

Amanda shook her head. "I swear, he knows something like this and doesn't even think it's important enough to share with me."

"Don't be so hard on him. It was by my request he not tell anyone," I assured her.

Amanda wasn't appeased, but she shrugged. "Well, I don't think I'll ever forget my shock when you stepped out of his car holding his hand. I swear, I thought I was hallucinating."

I laughed, and Jax chuckled beside me.

"I'm going to introduce them to some other people," said Amanda to her friends. "And I'm sure they're hungry. See you girls later."

Over the next hour we were introduced to so many people, I knew I couldn't remember them all. But I had no doubt they'd remember me. I somehow appeared famous in their eyes. But I happened to like *not* being the center of attention. It worried me that I wouldn't be able to deal with the way this changed my life. We sat down by the bonfire and listened to the boys talk about the upcoming football season. They all seemed excited and ready for it to begin. They were trying to impress Jax with their stories, and a couple even broke down and asked Jax about his tour and his playing guitar by ear. He answered their questions as if he'd known them forever. His ability to act comfortable in any situation amazed me. We drew a small crowd when others began to realize he was answering questions and talking. This crowd didn't seem as crazy as the earlier one, just curious. I ate a hot dog Jax roasted for me while he talked. He'd fixed it for me as he answered questions about Star. The guys all seemed to have questions about the pop princess.

When we finished eating, he stood up and took my hand. "If you will excuse us, I want to go dance with Sadie."

Their faces shone with disappointment, and I think I even heard someone sigh. We walked close enough to hear the music.

He reached down, slipped off my heels, and placed them beside his discarded shoes. He pulled me out of the light and onto the moonlit beach. He nodded to the DJ who had taken over for the band, then back at me. The song began, and I instantly recognized the voice coming over the speakers. Jax held me closer as his smooth, velvet voice sang softly.

*"Let me hold you close just for tonight.*
*When you're not in my arms, nothing seems right.*
*Just to see your smile lights up my darkest night.*
*So, baby, please dance with me in the moonlight."*

Jax leaned back and tilted my face to his.

*"Your touch is my only addiction.*
*Your heartbeat takes my breath away.*
*You'll break my heart if you don't stay.*
*Your whispers sing to me each night,*
*and your laugh is my only sun.*

*"Hold me and whisper you love me.*
*Hold me and tell me there's no world without you beside me.*
*Hold me, I need you to guide me.*
*I can't live without you.*
*Hold me and whisper you love me.*

*Hold me and tell me there's no world without you beside me.*
*Hold me, I need you to guide me."*

The song ended, and I stood in Jax's arms, unable to look away from his steel-blue eyes darkened with emotion.

"I've never understood those words until tonight. I sang them, but I didn't write them. I didn't want to record the song, but I lost the battle. Now when I sing those words, I'll have a face to put behind them." He paused and traced a line from my ear to my chin. "I just hope I'm able to get through those words when you're a thousand miles away."

I swallowed the lump in my throat. I didn't want to think about him being a thousand miles away. I laid my head against his chest, and he pulled me closer.

# Chapter Twelve

**JAX**

I managed to sneak Sadie out of the party without anyone noticing. Lifting her into my Hummer, I pressed a quick kiss to her lips before closing the door and running around to get in on my side. I hadn't been kidding about taking her back to my room. Even if we just talked all night, I wanted more time with her. I wasn't ready to take her home.

"Do you have to be home at a certain time?" I asked, glancing over at her before cranking up.

Sadie let out a short laugh. It sounded more sad than anything, and my chest squeezed. "My mother is sound asleep by now, and she won't check to see if I'm home all night long. She wouldn't have a clue if I stayed out all night."

There was a bitterness in her tone that surprised me. I knew enough about her mother to know she was pregnant and unwed and that Ms. Mary wasn't a fan. The idea that no one checked on Sadie and made sure she was home safe bothered me. No, it scared the shit out of me. What would happen when I left? Would she be safe?

"My mom is just very pregnant right now. She's tired," Sadie added.

"Then are you up for going back to my house? We can talk. I don't expect more. I just don't want to take you home yet," I explained.

Sadie shifted in her seat, then turned to me. The smile on her face was one I hadn't seen yet. She looked like a naughty little girl with her innocent smile. "I would love to come back to your house . . . and room . . . but I don't want to just talk."

I needed to adjust myself. Sadie going all sexy on me made everything harder. "Are you sure about that?" I asked, wanting her to tell me yes but knowing she really needed to say no. We didn't need this. I was already addicted to her. I wasn't sure how I could leave if we got any closer physically.

"Very. I've thought of nothing else every night since."

*Ah, hell.* I was a goner.

I drove the short distance back to the private island my summer house was safely tucked away on. Pulling into the driveway, I watched as Kane, who normally followed me everywhere, scowled at me and walked out to the Hummer. I'd snuck away from him tonight. I hadn't wanted him tagging along once he found out where I was headed. He would really be pissed if he knew I'd just gone to a public party with crazed teenagers.

I shot a smirk at the angry bodyguard who had been close by for most of my career and put the Hummer in park. Kane was opening Sadie's door and helping her out before I got around to her. He needed to stop that. "I got this, Kane," I told him, and reached for Sadie's hand.

He only grunted in reply and walked around to the driver's seat.

"I'm surprised he didn't come with us tonight," Sadie said.

"Yeah. So is he," I replied with a grin, and led Sadie up to the stairs and inside the house.

Luckily, my parents were in bed already. They weren't big night owls. It wasn't that I wanted to hide Sadie from my mom . . . No, it *was* that I wanted to hide her from my mom. I would be lying if I said it wasn't. Only because she might possibly say something to hurt Sadie. My mother didn't think about others' feelings when she spoke. Then I'd have to kick her out, and it would cause all kinds of drama I didn't want to waste my time with.

Sadie glanced around nervously as we walked over to the stairs. She was wondering about my mother too. She didn't want to meet up with them either. Smart girl. I put my hands on her hips and walked up the stairs behind her, not even pretending not to be enjoying the view of her perfect backside. We made it upstairs and to my room without any run-ins with family members.

I closed and locked the door behind us, and Sadie walked over and sat down on the end of my bed. Yeah . . . I wasn't going to be able to get the picture of her lying back on that bed out of my head.

"You look nice on my bed," I said honestly.

She smiled sweetly and scooted farther back, then crooked her finger at me. Damn. When had innocent little Sadie gotten good at bringing a man to his knees?

I walked over to her and decided then that we'd talked a lot tonight and if Sadie wanted to do other things for a while, I wasn't going to argue.

Sadie slightly parted her knees, and I came down over her until she was lying back and I was holding my body up with a hand planted firmly on each side of her head. God, she was gorgeous. And I'd have to leave her soon. The idea of someone like Dylan touching her or just getting to spend time with her while I was in other countries onstage . . . cold . . . alone . . .

I didn't want to think about it anymore. Sadie's hands lifted and wrapped around my neck, pulling me down to her. I needed this right now. Even if it was going to be hell on me when I left, I needed to be close to her like this now. It was the only thing that was going to get me through this tour. Remembering.

Sadie opened her legs farther, and I settled between them until my raging hard-on that she always seemed to cause was pressed up tight to the warmth between her legs. Fucking amazing was the only way to describe it. Just on the other side of her tiny bathing suit bottoms, she was all skin. Long, bare legs slid up my sides, and I couldn't touch her enough. I ran my hands down her smooth legs and took each ankle and wrapped her legs around my waist.

"Oh!" she cried out, and closed her eyes as the movement put more pressure on her. I knew what I was doing. But I had to see her come again. It'd been intoxicating.

"Tell me if you want me to stop," I whispered as I trailed kisses across her jawline until I claimed her mouth with mine.

She shook her head and held on to me tighter. That was all the encouragement I needed. I rocked my hips and let out a groan as the silky fabric of her bikini bottoms easily slid back and forth. I needed to touch her.

Pulling back, I slipped my hand down and then slid one finger inside the small piece of fabric keeping me away from what I wanted a taste of, and she bucked against me.

"Sadie," I said, looking down at her. My voice cracked.

She was watching me, and her eyes lifted from my hand to my eyes. "Yes?" she whispered.

"Can I take these off?" I needed her to say no. But I was willing to beg her to say yes.

She simply nodded, and my greedy heart couldn't ignore it. I grabbed them and started pulling them down as she lifted her hips so I could ease them down her bottom.

I'd seen a lot of girls naked. I'd even seen some women who were a few years older than me naked, but the sight of Sadie lying on my bed like this was causing my heart to slam against my chest.

She had pressed her knees back together, and I knew that if I was this nervous, she had to be ten times worse. I covered both of her knees with my hands and held her gaze as I slowly opened them. Sadie closed her eyes tightly, unable to keep looking at me, so I lowered my gaze down. A small triangle of pale blond hair barely covered up anything. And fuck, she was wet.

I pressed a kiss to her knee and began making a trail down the inside of her thigh. I could hear her quick intakes of breath, but I couldn't take my eyes off this newfound treasure. I was obsessed. I needed to touch her and taste her. In some way I felt like I could claim her. Make her mine. Even if we both knew it was impossible.

I inhaled deeply and took in the sexy smell that was Sadie. Then I pressed one more kiss to the tender skin at the top of her thigh. Sadie trembled underneath me. I ran a finger through the warm wetness that was no longer hidden from me, and she cried out and moved her hips against my touch. I wanted inside her. More than anything I'd ever wanted in my life. But I knew I could never do that. Sadie deserved more than I could give. I wasn't the guy who could be beside her, cherishing her, protecting her. I didn't deserve to be the one who found heaven inside her.

But I would claim her tonight. If even just a little. I lowered my head and took a long, slow taste of those wet folds I'd only touched until now.

"Jax!" Sadie cried out my name, and it only inflamed me more. I could do this forever.

I held her open so that I could see the swollen red clit that needed my attention. When my lips touched it, Sadie went off like a rocket. Her cries were muffled, but her body twisted underneath me as she trembled. I was going to have to take one hell of a cold shower after this, but I wasn't done yet. I glanced up at her. She had taken one of my pillows and covered her face. I watched as she slowly came back to earth and moved the pillow from her mouth and looked down at me.

Grinning, I took another long taste, and her blue eyes went wide again as she watched me.

**SADIE**

Jax made me promise not to come to work the next morning after he didn't bring me home until three. The sun was getting brighter, and my white mini blinds didn't do much to block out the light. I stretched and smiled into my pillow as

I thought about last night and all Jax had done to me. I could feel the blush rising up my neck at the memory of how wild I'd been in his bed, but he'd just kept on. I couldn't seem to catch my breath from one orgasm when he was sending me into another one.

He had never pressed for more. Later he had excused himself to go to the bathroom, and when he'd come back he had lain down beside me on the bed and pulled me against his chest. Then we'd talked. About everything. I'd wanted to touch him and make him come apart for me, but he refused. He said that watching me and tasting me had already given him a release. I had no idea what that meant, but it made me smile.

I knew Jessica would wonder what I was still doing in bed this late, so I didn't wait on her to come in here and interrupt my happy thoughts. I got up and pulled on a pair of shorts. It was time I talked to Jessica about Jax anyway. If I wanted to go with him to that auction fund-raiser, I needed to ask her.

I peeked inside Jessica's room, but she was already up. When I walked into the kitchen, Jessica stood fixing a bowl of cereal.

She frowned at me. "You better not lose that job due to oversleeping. What time did you get in, anyway?"

Not sure where to start, I sat down at the table. "We need to talk about something."

She set her bowl down on the table. "Girl, if you tell me you're pregnant, I think I might go mad."

I laughed. "That's not gonna happen. And no, that's not what this is about."

Jessica tilted her head to the side. "Is this going to answer my question about what time you got in last night?"

I nodded.

She motioned her spoon at me to proceed, and then she took a big bite of her flakes.

I took a deep breath. "I'm not real sure where to start."

Jessica paused with her spoon in midair. "You mean this is going to be that good?"

I rolled my eyes. Sometimes I wished she could be a normal mother, but then, I was not normal, so why should I expect her to be? "Okay, when you worked for the Stones, did you know *who* you were working for?"

She nodded. "Sure, the teen rocker Jax Stone. I couldn't miss his pictures on the walls."

I sighed, relieved she at least knew that much. "Well, I'm dating him." I stopped and waited.

She swallowed her mouthful, and then her jaw dropped. "No way."

I'd hoped for a more in-depth reply from her. But then, depth wasn't really Jessica's thing.

"We've been seeing each other, and, well, he has to go back

to Hollywood for a fund-raiser next week and he wants me to go with him as his date."

This got Jessica's attention.

"He wants you to go to Hollywood?"

I nodded, and she chewed on her flakes a few minutes. "I don't think it's a good idea," she finally said.

I hadn't expected her to care if I went or not. "Can I ask why?"

She sat back in her seat and sighed. "Sadie, until this Jax Stone, you have never dated anyone. You're beautiful, but you're young and naive. His world isn't something you're ready for. Sure, dating him here is one thing, but walking into his world is another. I know I'm not the best mother in the world, but I love you, and I'm going to say no to protect you. You're not ready for this, and the heartache this is going to cause will be like nothing you've ever experienced. A relationship with him for any reasonable amount of time is impossible. You're just going to fall in love with him and he's going to leave. He has to. He can't be Jax Stone in Sea Breeze, Alabama."

I wanted to argue, but I knew she was right. "I already love him," I whispered.

She stood, walked over to me, put her hands on my shoulders, and squeezed. "Ah, baby, you're about to find out how bad love really does hurt." She kissed my head and left out the back door.

I couldn't go, and it disappointed me, but somehow I knew it would be for the best. I wouldn't fit into his world in Hollywood. I couldn't even handle something as simple as high school.

Jax didn't take my mother's decision well, but he accepted it.

Saying good-bye even for a little while made my chest hurt. I dreaded it all day. If this was what it felt like to watch him leave for a short time, how much worse would September be? I heard him walk up behind me before he said anything. I stood up from my work with the roses and turned to him. He looked like someone out of a magazine, and I fought the urge to reach out and grab him and hold on to the Jax I loved, not this stranger standing before me.

He reached out, took my hand, and slipped my garden glove off. "I already miss you," he said as he began kissing my fingers. "This is going to be two very long days."

I forced myself to smile. "It'll be over before we know it."

He frowned and pulled me closer. "God help me if they ask me to sing a love song. I don't know if I'll be able to get through the lyrics."

I smiled and reached up to run my fingers through his thick dark hair. "You'll have them all eating out of the palm of your hand. All you have to do is smile."

He grinned. "I think you're a little biased."

I laughed. "No, I'm not. I've witnessed you charming a room full of girls with one simple smile."

He frowned and leaned down to kiss my cheek, then kissed a trail to my ear before whispering, "You're the only one I care about charming."

I sighed. "Well, don't worry, I'm completely charmed."

He leaned back and reached into his pocket. "I have something for you, but it's really for me. I need you to take it so I'll be able to get some rest while I'm away."

He held a slim, flat cell phone in his hand.

"Please keep it on and with you at all times, so I can hear your voice whenever I need you." Somehow he had managed to say the only words that would make me take a gift like this from him.

"I don't know if I can use it. It seems complicated."

He grinned. "It's a touch screen. When you touch the screen, all your necessary buttons appear."

I did as instructed, and the screen came to life. "It's like the iPod you gave me."

"That's because it's an iPhone."

I slipped it into my pocket. "I'm just a phone call away."

Jax smiled sadly. "I hate this."

I didn't want to make things harder on him, so I made myself smile. "You'll be back soon."

He stepped closer and leaned down to kiss me. I didn't want

to close my eyes. I wanted to see him while he made my world spin. The moment his hand traced my face, I lost all concentration and just enjoyed being in his arms. He stepped back and broke the kiss.

"I'll be back as soon as I can," he said in a raspy voice. I liked knowing our kiss had affected him.

"I know."

He gave me one more grin and walked away. I watched him until he was almost out of sight. He turned back around and stopped to look at me. He lifted his fingers to his mouth and blew me a kiss before walking around the corner. The slim phone in my pocket reminded me he would call soon and I would hear his voice. It would have to be enough to get me through.


Marcus took me home after work. Jax had left a car, but I couldn't bring myself to ride home in his Hummer without him.

"What do I gotta do to make you smile?" he asked when we pulled up beside the apartment.

I sighed and forced a smile. "Nothing."

He leaned back against his seat and closed his eyes. "I hope he knows what he's got."

I glanced at my friend, not sure what to say. I dropped my hand from the car door. Apparently, he wanted to talk. "I'm the one who has been given something special. Jax isn't like people think. He is this wonderful guy who is kind and polite and sweet.

He makes me laugh and is happy just holding me. In his arms I feel safe. It's like I have finally found somewhere I belong."

Marcus let out a short, hard laugh. "Sadie, holding you isn't a hardship for him, I can promise you. And how do you know you can't find all those qualities in someone else? Jax isn't the only guy on earth who is kind, polite, and sweet."

"I'm sure you're right. But no guy I've ever met has made my heart go on a frenzy and my skin tingle just from him walking into a room. Somehow he's the only one who has ever been able to touch my soul."

Marcus sighed and shook his head. "You're right, it isn't something just anyone can do to you. It just sucks Jax Stone is the one to make you tingle."

I let out a small laugh. "I'll always love him. But I know soon I'll have to learn to live without him and move on. Right now just isn't the time."

Marcus nodded.

I opened the door and got out. "Thanks for the ride."

He smiled. "Anytime."

I walked inside. Marcus was a great guy, and if I didn't love Jax so much, maybe I could feel something for him. But my soul was already taken.

I didn't want to fall asleep for fear I would miss Jax's call. I swept the kitchen and scrubbed the bathroom before finally getting in the shower. I left the cell by the sink just in case the phone rang. When I finished, I put on my nightgown, and then I turned to my bed and fought the urge to crawl in. I knew if I did, I would fall asleep. Closing my eyes was out of the question even though my lids were very heavy. I sat down on the edge of the bed and thought about the likelihood of him calling me tonight. I'd just about convinced myself he wasn't going to call when I heard Jax singing "Wanted Dead or Alive." I hadn't expected a one-of-a-kind ringtone, and I laughed as I answered the phone. "Hello."

"Hey, beautiful."

"Do I happen to have the only recorded version of Jax Stone singing 'Wanted Dead or Alive' as a ring one?" I asked, unable to get the silly grin off my face.

"Yes, you do. When I tried to think of a song to play when I called you, I realized I'd never recorded a song you liked, so I went into my studio at the house and recorded the only one I knew you would enjoy."

I smiled and crossed my legs on the bed. "I happen to have become an obsessed fan. You could have put any of your songs on there, and I would've been happy."

"Is that so? I wish you'd told me you were a fan. I would've left my door unlocked so you could sneak in and squirt perfume on my pillow."

I laughed out loud, and then covered my mouth so Jessica wouldn't wake up and come in. I hadn't discussed Jax with her again, and I hoped I wouldn't have to.

"I don't wear perfume."

"You mean you smell that good without help?"

"I guess I do."

"Hmmm ... Well, how about I autograph one of your body parts. ... I get to pick." He chuckled into the phone.

I blushed, and the silly grin stayed on my face. "Okay, maybe I am not that crazy a fan, but I am a fan. I listen to your music every night while I go to sleep."

He groaned. "Sadie, did you have to remind me? I have a hard enough time closing my eyes to go to sleep. I don't need images of you all curled up in your bed with your hair spread out around you, listening to me sing in your ears."

"Sorry, but I don't want you to think I prefer Jon Bon Jovi's work over yours."

"Thank you."

"You're welcome."

"I miss you."

"I miss you, too."

"Go to sleep. I'll see you soon."

I sighed and wished I had a poster of him on my wall. "Good night, Jax."

"Good night, Sadie."

I pressed end and slipped under the covers with Jax playing in my ears.

Ms. Mary stood over Henrietta, who appeared to be making bread, when I entered the kitchen the next morning.

"Now, Mrs. Stone said she needs it to be whole wheat, but she wants it light and fluffy, not heavy."

Henrietta nodded and continued kneading the dough in front of her. I grinned and walked toward the laundry room to change. Today wasn't going to be easy with Jax gone, but at least I was at his home, near his things. It was better than nothing. I slipped into my uniform and went back to the kitchen.

"Go ahead and get some of the fresh bread over there. Henrietta made it for lunch today, but it is really good with some butter on it while it is still warm."

I didn't have to be told twice. My stomach growled. I sliced off a piece and buttered it. The fresh homemade bread melted in my mouth.

"Hey, don't eat all the good stuff." Marcus poked me in the ribs and grabbed the knife to slice himself off a piece too. I smiled up at him.

"Good morning to you, too."

He grinned and took a bite of his bread. Marcus closed his eyes and moaned loudly, and poor Henrietta jumped.

Ms. Mary rolled her eyes. "Boy, can't you eat any quieter?"

With a chuckle, he shook his head.

I wiped my hands on a paper towel and turned to Ms. Mary. "What do you have for me today?"

She smiled and pointed to the pantry. "I need you to go through and check all the expiration dates for me. We need to throw out anything that's old and replace it."

I nodded and went straight to work. With Jax singing in my ears, the morning flew by.

Marcus joined me at lunchtime. "How's it going?" He grinned down at me and sat at the table with his plate full of food.

"Good, thank you. And you?"

Marcus shrugged "Same ol', same ol', I guess." He studied me as if waiting for me to do something.

I frowned. "What?" I asked, before taking another bite of my Reuben sandwich.

"Nothing, I just thought you might be a little upset. You didn't talk much this morning, and I figured you knew."

I frowned and set my drink down. "What?"

It looked like he was trying to decide whether or not to answer me.

"Well?"

"Um, why don't we go outside and eat . . . and talk."

A nervous knot formed in my stomach, but I wanted to know what Marcus knew and I didn't. I picked up my food and followed him out to the gazebo. "All right, tell me what this is about."

Marcus didn't sit down. He walked over to the edge of the

gazebo and leaned a hip against the railing. "Amanda has e-mail subscriptions to several teen news websites. This morning she came running into my room before I left, asking me if you were still dating Jax. I told her yes, and she showed me the *Star Follower* website. It has photos of Jax taken last night out on the town with the actress Bailey Kirk."

My stomach quivered, but I'd been through this before with Jax, and I knew he couldn't help the publicity photos and what the news reported.

I forced a smile. "It's not a big deal. He has to take those photos for publicity reasons. I'm not concerned."

Marcus sighed and reached into his back pocket to pull out some papers. "I printed it out."

I took the papers from his hands and sank down into my seat with images of Jax holding hands with a beautiful dark-haired girl. One photo showed him leaning down and laughing at what she was saying. The other showed him with his arm around her shoulders while he was pointing at something and smiling. I didn't want to read the words, but I found myself reading anyway. *Last night Jax Stone was seen out for the first time in weeks, on the arm of Bailey Kirk (*The Dream Date *and* Winter's Way*). Both appeared very interested in each other. We guess the rumors that Jax has been hiding out with a new lucky lady are untrue, because he seems very interested in Miss Kirk.* I handed the paper back to Marcus and stood up. "I'm not hungry anymore. I need to get back to work."

He grabbed my arm when I walked by him. "He doesn't deserve you."

I didn't want him to see my face, because tears were threatening to fall at any moment.

"I'm not a part of his world. He has another life outside of his life here with me," I choked out in a whisper. I pulled free and started back to the house.

Marcus came up behind me and grabbed my hand. "Stop, Sadie."

I stopped but didn't turn around. Tears were rolling down my face, and I didn't want to humiliate myself.

"I know I've said this before, but you're worth more than what he gives you. You're beautiful and smart and kind and funny, and you don't care if your hair is messed up or if you break a nail. You're not too busy to play chess with an old man, and you're raising your mom and never complain." He sighed, took my face, and turned it toward him. "Why can't you see how special you are?"

I kept my eyes down.

He wiped my tears. "I should kick his ass for making you cry."

I shook my head. "I chose this. It's my choice. I chose him. I can't help what my heart feels."

Marcus clenched his jaw and nodded before dropping his hands and stepping back as if I'd burned him. He was such a good guy. I hated that the truth hurt him so much.

I closed the gap he'd created, and reached up to touch his face. "You're special too, and one day someone is going to steal your heart and become one lucky girl." I dropped my hand and turned to walk away.

"What if she already has, but her heart is taken?" he asked in a hoarse whisper.

I closed my eyes and took a deep breath, then turned to glare at him. "Then she isn't the right one."

He walked toward me in one long stride. "But what if she's wrong?" he asked, right before his mouth came down on mine.

I was stunned at first, and then I panicked. I couldn't be doing this. I put both my hands against his chest and pushed him away before turning and running. I ran straight to my bike and pedaled home as hard as I could.

The phone rang. I'd just reached my road and was out of breath from pedaling so fast. I pulled over, sank down against a tree, and took a deep breath. I needed to answer this. I would talk to him about the actress when he got home, but I wasn't going to jump to conclusions while he wasn't here to defend himself. Even if the pictures were rather incriminating.

"Hello," I answered.

"Where are you?" Jax's voice sounded hard and strained.

"Uh . . ." I realized it was two in the afternoon and I was

almost home. How could I explain this?

"Well, I'm pulled over on the side of the road talking to you," I said in the lightest tone I could muster.

"Why are you not at my house?" His tone sounded a little less hard, but still very strained.

"Well, um . . ." I did not want to lie, but I did not want to tell the truth, either. At least, not over the phone. "I'm going home early."

He paused for a minute. "Are you going to tell me why?"

"Do I have to?"

"Yes, I think you need to."

"I have a headache." It wasn't a lie.

"Jason just called me. He witnessed something from his window about thirty minutes ago."

I sighed and laid my head back against the tree.

"This is something I wanted to wait and discuss when you got home."

"It can't wait. He said you were crying and he said . . . he said Marcus kissed you."

The last part sounded so hard and angry I feared for Marcus.

"There's a lot more to it."

"Then tell me."

I knew this wouldn't end until I told him everything.

"Marcus's sister, Amanda, saw pictures of you online taken

last night with Bailey Kirk, and you were really very friendly and touchy in them. You seemed happy. I had a hard time with the photos, and Marcus said a few things about our relationship I didn't want to hear, and I cried a little. He stopped me and tried to console me, and I started to leave again and he just . . . he just kissed me."

Jax didn't say anything for what seemed like a lifetime. "He's fired, and I'm on a plane home now."

"Jax, no! He, he . . . I think he's in love with me."

Jax let out a hard laugh. "I know."

"Well, he's just worried about me, and he was trying to convince me someone like him would be a much better match for me."

Jax hissed. "He's fired *now*! I told you I wouldn't fire him unless he said something against you, and he did. He tried to convince you I don't love you."

I sighed. I couldn't stand this. It was all my fault. "I didn't kiss him back, and I pushed him away quickly. No harm done."

"I know you didn't, and I know you pushed him off. Jason saw all of it. He also saw you run like hell and fly down the driveway on your bike at a breakneck speed. He called me immediately and told me. I walked out of a photo shoot and called my pilot. I'm on my way to you now."

"You have explained the photos to me before. I just wasn't prepared to see it firsthand, and reading the reporter's words wasn't much fun either. I tried to handle it without getting upset."

Jax sighed. "Every one of those photos was taken last night by her publicist. She's going to be in a new movie, and they needed the buzz. They told me what to do in all those pictures."

Relief washed away the pain, but guilt still weighed on me because Marcus was going to be out of a job.

"Thanks for explaining everything to me."

He chuckled this time, and it was the warm sound I loved so much. "Wait up for me. I will see you soon."

"I will."

# Chapter Thirteen

**JAX**

I knew posing for those photos last night was a bad idea. But I'd agreed hoping it would end the gossip about some girl in the south keeping all my attention. I'd been afraid they'd find out about Sadie and completely bombard her world. I liked keeping her safely tucked away from the media and the cruel life that comes with it—no privacy. I couldn't let them do that to her. So I'd posed for the pictures with Bailey to stop the rumors.

The idea of Sadie seeing them and thinking I was even remotely enjoying myself was painful. All I had been able to think about was getting back to her. Nothing about Bailey interested me. She was just another girl fighting her way to the top. I met her kind daily. They all thought getting a piece of me was their ticket to fame. I was just a ticket for them.

With Sadie none of that mattered. She didn't care about who I was to the world. She just wanted me. The guy no one else knew. The guy I'd thought I'd lost.

Going to Sadie first was what I wanted to do, but I also needed to face Marcus. Ms. Mary had called me and said Marcus was waiting on me in the kitchen. I couldn't let that wait.

I was ready to murder him for touching Sadie, but I took several deep breaths before walking into the house and making my way down to the kitchen to face him.

## SADIE

Jax didn't have to fire Marcus; Marcus quit. Ms. Mary said it was for the best and for me not to worry. Marcus would have no trouble finding other work for the few weeks of summer remaining before he would have to go back to college. However, William quit too, and it left Ms. Mary with a problem. No servers.

Ms. Mary stood over a pile of résumés in front of her. "I've seen two applicants today, and only one is suitable. But he is going to need some help for his first time."

"I'll do it tonight. I know how. The one suitable applicant can help me."

Ms. Mary cut her eyes at me and frowned. "I don't know about that. Master Jax won't like it much. He's already grumbling about you working out in the sun, and he made me promise not to make you touch shrimp or oysters again since he found out how much you hate them."

I laughed. "Well, he will get over it. Besides, what else can you do?"

Ms. Mary chewed on her bottom lip, then nodded. "Well, I guess you're right. You're my only way out of this mess."

The door opened, and Jax walked in with a grin on his face. "Ah, just who I wanted to see." He leaned down and kissed my nose, then gave Ms. Mary his charming little-boy grin. "Do you have any sweet tea?" he asked her.

"You know I do. Just made some fresh." She stood up to go fix his drink. "While you're here, I wanted to go ahead and let you know that since you ran off my servers, Sadie here will be serving tonight with the new guy so she can train him."

Jax frowned. "No, she isn't."

"Jax, I don't see why not. Ms. Mary needs help." I stood and put my hands on my hips, ready to wage a war.

He grinned and slipped his arms through mine. "The family will be dining out tonight, and I will be busy. We won't have need of servers." He turned to Ms. Mary and smiled. "Take the night off." He looked at me. "Will you do me the honor of going to dinner with me?"

Ms. Mary chuckled, and I smiled.

"I would love to."

He took my hand and led me toward the entrance to the

main part of the house. "Good night, Ms. Mary," he called over his shoulder.

We walked to his room.

"I had my stylist buy you clothing for the trip you didn't get to take with me. If we want to enjoy a fan-free meal, then we're going to have to go eat somewhere where the dress code is a little more strict than most." He went inside his massive walk-in closet and came out with a long white box. "For you," he said, smiling.

I didn't like the idea of him buying me clothes, but the eager smile on his face made me bite my tongue and get over it. I laid the box on the bed and opened it up. Inside lay a pale-blue dress that appeared to be made with fabric so delicate it would tear when I touched it.

"I'm afraid I'll hurt it," I whispered, and looked at him.

He chuckled and walked over to stand behind me. His breath caressed my ear. "All you're going to do is make it the envy of everyone around you." He returned to his closet and came back out with a shoe box. "You'll need these, too."

I opened it. A pair of strappy silver stiletto heels lay inside. "I hope I can walk in these." My voice sounded nervous, even to me.

He took one, slipped his finger through a strap, and let it dangle. "These do seem complicated, but I can just imagine them on, and the image I'm getting is making me sweat. We need to get you away from me." He took the dress and led me to a guest bedroom. "You have a bathroom at your disposal, and you'll find it has all you could possibly need to get dressed for tonight."

"Okay," I said as he lay the dress on the bed and walked back to the door.

He gave me a cocky grin. "I'll pick you up at seven, if that's all right."

I glanced at the clock on the nightstand. It showed a quarter to six now. "See you then."

He bowed and closed the door behind him.

I walked into the adjoining bathroom. Makeup, bath gels, soaps, salts, creams, and as many different body lotions, splashes, and powders covered the marble countertops. I bit my lip to keep from laughing out loud. He'd been prepared for me to say yes. A piece of paper lay on top of the towels, bath cloths, sponge, loofah, and some other item I'd never seen before. I picked it up and smiled when I realized it was from Jax.

Sadie,

I had no idea what you would need. I took the liberty of buying everything I thought smelled good. Not any of it smells as good as you, but the saleslady assured me all women want to feel pampered in the bath. So I just bought it all. As for the makeup, you don't need any. Your natural beauty is enough to bring me to my knees, but I wanted you to be happy, so I had a saleslady give me everything a "gorgeous blonde with incredible skin and amazing blue eyes with lashes that are long and curly without any help" might need. She said it sounded like you didn't need anything, but she gave me a few things she believed would make you happy.

I love you,

Jax

I laughed and tucked the note safely into my purse. Then I picked up the first bottle to test the smell and decide which fragrance I wanted to use. The bathroom door opened behind me, and I spun around to see Jax standing there, staring at me. Before I could ask him what he needed he closed the distance between us and grabbed my waist to pull me up against his chest. The bottle I'd been holding fell to the plush rug below right before his mouth came down over mine.

"I'm sorry, but I suck at being good," he murmured as his tongue tangled with mine. I was completely consumed by his taste. I grabbed his shoulders to hold on to something while he made my world spin with one extremely hot kiss.

He pushed me back until I was pressed against the edge of the marble counter, then he picked me up and sat me down on it without once breaking our frantic kissing. Jax stood between my open legs, and the idea of what he'd done to me the last time he'd been between my legs made my body shiver. Both of his hands slid slowly up the inside of my thighs. I knew where he was going and I wanted him to hurry. He'd made me weak when it came to his touch.

Jax's lips left mine and he trailed kisses across my jawline. Then he focused on nibbling and licking the spot behind my ear until he had me trembling in his arms as he moved his kisses down my neck to stop just at the edge of my cleavage.

Both his hands moved up to take the hem of my shirt as his eyes lifted to meet mine. "Can I?" he asked as he began easing my shirt up over my stomach. I managed to nod in response. He made quick work of discarding my shirt, and his mouth was back on the tops of my breasts as his talented fingers reached around me to find the clasp of my bra.

In the back of my head I knew this was getting more and more out of hand. I couldn't be my mom. I didn't want to be like her. But Jax's touch made everything else seem unimportant. I was lost in the sensations he stirred in my body. They controlled me.

The lacey straps to my bra fell down my arms and Jax pulled it the rest of the way off, dropping it to the ground beside us.

"Your body is so damn perfect. I can't get it out of my head. I think about touching you . . . and tasting you . . . and being inside you all the time. I don't want to scare you or do anything you're not ready for, but I just need to touch you more."

The pleading sound in his voice was like warm butter. I was ready to strip down and let him do exactly what he wanted to do. I wouldn't though. There was a line I just wasn't sure I could cross. He'd be leaving me soon. Could I give that part of myself to him knowing there were no promises between us? No. I couldn't. Instead of telling him any of that, I reached for his shirt and pulled it up until he raised his arms to allow me to completely pull it over his head. I wanted to touch him too. Especially his chest. It was beautiful. I ran my nails across his abs, and his body tensed under my touch. I smiled up at him and his heated stare only made my body ache more. How could I stop him if we went too far? Seeing him like this made me want to get closer to him.

"Can I—" He swallowed hard and his breathing grew heavier. "Can I take a shower with you?"

Oh my. I wasn't sure I could do that. Naked and vulnerable in a shower with Jax.

"Please. I'll be good. I'll try to be. I want to wash your hair . . . and I want to wash you."

My heart was slamming against my chest as I glanced back at the large shower behind him. It was surrounded in glass and was the same marble as the counter I was sitting on. I wanted this. I did. But was it smart?

"Please, Sadie," Jax pleaded.

I was weak. I couldn't tell him no. I nodded and his hands tightened their grip on my waist before he pulled me off the counter and began undressing me the rest of the way. I didn't know what to do, so I let him. He unsnapped my shorts and pulled them slowly down my legs. I was standing there in my panties when he glanced up at me. His eyes never left mine as he reached up to slip his thumbs into the sides of my panties. But the moment he began pulling them down he lowered his gaze and I wanted to cover my face. Even though he had been very up close and personal with that part of me, something about standing here in front of him naked was completely different. There were no barriers.

I stepped out of my discarded clothing and Jax slowly stood up never taking his eyes off my body. When his hands went to the button on his jeans I wanted to do that for him, but I couldn't bring myself to reach out and take over. I just watched him as he stripped. I'd never seen a man naked before, so my curiosity was taking over.

Jax dropped his jeans and boxer briefs at the same time, then he stepped out of them. I didn't want to stare at him there but it was really hard not to. I was fascinated.

"If I'm gonna be good you can't look at me like that," Jax

said with a smirk before turning to go turn the shower on. His backside was just as perfect as his front. The urge to touch him was becoming overwhelming.

Jax turned around and held out his hand. "It's warm enough now. Did you decide on a body wash?"

I hadn't had time to decide on a body wash and right now that was the last worry on my mind. I reached back and picked the closest one to me up then I slipped my hand into his and he gently pulled me into the shower with him. My heart was racing in my chest. The water hit my cooled skin and I shivered.

"Give me the bottle. I want to wash your body," he whispered in my ear. I couldn't respond so I just held the bottle up so he could take it. Jax took my hair and moved it all over until it was hanging over my left shoulder. Then the bath sponge touched my back and I closed my eyes tightly. How much would he wash? Or more importantly would I make embarrassing moans when he touched me in intimate places?

As he stood behind me, the sponge thoroughly cleaned my back, but it felt more like a caress. Then he moved down over my bottom and spent extra time cleaning me there before moving down the backs of both my legs. When the sponge moved around to the front of my legs and started making its way upward I trembled with anticipation. He was getting closer to the places that I needed him to touch now. Except he ran the sponge up the front of my thigh and it went directly to my stomach, which he cleaned a little more than it actually needed before both his hand holding the sponge and his empty hand each covered one of my breasts.

I let my head fall back to his chest as his hand cleaned my breasts and his free hand tugged gently on my nipple, causing me to make sounds of pleasure. The sponge began to move back down over my stomach. Jax's other hand moved down beside it and then slipped down between my legs and shifted them further apart. His breathing was heavy and fast in my ear as the sponge moved between my legs. I put one hand on the bathroom wall for support and the other hand grabbed Jax's arm. My legs were trembling. The moment the sponge fell from Jax's hand I heard it, and I knew what that meant. He moved in closer behind me and his hardness was pressed firmly against my back. I wanted to move against him but his fingers chose that moment to slip inside me, and I could only think about the pleasure that would come from this.

"I want inside you, Sadie. So bad. I want to be as close to you as humanly possible. But I don't want you to ever regret it," Jax's words almost sounded as if he were pleading. My head knew what the right thing to do was, but my heart wanted something else entirely. I turned in his arms and slipped both of my hands up his chest and then into his hair.

"I love you, and I want that too."

Jax closed his eyes tightly and swallowed hard. "Are you positive?"

I ran the pad of my thumb over his bottom lip and then stood on my tiptoes so that I could kiss where I'd touched. "Yes."

Jax reached around me, turned off the shower, then opened the door and grabbed a towel. He wrapped it around me, then lifted me into his arms and carried me into the other room. He put me down on the bed, then stood back and looked at me a moment before walking over to open the bedside table. The fact he had condoms in there was a little surprising.

"Don't start thinking what I know you're thinking. I've never been in this room with a girl. Jason uses this room when he has dates he brings home. His last girlfriend stayed in here, so I knew it would be stocked."

The bucket of ice water I'd been expecting was stilled by his words. This wasn't some room Jax brought his dates. I was special. I had to believe I was special.

Jax ran a finger over my eyebrow. "Why the frown?" He asked leaning down over me.

I was about to give him something I'd never be able to get back. I needed honesty right now.

"Am I special to you? Or am I just another girl? Another summer?"

Jax dropped the condom on the bed and his body moved over until he was beside me. He pulled me into his arms and held me a moment. I was beginning to think he wasn't going to answer when he buried his face in my damp hair. "You will never be just another girl. You will be the only one I ever think about. I'm in love with you, Sadie. I've never been in love with anyone before."

I thought about Jessica and the lifestyle she'd led. The guys who had used her and tossed her aside. None of them treated her the way Jax treated me. This was different and I was smarter. I reached for the condom he'd dropped and I opened the small package. "I want this. With you."

Jax reached for the condom without a word and I let him take it. I didn't know how to put that thing on him. I watched transfixed as he rolled it down his length then I lifted my eyes to meet his steady gaze.

"Are you sure?" he asked in a hoarse whisper.

"Very," I replied. Jax leaned down and kissed me softly before settling between my legs. He brushed his lips against my neck and whispered promises in my ear that I believed. He ran his fingers through my hair and with each sweet caress my body relaxed. Then I felt him at my entrance. I couldn't help but tense up. As much as I wanted this to be with Jax I was still nervous.

"I'm going to go easy. I promise. You tell me if you want me to stop."

I only nodded my reply. Then with one shift of his hips Jax

was inside me. The pain was sharp, but brief. The muscles in Jax arms flexed as he held himself over me. I wanted to kiss the vein standing out in his neck. He was holding himself completely still, but his breathing was fast and heavy. It was the sexiest thing I'd ever seen.

I reached up and cupped his face and ran my thumb over his lips. "You can move," I reassured him. The excitement and passion in his blue eyes made everything tingle. I wanted to feel him move inside of me. He eased out and then slowly back in with a smooth rock of his hips. It was building inside me. The pleasure was there and I wanted to feel that again.

"I want you. I want you to come, but I don't think I can hold off much longer," Jax said through clenched teeth.

A powerful feeling coursed through me that only intensified the hot ache getting ready to explode. "I want to see you . . . come," I told him.

I watched his face and the heat in his eyes flared.

Jax ducked his head and pulled one of my nipples into his mouth and began to suck. Acting on instinct I lifted my legs and pressed my knees against his sides just as the wave I had wanted to experience while Jax was inside me crashed through my body. His name tore from my lips and I grabbed his arms and held on as I arched my back off the bed and clung to him.

"Oh fuck," Jax groaned. Then his body began to tremble and he cried out my name as he jerked over me several times. I loved him. There was never a doubt in my mind. But now, that we had been this close . . . Jax Stone completed me.

Jax knocked on my door at exactly seven-thirty, and I slipped on the sexy silver heels. They fit me perfectly. He had really done his homework. I opened the door, and my heart skipped a beat. Seeing him in a black tuxedo wasn't as beautiful as seeing him naked, but it was a close second.

"You really should warn someone before you unleash yourself on them dressed like that," I said with awe in my voice. It was then I realized he was staring at me—well, my body—and his gaze stopped at my feet.

"I think I'm going to give my stylist a raise."

His eyes met mine, and he smiled a slow, sexy smile that didn't help my weak knees.

"You're incredible," he finally said, reaching for my hand and pulling me against him. His warm, clean smell of soap, mouthwash, and Jax set the blood in my veins racing. Even though we had just spent the last hour together, I wanted more of him.

His lips touched my ear. "I want to hold you, kiss you, and enjoy you in this dress right here in this room all night, but I can't."

I shivered.

"Please don't shiver. It does something to me," he said, against my ear again.

I smiled. "Well, stop whispering in my ear and tracing patterns on my naked back, and I'll stop," I forced out through the desire clogging my throat.

He grabbed my hand and started walking. "I have to get us around people. Now," he said with a sense of urgency I completely understood.

Kane stood at the door of the Bentley I'd only seen Mrs. Stone use. He nodded. "Miss White, Mr. Stone," he said with no emotion as we stepped inside. Jax put his arm behind my back.

"I have it on the best authority you don't like most seafood."

I grinned and nodded, knowing the authority was Ms. Mary.

"So I'm limited to two choices. This area is for the tourists—the casual, everyday tourists—but there are a few establishments harder to get into. Have you ever heard of Le Cellier?"

I hadn't, of course. I shook my head.

"I've been there a few times. It's good, but more important, it's somewhere we can enjoy a meal out together and not deal with fans."

I let out a happy sigh and leaned back against the seat and crossed my legs. Jax cleared his throat and I looked up at him.

"Could you try to not flash me any leg while we're alone? I'm having a hard time with it." His smile was strained, and I bit back a smile.

"Sorry," I said softly, and tucked my crossed legs back toward the seat.

We pulled up to the establishment, and there were men waiting to open our door. Jax took my hand and walked us up to the hostess, who immediately noticed him.

"Mr. Stone, we have your table ready. Right this way."

Jax was right. The other diners were not going to come ask for autographs, but they did notice him as we walked by. Several whispered, and their eyes followed him. We were seated at a table away from the main dining area, where there were no other people around us. Jax pulled my chair out for me and I sat down, glad we weren't going to be in view of curious eyes.

Jax grinned. "Do you read French, or should I order for you?"

"The menu is in French?" I asked, surprised.

He nodded. "Yes, and I know to stay away from oysters and shrimp. Are you okay with veal or lobster?"

I wasn't really sure what I was okay with. The nicest restaurant I'd ever been to had a menu in English and nothing cost more than fifteen dollars.

"Just order whatever you think I'll like."

He chuckled. "Okay."

A server appeared, and Jax ordered in French, of course.

I watched him, mesmerized by his voice and the way the foreign words flowed from his mouth with such ease.

He stopped. "What do you want to drink?"

I frowned and almost hated to ask. "Do they have Coke?"

He grinned and went back to speaking in French.

Once we were alone again, he leaned toward me and whispered, "I ordered you lobster because I know it is good here. It also tastes nothing like shrimp or oysters."

Before I could reply, a Coke appeared in front of me and in front of Jax.

He took a sip and reached out a hand toward me. I slipped my hand in his and sighed.

"It's hard to be near you and not be touching you in some way," he said.

I knew exactly what he meant. The thought should have been a happy one, but it reminded me how short summer was and how close I was to not being able to touch him any longer.

"That wasn't supposed to make you sad," he said softly.

I made myself smile. "It doesn't. I was just thinking about how quickly summer will be over. How fast it's already gone."

His eyes showed emotion I didn't understand. "I know," he said, and tightened his hold on my hand. He looked at the drink in front of him, then back up at me with a sadness in his eyes. "I can't think about it right now. Leaving you will be the hardest thing I've ever had to do. I'm just not sure how I'll be able to." He broke off and turned his gaze away from me.

I wish I hadn't brought up our very near future. I hated seeing the pain in his eyes. "We'll figure it all out. Let's not let it get us down now. We still have a month and a half to go."

He forced a smile and nodded. "You're right."

Jax stood up, came around the table, and held out his hand. I stared at him in his tuxedo and my breath caught in my lungs. He really was breathtakingly beautiful.

"Would you dance with me?"

I slipped my hand into his and followed him into the main room, where a band played. I stepped into his arms and wished I could stay there forever. His hands rested on my lower back, and I slid my hands up his arms and rested them on his shoulders. With my extra height thanks to my killer heels, I was much closer to his six feet two inches. He leaned down until the warmth of his breath tickled my ear and neck.

"I love having you in my arms," he told me. I shivered and slipped a hand behind his neck. "However, if the old gentleman at the table to our left doesn't stop ogling your legs, I'm going to have to go take him out."

I bit back my laugh and turned my head to see the offending old man. "You're crazy," I whispered.

He nodded. "I've been crazy since the day I walked upstairs to my bedroom and found you wiping something off the floor. I'll never forget thinking, 'I don't care if she snuck in here to get close to me. If she'll let me lose my fingers in those curls and stare into those baby-blue eyes, she can get as close as she wants.'"

I hadn't realized he had felt anything for me that first day.

"Really? I thought you were aggravated some crazed fan had slipped through."

He grinned wickedly. "How do you suppose someone gets aggravated at someone who could have fallen out of heaven?"

I blushed and laid my head against his chest. We finished the rest of the dance in silence. I memorized his heartbeat and closed my eyes to commit the moment to memory. I knew one day soon I would need to remember how right this moment had been. When it was all over, I never wanted to think I had made a mistake by loving him. I wanted to always remember how he'd made me feel, so I would know the pain was worth it.

Jax walked me back to my seat before taking his. I took a drink of my Coke and noticed there was some kind of bread on a silver platter in the middle of the table. Jax sliced the bread, then put something that looked like oil on a piece and handed it to me.

"Their bread is really good," he assured me.

I took a bite and decided the strange oil tasted much better than butter. He had slathered the yummy oil on a piece for himself and somehow managed to be sexy while eating bread. I wondered if they gave lessons to rock stars on such things. And if so, could I get in on one of those lessons?

"What are you grinning at?" he asked.

I hadn't realized my thoughts showed on my face. I shrugged.

"I'm thinking about the way you make things as simple as eating bread attractive."

He gave me a crooked grin and leaned toward me. "Maybe the same way you make breathing sexy."

"What?" I asked, confused.

He raised his eyebrows. "When you breathe, it gives me chills."

I laughed and shook my head. "You're really good with words."

He winked at me, then sat back in his seat and took a drink of his Coke. "You make me feel poetic."

A server came up behind Jax, and I heard one behind me so I sat up straight and waited for them to serve our salad.

"The wonderful thing about Alabama is you get pecans in your salad," Jax said as the servers left.

I had to agree with him. I loved pecans, but I'd never thought to put them in my salad before.

Once our meal was finished and Jax had paid the bill, we went outside to Kane and the Bentley waiting for us at the front door. How Kane did that I would never know, but he was always on time. We rode to my apartment in silence. I sat snuggled up in Jax's arms, and he played with my hair. It was one of those times when words weren't needed.

Kane slowed and parked right on the street in front of my apartment.

"Thank you for tonight."

Jax smiled down at me and tilted my face to match his before gently kissing me. I closed my eyes and pressed closer to him. He pulled back just enough to look into my eyes.

"I love you, Sadie White," he whispered in a raspy voice.

I smiled and kissed his face softly. "I love you, too, Jax Stone."

He groaned, pulled me closer, and buried his face in my hair. I wanted to stay this way forever. I never wanted September to come.

"You're every song I have ever sung. I'll never let anything hurt you again. For the first time in my life, my dreams aren't about me." I lifted my eyes up to meet his, and he smiled. "They're about you."

# Chapter Fourteen

**JAX**

The banging on my bedroom door woke me, and I sat up, ready to yell at whoever had decided it was okay to wake me up so damn early. But my eyes registered the panicked look on my brother's face as he came barreling into the room.

He didn't speak. He just grabbed the television remote and turned it on. "You need to see this" was the only thing that registered when images of me and Sadie flashed on the television screen. What the hell had happened? They'd found me. And my worst nightmare had come true. Sadie's private life was being broadcast for the world to see. I hated anyone seeing her face. I hated the way they talked about her like they knew her. They didn't know anything.

I'd done this. It was all my fault. I hadn't protected her from this. I'd walked her right into it.

## SADIE

Sunday morning I slept late again. I could hear Jessica up and about in the kitchen. I stretched before standing up, reaching for my phone, and slipping it into the pocket of my pajama pants. I was supposed to be meeting Jax this afternoon to go surfing, something I had never tried. I walked down the short hallway into the kitchen and saw Jessica leaning against the bar drinking a big glass of milk.

"It's about time Sleeping Beauty woke up."

I stifled a yawn and shrugged. "So I slept late. I get up early every other day of the week."

Jessica nodded. "Yes, but today is the day you get to find out what happens to girls who date rock stars."

I frowned at her. "What're you talking about?"

She pushed off from the bar and threw the Sunday paper on the table in front of me.

"Good thing I have thick skin, because this ain't flattering." She turned and walked out of the room. I stared down for the second time at a photo of Jax with a girl, but this time it was my waist his arm wrapped around. He appeared to be whispering in my ear or kissing it. I sank down into the chair when I realized I was wearing my swimsuit. The picture had been taken at the July Fourth party while we were dancing. Above our pictures the headline read THE PRINCE OF ROCK IS SNAGGED BY HIS MAID. My stomach dropped.

Jax Stone has been living semi-undercover here in Sea Breeze this summer, courting his hired maid, Miss Sadie White. The couple was seen together at a party held at the house of Mayor McCovey. Mayor McCovey's son, Dylan McCovey, held his annual July Fourth party at his parents' home on Seagull Drive, and Sadie White was an invited guest.

When we spoke to Dylan, he said, "No one was expecting it. Sadie is just a girl who moved here this year. We had no idea she was dating Jax Stone. But the two were inseparable." Sadie is an employee of the Stones', and she rides her bike to their house on Sea Breeze's exclusive island, where only the extraordinarily wealthy have summer homes. She works in his kitchen and serves him his food. Apparently, he takes her home after work.

Sadie lives with her mother, Jessica White, in an apartment here in Sea Breeze. Her mother is a single mom who is expecting a baby any day. Sadie seems

> to be the only one with a job. Interestingly enough, she somehow managed to be Jax Stone's summer girl.

I closed my eyes and laid my head on the table. I couldn't believe the local newspaper had gotten wind of this. They'd painted Jax as a cold jerk who took advantage of his employees.

"You'd better come in here, Sadie," Jessica called from the living room. "Things seem to be getting better and better."

I looked up. She was staring at the television. I knew deep down I didn't want to see what she was watching, but I stood up and forced myself to walk in there.

"*Star Follower* has the scoop on everyone's favorite teen rocker. Jax Stone, who was spotted with Bailey Kirk just last week here in Beverly Hills, has been located in Alabama. That's right, fans. He has been spending his time this summer on the coast of Alabama, and not alone, either. He has been dating his hired help. The kitchen maid." Photos of me with Jax appeared on the screen. "Our insider source says she rides her bike to his home, where she is employed to work in the kitchen and in the garden. When Jax has any free time, he spends it charming this Alabama local. It seems the girl who lives in a small apartment and takes care of her single, yet pregnant, mom has climbed up the ladder and found herself a way out of poverty. We are left to wonder if she will manage to squeeze out a better way of life from this smitten rock star. Jax Stone really is a bighearted guy. It's one of the reasons he is so incredibly edible!"

I felt sick. I ran from the room and went straight to the bathroom. After I emptied everything inside me, I splashed my face with water, then sank down to the floor and laid my head on the tub.

This wasn't something I'd been expecting. I had been prepared for a lot, but this wasn't something I ever feared. Now my life was being splattered all over the media. Either I sounded like a gold-digging tramp, or Jax sounded like he was taking advantage of a stupid, naive southern girl. There was a knock on the bathroom door. I couldn't face Jessica right now. I just needed to be alone.

"Throwing up isn't going to make this better. You might as well come hear the other versions on other news channels. Some of them don't paint us like white trash."

I groaned. "No."

I stayed on the floor of the bathroom until I heard someone at the front door, and I knew without a doubt it was Jax.

"Sadie, honey, you got company," Jessica called from outside the door again.

I didn't want to leave him out there with her, so I stood up and stared at myself in the mirror. My eyes were bloodshot, and there was nothing I could do about it. I opened the door and there, instead of Jessica, stood a very upset Jax.

He grabbed me and pulled me into his arms. "I swear, I'll kill whoever did this."

I began to cry again. I didn't want to do this to him, because he was obviously beating himself up about it.

He pulled back just enough so I could see his face. "Will you come with me?"

I nodded.

Jax led me with his arm firmly around my waist. "Ms. White, I'm just going to take Sadie for a little while. I'll bring her back soon."

Jessica snorted. "Just make sure you bring her back happier than she is right now."

He frowned, and we walked out to his Hummer. Kane sat in the driver's seat, and I was glad Jax didn't have to drive, so I wouldn't have to give up his arms. A flash went off, and Jax put himself in front of me. "Hurry, get into the car." He slid in behind me, and we were behind the protection of dark tinted windows.

"Sadie, I'm so sorry," he whispered again.

I sniffed and wiped my eyes. "It's not your fault."

He gave a hard laugh. "Yes, it is. I was careless. I wanted everyone to know you were mine, and I put you in the way of danger. The media are like hungry vultures. They pick you clean. This isn't going to just disappear."

I shuddered at the thought of more of my personal life

being shared with the world. "How do you do this? How do you handle the invasion of privacy?" I whispered through my tear-clogged throat.

He sighed. "It's all I've known for a very long time."

"This is hard," I admitted.

His eyes were haunted. I hated that I was the cause of all this. Being with me seemed to only bring him trouble.

"I'm tough." I forced a smile. "I can live through this."

Jax didn't say anything for a few minutes. He reached over and pulled me into his arms, and we sat in silence.

"I promised you I would never let anything hurt you again." He closed his eyes tightly and whispered, as if the images in his head were too much, "And instead I've not only hurt you, but I've hurt your mom."

I touched his arm, hating to see him so torn up inside. "I told you I was tough. It isn't your fault."

He dropped his hold, pulled away from me, and leaned forward on his knees. "No, Sadie, *no!* This is all my fault. I am the world's favorite teenage rock star. I live in the media. But to hear them"—he stopped and his jaw clenched—"to hear them talk about you that way . . . I need . . . I want to hurt someone."

I scooted up on my seat to get closer to him. "Jax, please, I should've known something like this would happen. Yes, it hurts, but I can live through this. I can live through anything as long as I have you."

He shook his head violently. "Don't you see, Sadie? This is just the beginning. Your life will never be the same. I knew this when I first realized I wanted to be with you. My life isn't made for relationships. Only girls in the spotlight can handle it, and I have never found one I wanted. Then came you. Sweet, gorgeous, selfless . . . everything I had never known. I was selfish to allow this to happen. I was selfish when I decided to charm you, and when it worked, I was selfish to want to hold on to you."

He took my hands in his. "I love you more than anyone or anything I've ever known. You've somehow become the song inside of me. It's because I love you so much I'm going to walk out of your life and allow you to heal and find someone worthy of you. Someone who can take you to the movies and out to get a pizza and not have to worry about being mauled by fans or getting your picture taken and splashed all over the news. I want you to have more than I can give."

I glanced out the window and realized we were sitting outside my apartment again.

"I'm not strong enough to do this, Sadie. If you love me, you will get out of the car and walk away."

My heart shattered, and I couldn't take a deep breath. My eyes were blurry with unshed tears. But I didn't move. I couldn't.

"I don't want to walk away from you. I love you, but how can you ask me to do this?" I whispered.

He studied me with hard eyes. "Sadie, I was leaving anyway

in a few short weeks. We couldn't have kept seeing each other after I left. This, and more, would happen if I tried to come back here during my free time."

"But you said you loved me."

His laugh sounded hard and mechanical. "Sometimes, Sadie, love isn't enough. This is one of those times."

The door on my side opened, and Kane stood with his hand held out to me.

Jax's eyes seemed void of emotion.

"Good-bye, Sadie."

I always knew he would have to be the one to end this. I could never walk away from him any other way. But he wanted me to now. He wanted me to leave. I was a hindrance to his life. I couldn't fit in. I hated myself for my weakness and my emotions. But I knew they were a part of me, and I couldn't help it. I couldn't be what he needed. I stepped out of the car and headed toward the door, where my mother stood waiting on me. She had known somehow I would be coming back this way. The tears rolled down my face as I made my way to her, and for the first time since I was a little girl, I hurled myself into her arms and wept.

# Chapter Fifteen

**JAX**

"So you're really going to just leave her?" Jason asked, staring at me as I handed Kane my last suitcase.

"Yeah, I am. What the *fuck* do you expect me to do? If I stay here, the media will descend and her life will just get harder. I can't do that to her, Jason. I just can't. Everything with us has been selfish on my part. I wanted something I should have cherished enough to leave alone, but I was weak. Now Sadie is paying for my need to be near her. I hate myself and my damn weakness." I slammed my fist against the wall and closed my eyes tightly. I would not cry. I couldn't. Especially not in front of Jason.

"But I've seen her. She loves you. You're different with her. You're . . . *you*. I've missed you."

If Jason had sliced me open with a butcher knife, it would have hurt less. I shoved past him and stalked out to the limo that sat waiting to take me to the airport. I needed to get back to my old life. The one where I lived each day numb to emotion and I just sang. I could do that again. If I refused to let myself remember how sweet Sadie tasted and how good she felt in my arms. If I could ever forget how she gave me a reason to want to live.

## SADIE

I'd never been empty and void before. Even during hard times, I'd had a dream for my future. To live without a daydream or hope for happiness was like walking around dead. There was no future I could see that gave me reason to daydream. I hadn't left my room for days—I'm not sure how many, but I couldn't bring myself to get up. Jessica stood outside my door every day and talked to me. She left food that I didn't eat, and she threatened to have me hospitalized. But when someone doesn't care if they take their next breath, threats mean nothing.

Jessica had begun leaving the house for hours at a time. The sound of her car starting up let me know she had left. After sunset her car returned. She always asked me if I was okay and encouraged me to eat. But I couldn't eat. My appetite had gone. I knew without my working we would run out of money, but I couldn't bring myself to care. Something inside me wanted to stay in this room and not move. If I moved, it hurt, and I couldn't deal with the pain again.

Somewhere in my darkness a phone rang. The ring of a familiar song that sent arrows through my heart. I knew it was for me, but I couldn't answer it. His voice on the line would open the blackness I had wrapped around me. I needed the blackness—it kept out the pain that wanted in. So I let it ring. The song eventually stopped, and I knew I'd never hear that ring again. I had the darkness to hold on to. That kept the pain out. It was so much easier this way.

A knock on my window startled me, and I jumped. The window opened, and I sat motionless, unable to stop the intruder. The fight in me was gone. I watched as my intruder stepped into the darkness. The familiar face of a friend broke through the dark blanket, and my tears began to fall.

Marcus sat down beside me against the wall and pulled me into his arms. I went like a child and curled up in his lap and cried. He didn't speak. He just held me, and his silence and acceptance soothed the pain. When my crying eventually mellowed, I stared up at him and touched his face. He was real, and he was here. Even after I had been the reason he'd lost his job, he had come to me in the darkness.

"Sadie," he whispered, as if his words might be too much for me. "I need you to eat for me." He shifted me so I sat beside him.

I frowned at him, confused. Why was he talking about food?

"Sadie, listen to me. You have been in here for three days without food or drink. You have to eat, sweetheart, or I'm going to have to take you to the hospital."

There they went again, threatening me. I shook my head. I didn't want food. Marcus held my face in his hands as if I were fragile and might break at any moment.

"Sadie, do you want to get better?"

Even in the darkness, I knew I didn't want to get worse. I did want to get better. I wanted to have a reason to smile.

"I know you do. Now, I have some water and bread, and I'm going to sit right here with you, and I want you to eat for me, okay?" He held the glass of water up to my mouth, and I obediently drank. It wasn't going to make me better. I knew water wasn't the answer to the pain, but I drank it anyway. I wanted to take the scared look out of his eyes.

"Good girl," he said softly, and he broke a piece of bread and held it up to my mouth. "Now take a bite for me."

I did, and he broke into a grin. Seeing him smile reminded me that I might never smile again.

"That's good. Now take another drink."

I did, and he seemed thrilled. So I ate more as he offered it and drank from the cup in his hands. When I had finished what he'd brought, he grinned like he had won some kind of medal.

"You did wonderful. Now, why don't we get you cleaned up, and we can go down to the beach and watch the waves?"

I realized I wanted to get out of this room with the darkness. Maybe I could find another way to deal with the pain. The ocean was always soothing. I liked the ocean. I nodded, and he stood and pulled me up. My legs wobbled, and I held on to his arms for support.

"That's my girl. Now, hold on to me."

I walked with him into the hall, and Jessica was standing there with relief in her eyes.

"Did she eat?" she asked Marcus, and he nodded. "Oh, baby, that's wonderful. Now let's get you all washed up."

She took my hand, and I stiffened. Some sort of pain tried to break through.

"Uh, maybe I had better get her in there first, and we will see how it goes from there."

Jessica nodded and stepped back. Marcus walked me into the bathroom and stood me in front of the mirror. The pale girl with dark circles under her eyes who stared back at me scared me. I shivered.

"Now you see why you need to go out with me. You need fresh air, and the sea breeze is the best thing for you. But first you have got to let me wait outside the door and let your mom in here to help you. You're weak from no food, and you're dehydrated."

I wanted to be me again. I didn't like the stranger in the

mirror. I nodded, and then he let me go, and Jessica came into the tiny little room. I let her help me shower and fix my hair. Once we finished, the face in the mirror appeared less scary, but it still wasn't me.

The fresh salt air smelled wonderful. I stood on the sand and inhaled as the waves crashed in front of me. Water splashed my ankles and calves, but I stood and gazed out at the water.

"I would have come sooner if I'd known," Marcus said from behind me.

I didn't want to talk about it. "It wasn't your problem."

His hands gently touched my arms. "I know all you need is a friend right now, and I want to be that for you."

I wanted a friend too. "I'd like that."

He softly squeezed my arms. "I'm not going to make you talk about anything you're not ready to."

"Thank you." I didn't want to need the darkness.

"Ms. Mary called me yesterday. She's worried about you, and she misses you. She said to tell you that you're always welcome at her house." It eased the pain to know I hadn't lost everything. "And Mr. Greg wants me to bring you over for chess as soon as you are up for it." I wanted to smile, but I couldn't. "The gossip is starting to die down now. But I'm afraid you will be the most sought-after girl at Sea Breeze High." I stiffened. I wanted to go back to being unknown and overlooked. "Hey, don't go getting all tense. It's not a bad thing."

I shook my head. "I don't want to think about school."

He sighed. "Sadie, you're going to have to pick up and move on. Not talking about any of it is going to keep you from having a life."

I knew he was right, but the pain that the thoughts evoked was so intense I didn't think I could do it. "The pain . . . I can't breathe when I start to remember."

He didn't say anything right away. We stood watching the waves together. I could breathe without the pain for the first time since Jax had gone.

"I hope one day I can evoke in someone as amazing as you that kind of love and need."

I turned my gaze to him. "It's the most amazing thing in the world when you're together, but when it's over, it hurts. It hurts more than you could ever imagine." I heard the words come out, and I was surprised at myself for speaking my thoughts aloud.

"Would you do it differently if you could, now that you know how it ends?"

I allowed myself to think of Jax's smile and his arms around me, and I knew I wouldn't change anything. Our last dance that I had memorized every second of came back to me, and with it came the pain. My knees buckled, and Marcus's arms came around me and held me up. I fought the pain with the happiness I had known, and that seemed to ease it. No, if I could go back and do it again, all I would do is just try to be stronger or . . .

just more. I would try to be someone who could hold on to him. Someone who could deserve him.

"No," I whispered, and I knew I wouldn't miss a moment. Saying it out loud and knowing I would never forget it, or give up the memories, eased the pain a little more.

"He loves you too," Marcus admitted into the darkness.

I wondered if he was saying those words in hopes of making me feel better, or if he truly meant them. "He didn't love me enough," I said into the night breeze, and turned my attention back to the water. It helped soothe me.

"What is enough?" Marcus asked.

I sighed and closed my eyes. "Willing to get through the hard stuff together." The words made sense, but I hated that it sounded as if I were betraying Jax with them.

"I don't know why I'm defending him, but I believe he left to protect you. For the first time since he'd met you, he put you first."

I let out a hard, cold laugh that didn't sound like me. "How can taking away the reason my heart beats be good for me?"

Marcus took my arm. "Jax knew when he met you he wouldn't be able to keep you. He knew you wouldn't fit into his world. I blame myself for pursuing you in front of him, because that is what broke his resolve to stay away from you. He couldn't handle the jealousy. For the first time in his life, he wanted something he could not have, and he fought it for you. I watched him. But then he caved, and when he did, it was the beginning of the end. I hate him for not being strong enough. I hate him for hurting you. But more than any of that, I hate him because he stole your heart and I don't think it'll ever be the same."

I didn't want to fight with Marcus. He had come to get me out of the darkness when no one else had. He was a friend. My first friend ever. I knew he would never understand that I didn't regret one moment I'd spent with Jax. The pain I was enduring now was worth every moment of the time I'd spent with him.

So I touched his arm and turned away from his sad face. "You're right about one thing. My heart—he took it with him."

The next few days, my darkness slowly faded. My memories began to brighten the darkest spots. I couldn't go back to Jax's house and work. My time there was over. After a week of being home, Jessica came to my room.

"If we're going to eat, we need money. No one is going to hire me when I'm ready to give birth at any moment. I know you're hurting, but you're going to be starving and hot if you don't find a job."

I had been expecting this. I knew our cash was low, and Jessica was right, she couldn't work. I was the able body around here. She brought me a piece of paper.

"Call Ms. Mary. She said she could get you a job if you wanted her help. What she can get you is going to be tons better than anything you can find on your own. Also, the Stones left all their summer employees severance pay since they were all laid off a month and a half early. Ms. Mary said she was mailing the check."

I flinched, and Jessica sighed and sat down on my bed. "I know thinking about him hurts, and you're so full of pride that taking money from him is hard for you, but right now, with me about to have a baby, we need this money."

I pulled my knees up under my chin. "Yes, but the family left early because of me. Why should they have to pay me because I forced their departure?"

Jessica sighed and shook her head. "You didn't do anything wrong but fall in love with a rock star. I can't say I blame you—he was a hottie—but a relationship with someone like him was impossible from the beginning. They left early, and you lost your job because of it. They owe you like everyone else."

I shook my head. "No, they owe me nothing!"

Jessica stood up. "Well, regardless of what you think, we will take the check and pay our bills, fill our kitchen, and go buy diapers. Stop being so selfish and open your eyes to the facts, Sadie. We are about to have another mouth to feed, and no amount of your whining and wallowing in self-pity or pride is going to supply our needs. So stop it and move on."

Jessica turned and left my room. One thing I agreed with was that we needed money. So I got up and got dressed because I was off to find myself a job.

# Chapter Sixteen

**JAX**

I sat on the bed in my suite and held my phone in my hands. Ms. Mary had just called and told me she had gotten Sadie a new job. One she could work at even after school started back up. She'd said Sadie had looked good the last time she'd seen her and that she was spending a lot of time with Marcus.

The idea of her falling in love with Marcus and moving on made it hard for me to breathe. I closed my eyes and buried my head in my hands. She was going to move on. Maybe not now, and maybe not with Marcus, but she would one day. And our time together would be nothing but a memory for her. One she would probably work hard to push away.

Tears stung my eyes and I let them fall. There was no one around to see me cry, and I needed to cry. I needed to mourn. I'd lost it all. My chance at ever really being happy. I'd found it for a moment with Sadie, but now it was gone.

## SADIE

Ms. Mary was well connected. For three weeks I'd been doing the filing at a local lawyer's office. Apparently, Ms. Mary's neighbor worked for a lawyer, and the lawyer needed someone to assist his secretary. With Ms. Mary's glowing recommendation, he hired me and was paying me exactly what I had been making before. When school started, I would go directly to his office after school and work until six each night. Mary Ellis, his secretary, was around Jessica's age and easy to work with. I enjoyed the work, and at times I even got so busy I didn't think about Mr. Greg and his war stories, or Ms. Mary and her laughter. I had finished my third week, and my paycheck was in my hands. It wasn't really needed yet, considering that the severance pay from Jax had been ridiculous and Jessica had refused to let me dispose of it. Ms. Mary had assured me everyone's had been just as ridiculous. It mollified me a little, but not enough. Somehow I still felt bought off. I hated thinking of it that way, but I did.

I parked my bike by the door and heard a scream from inside the house. My heart started racing. I jerked the door open and ran inside. Jessica was bent over in the kitchen, and bloody water was running down her legs and pooling on the floor. "What's happening?" I asked, panicked.

"Call 911 *now!*"

Her cell phone was lying on the countertop, and I grabbed it. She screamed again. My hands shook so badly it was hard to dial. Something was terribly wrong.

"Nine-one-one, what's your emergency?"

"My mother, she's bleeding and in a lot of pain, she is screaming. She's eight months—maybe almost nine months pregnant. I think, I'm not sure." My words were so rushed I hoped they made sense.

"Help is on the way now. Tell me what your mother is doing." The voice sounded so calm.

"She's breathing hard and sitting in a chair."

"Ask her how she feels."

I looked at her. All color had vanished from her face. Her eyes were big and scared. Seeing my mother worried and in pain made me want to panic.

"How do you feel?" I asked shakily.

"It's okay right now, but that doesn't mean anything. It'll come back." She gritted her teeth and closed her eyes.

"She's fine now, but she said it would come back."

"She's correct, it will come back. Your mother is in labor. Now I need you to remain calm and get her a cold wet wash-cloth and wipe her face. It'll help soothe her."

I did as the voice told me. Jessica sat silently while I washed her face.

"How is she?" the voice asked.

"She's okay. I washed her face, and she is breathing easier."

"That's good. The baby isn't coming too quickly. Now, if you'll get her some ice chips to suck on, or crushed ice in a cup, this will also help."

I started to go get some ice cubes and crush them when I heard the ambulance sirens outside.

"The ambulance is here," I told the voice on the phone.

"Good. Then everything is going to be fine, and you did really well. I'll let you go and talk to them."

"Thank you," I said hastily, and hung up the phone. I ran to the door and threw it open wide, just as a guy was about to knock. "She is right here."

I motioned, and he came in quickly with a lady behind him. They talked to Jessica and checked her pulse and temperature. When they'd finished with their examination and questions, they got a stretcher, laid her on it, and slid her into the back of the ambulance. I stood frozen and unsure. Jessica wasn't the best mother in the world, but I loved her, and tears ran down my face. I didn't want to think about anything happening to her.

The lady said to me, "Oh, honey, everything is just fine. Your mom is just in labor. Come on, now, wipe those tears before she sees you. The last thing she needs is to see you upset."

I did as she said. Suddenly I realized if I didn't drive, we would be without transportation when we needed to come home. And then the fact that I needed to get the car seat and all the other things she needed for the hospital occurred to me.

"I . . . we will need our car, and the stuff for the baby."

The male paramedic walked up, an easy smile on his face. "You go ahead, then, and get the things your mom and the baby will need and bring the car. When you get to the hospital, go to information, and they'll direct you to her room."

I stared at the lady as she climbed into the back with Jessica.

"Don't forget her things too," the lady said. "She will need toiletries and nightgowns, and then of course something to wear home."

I nodded, and the doors were closed. I couldn't believe this was happening already. I watched them drive away, and then I rushed back inside to pack up everything Jessica and the baby would need. First things first, I mopped up the blood and water from the floor and the seat she had been sitting in. Having a baby really was gross stuff. After the kitchen was clean, I went to Jessica's room and found the infant car seat she had bought from a secondhand store before we left Tennessee.

Ms. Mary had sent bags of baby girl and boy clothing to my workplace last week. She had kept almost everything she had bought for her grandchildren as they outgrew them. I sifted through the baby-scented clothing and found the smallest item in there. It was a soft yellow outfit with feet, and with snaps up the front. This should be safe for a boy or a girl. I grabbed it and quickly snatched up a diaper bag for the items Jessica had bought for the baby. With no idea what all of it was used for, I figured if I took it all, we should be good. After I had the baby stuff ready, I packed Jessica a nice, stretchy sundress and underthings, as well as a few nightgowns. She had very little in the way of modest sleeping attire, so I stuffed in a few T-shirts for her to slip on over her nightgowns. Once everything was packed, I headed out to the car and loaded it up. I wanted to be there when the baby was born. I wanted to experience its entrance into the world. It had been a stranger to me for nine months. Up until now, all I'd had was Jessica. Now I would have a sibling.

I pulled the sliding overnight bag back up on my arm as I stepped off the elevator. The waiting room was full of excited, hopeful people of all ages. Grandparents bounced children on their knee and pointed and gushed over the babies in the window. This was a happy place, where life started. I walked toward the double doors that led to the delivery rooms. I passed new dads, or almost new dads, standing around the coffeepot, sharing horror stories of wives who had morphed into monsters. A few had decided that hiding out here was a better idea than witnessing the birth of their child. I wondered if Jessica had become one of these crazed monsters as I searched for room 321. I spotted it and took a deep breath before walking in. I was all Jessica had.

There would be no one else standing by to hold her hand. It was just me, and I couldn't go anywhere.

"Sadie, oh good, you got all the stuff. I guess I should have packed, but I wasn't expecting this to happen so soon."

I nodded, set the bags down on a chair, and walked over to her. All sorts of cords were hooked up to her. She was wet with sweat, her hair clung to her head, and she remained pale. Other than that, she wasn't cursing and foaming at the mouth, which was what other women on this floor were apparently doing.

"Um, you look good," I admitted.

She grinned and shrugged. "Well, it ain't over yet, honey, and it gets worse. Right now my dilating has slowed, and I'm high on Demerol. I know there is pain, but I just don't seem to care at the moment."

I nodded, not sure what that meant. "Well, do you need anything?" I asked, wanting to be useful.

"More ice would be nice," she mumbled. I nodded and headed out to find ice. "Wait! You're gonna need my cup."

I turned around and went to get the plastic hospital cup sitting beside her bed. "I'll be right back."

Once outside the room, I went to find the ice and filled her cup up to the top. I wanted to make sure she was fine before I made the call to Ms. Mary. Once I had Jessica fixed up, I slipped out of the room and back outside the hospital. I called Ms. Mary.

"Hello." Her cheery voice lightened my spirits.

"Ms. Mary, it's Sadie. I just wanted to call and let you know my mom is having the baby."

"Oh, this is early, but don't worry about that none. I had both my girls several weeks early, and everything was just fine. I'm coming to see you as soon as I get off work. Now, how are you?"

I smiled at the warmth that filled me when Ms. Mary worried about me. Jessica loved me, but she had never really worried over me.

"I'm fine, and my mom's doing good. They have given her some Demerol, and she said it makes her not care that she is in pain."

Ms. Mary chuckled. "That is some amazing stuff, I tell you. Well, I'll be with you soon, and maybe there will be a baby to hold by then. You call me if you need me, do you hear?"

I couldn't help but smile. "I will."

"Good-bye, for now," she said in her jolly tone that always made it seem like everything was going to be okay.

"Good-bye," I replied before pressing end. I turned the phone back off and slipped it into my pocket.

When I neared Jessica's room, I heard the familiar screaming and hurried inside. Jessica was sitting up with her legs spread—with the covers draped over her, thankfully. A nurse, who appeared very calm and collected considering her patient was screaming profanities at her, smiled at me. I smiled at her apologetically and went to stand beside Jessica.

"Is she about to have the baby now?" I asked nervously.

The nurse nodded. "Yep, as soon as the doctor gets in here, she can begin pushing."

My stomach churned. The whole idea of pushing and where this baby was going to enter the world from made me slightly light-headed. However, another of Jessica's bloodcurdling screams was like a slap in the face, and I quickly shook the thoughts out of my head.

"What can I do?" I asked, anxiously staring at the nurse.

"You can lock me in my room if I ever decide to date again!" Jessica yelled, and grabbed my arm as another onslaught of contractions hit her.

I grimaced and fought the urge to pry her hands off me. As soon as it ended and she released her ironclad grip, I stepped out of her reach. The nurse grinned at me.

"That might be wise," she whispered as she walked past me to check the machine's beeping.

Jessica began screaming again, and this time the bed rail was her gripping post. I rubbed my arm, thankful to have put distance between us.

"Ah, the doctor's here." The nurse beamed, obviously ready to get this over with so she could escape the violence being spewed from my mother's mouth.

"Are you going to stay for this part?" the doctor asked,

frowning as he slipped gloves onto his hands.

Jessica panted and nodded. "Yes! She is!" she yelled, and then let out another fierce scream.

I nodded.

He shrugged and took his place down by her feet. "All right, Ms. White, are you ready to do this thing?" he asked jovially, and I wondered if someone had to be mentally off to actually be glad he was in the room with a screaming woman and about to extract a human from her body.

*"Get it out!"* she screamed.

He smiled at me. "She'll be back to normal real soon." He winked and nodded to the nurse.

I stepped back toward Jessica's head when he flipped the white sheet up over her knees.

"Okay, Ms. White, when the contraction starts, I want you to push as hard as you can," he instructed.

Jessica panted, then began screaming and pushing all at once.

"That's great! Keep this up, and we'll have a little one here in seconds."

She stopped to catch her breath before her face morphed into the monster those men had been speaking of earlier, and she screamed and pushed again. We went through this several more times before I heard a cry that was too soft to be anything but a baby.

"Beautiful! You can relax now, Ms. White. He has arrived."

The doctor had said "he." I no longer cared about the messy scene going on down by her feet. I just wanted to see this little life that was now a part of mine.

The nurse wrapped him in a blanket and smiled at me. "You have a brother." She handed the baby to Jessica, who, although exhausted, smiled down at the little life in her hands.

"Hello, Sam," she whispered.

I leaned down over her and studied his miniature features.

"Sam, meet your big sister, Sadie," she said, handing the little bundle up to me.

I stiffened and stared at her like she was crazy.

"Oh, come on. He's just a baby. Hold him."

I slid my arms under him and took him from my mother. His tiny little fist fought its way out of the blanket, and he swung it around in the air and let out a small cry. I laughed. He was like a little miracle.

"We need to go clean him and let the pediatrician check him over. However, we will bring him back to eat very soon." The nurse was standing in front of me with her arms held out.

"Okay," I said through the lump in my throat. Reluctantly, I handed over this new little person I already loved, and watched her take him away.

"Don't worry, you were ugly too when you first came out, but after a few days you were the most beautiful baby I had ever seen."

I glared at Jessica, who had laid her head back and closed her eyes.

"He's beautiful now," I countered. Already the little guy had me wanting to defend him.

She let out a laugh. "No, he looks like a prune. All new babies do."

I frowned and tried to remind myself that Jessica was not normal, so I should not expect her to treat birth normally.

"Excuse us, but we need to patch some things up for your mom and move her to a room. Why don't you go get something to eat and rest? This has all been very exciting for you, I am sure." The nurse, who had been there through it all with us, smiled at me.

I left the room. I was in a daze when I stepped into the waiting room and was immediately surrounded.

# Chapter Seventeen

**SADIE**

"Are you okay?" Marcus was beside me, touching my arm. I gazed into his big, worried eyes and smiled.

"Back up, boy, and give her some breathing room. She didn't just give birth, her mama did." Ms. Mary batted Marcus's arm and beamed at me.

"Is it as beautiful as you are?"

I laughed and shook my head. "No, *he* is more beautiful than anything I have ever seen," I answered truthfully. He'd looked nothing like a prune to me. He was perfect.

"I find it hard to believe any male could surpass you in beauty," came another familiar voice. Preston shuffled his feet and grinned.

I hadn't seen him behind Marcus. I smiled at him and

shrugged. "Well, believe it," I said, and they all laughed.

"Move out of the way, you bunch of vultures. I can't even see the girl, much less talk to her," Mr. Greg grumbled as he pushed Marcus out of the way.

"A boy, is it? Well, ain't that good news! Is he healthy and all?"

I nodded, glanced over to the nursery window, and saw him being brought in. "There he is. Come see."

I turned and went to the glass. He was all bundled up again, but this time nice and clean. The nurse who had come in to take him saw me and brought him over to the window so everyone could see.

"He is a beauty." Ms. Mary beamed.

"Look at the little guy. He already has his fist up ready for a fight." Marcus grinned at me.

I shook my head and laughed before turning back to my little brother.

"I guess if there was a pretty boy, then that would be one," Mr. Greg admitted from his spot behind me.

I couldn't agree more.

"Well then, how is your mama?" Ms. Mary asked, walking over to the side of the window so others could come see inside as well.

"She's doing great. She, uh, got a little loud and angry toward the end, but she is good now and was dozing off when I left her."

Ms. Mary chuckled and shook her head. "I guess you won't be wanting babies anytime soon after witnessing that."

I laughed. "You're right, I won't."

Marcus came up beside me. "Why don't you let me take you to get something to eat while you're waiting? You have to be hungry."

I was getting ready to turn him down when Ms. Mary nodded. "Let the boys take you for a bite. It'll be an hour before they let you back into your mom's room. Besides, when you leave tonight, it is going to be too dark to stop somewhere on your own."

"Sure."

I knew I wouldn't have to deal with any deep conversations with both Preston and Marcus there. I was hungry, and getting out of the hospital would be a good change of scenery.

Luckily, we didn't have to squeeze into Marcus's truck, because Preston had driven his Jeep. Marcus, however, was stuck in the back, and Preston seemed extremely pleased. We all agreed on going to grab a burger at the Pickle Shack. I hadn't had any free time since I'd started my new job, and my visits from Marcus were always short. I was glad we were going to get to sit and talk without my having to hurry off to work.

We slipped into a booth, and Preston shot Marcus a deadly glare when he slid in beside me. I was beginning to think that Marcus wasn't overreacting, and maybe Preston did like me. Not that it mattered. My heart didn't race at the sight of him, and the tingles didn't come. My knees didn't go weak when he smiled. He was just another guy. I knew that it would always be this way. I was getting better with dealing with the memories and the pain. Once I had accepted that I would never love someone the way I love Jax, it was a little easier to breathe. He would always be in my heart, whether he wanted to be there or not. I just didn't have enough room for anyone else. He was my air, my soul, and the keeper of my heart.

"So, you ready for your senior year?" Preston leaned on the table and grinned.

He had a good grin—even a sexy grin—but it did nothing for me. I sighed and shrugged, because the truth was, I didn't care anymore about school. I didn't think about my future like I had before the summer began.

"I guess I'm as ready as I'll ever be," I mumbled.

He frowned, "Your senior year is supposed to be the best year of your life. You have to be excited about it!"

I wasn't, and I knew they wouldn't understand, so I didn't try to explain that my reason for breathing was gone. I nodded as if to agree with him and just kept my mouth shut.

"I leave in a week to go back to Tuscaloosa." It was the first time Marcus had spoken. "I have to get me an apartment and get moved down before the semester begins."

Marcus's words surprised me. I hadn't realized realize he was leaving so soon.

"Really?" I asked, hearing the sadness in my voice. He nodded and looked away from me.

"Well, make sure to come tell me bye,'" I reminded him, thinking that at least this good-bye wasn't going to zap me of life.

He gazed at me with a strange expression on his face, as if he wanted to say something but was fighting himself about it. "Yeah. I will," he finally said halfheartedly.

"Well, the good news is, *I* will not be going anywhere," Preston said, "and you can call me anytime, and I will be more than willing to, uh, I don't know, take you to dinner, a movie, or a— Ouch!"

I jumped, and Preston shot daggers at Marcus. "What did you do that for?" he challenged.

Marcus rolled his eyes. "I stopped you before you made an even bigger idiot of yourself."

Preston snorted. "Is he always this moody around you?"

I grinned and shook my head. "Nope."

Preston broke into a grin. "So, you don't like the competition, do you, big boy?" he teased, and Marcus glared at his friend and sighed before he turned to me.

"What he doesn't realize is that the competition isn't even at this table."

Preston frowned, and then, like a light went on, he sat back and grew serious, which was a first.

"Can I get you something to drink . . . Wait, *Ohmygod*, it's *you*! Ah, I can't believe it! Jax Stone's girlfriend."

The girl rummaged through her apron pocket and pulled out a piece of paper and handed me a pen. "Can I have your autograph, please?"

I was too shocked to respond, or to move, for that matter. I looked at Marcus, and I guess he noticed the panic in my eyes, because he took the paper and pen and handed them back to the girl.

"Uh, why don't you take our drink order instead?"

The girl's grin fell, and I dropped my eyes to my hands. I wasn't sure what to say or how to respond. This was not something I had seen coming.

Marcus ordered me a Coke, then took my hand. "I guess you haven't been around town lately?" he asked cautiously.

I shook my head but didn't meet his gaze.

He sighed deeply and leaned down toward me. "Things are going to be a little different for you, for a while, at least. You're still on the news some, and, well, around this small town, you're a star. No one has ever gotten as close to fame as you have."

I closed my eyes. This wasn't supposed to be happening. Jax had left me to keep this from happening. Was my life going to always be this way? When would everyone realize the rock star had left me? I was no longer his, and I was no longer interesting. I was just Sadie White.

"Sadie, look at me, please," Marcus whispered.

I met his eyes slowly and noticed the waitress pointing our way.

"Great, she's announcing my presence," I muttered.

Marcus turned around to see girls looking our way. He turned to Preston. "Could you go put those pretty-boy looks to good use and distract the 'OMG' squad over there?"

Preston nodded. "Sure." He went over to the girls, and almost immediately he had them giggling and smiling at him.

Relief washed over me. "Do you think he'll go to school with me and do that?" I asked quietly.

Marcus chuckled. "No, you'll be on your own there. But remember, they will get over it. It's just Jax recorded a new song, and it's rumored all over the news that it is about you. It hit number one its first week on the radio. The buzz is being fed a little more."

I swallowed the lump in my throat. "What does the song say?" I heard myself asking. Why I wanted to know was beyond me. This was going to be painful, but I still wanted to know.

Marcus dropped his hands from mine and shifted in his seat. "Enough for me to know it's about you," he said with no emotion in his voice.

I nodded and turned my attention to watching the world outside the window. Preston returned with our Cokes and set them on the table.

"Thanks for that," I said, nodding toward the giggling girls, who now only had eyes for Preston.

He shrugged and grinned. "Not a problem. I'm glad these good looks are good for something." He winked and took a sip of his Coke.

I relaxed and took a drink too. I had so much to take in today. Our two had become three, and I needed to get ready for a baby in the house. And then there was the fact that I was apparently well known by complete strangers. I let my mind go to Jax's new song, and my heart raced when I thought about it. I had watched him writing out at the gazebo as I worked in the gardens during the time we were together. Back then, I had never dreamed what he was working on was about me. If it was about me, what did it say? Were the words going to rip into me and bring the dark blanket back? Would Marcus have to come back into my room and force me out of my pain? I needed to know what the song said. I needed to know if he spoke of what we'd had with joy or sorrow. Did he find light in our memories, or were they fading for him?

I ordered my burger, and we ate with only simple small talk. Marcus and Preston talked about Rock's upcoming wedding and then football. Finally, once I knew I was strong enough to hear the answer, I asked Marcus, "Will the words hurt me?" I knew he was going to know what I was talking about.

Marcus smiled sadly and shook his head. "I don't think so,

Sadie, but that depends on what hurts you. He describes you and how he feels about you. If that is going to be painful, then yes."

I swallowed to keep my throat from closing up.

Preston cleared his throat. "What are you talking about?"

Marcus squeezed my hand. "Jax's new number one."

Preston's eyes widened, and he gawked at me and then back at Marcus. "That's about Sadie?"

Marcus raised his eyebrows as if to dare him to say more. "Yes, it is." He threw his words out like a challenge.

"Hell, no wonder people want her autograph," he mumbled, and took a bite of his sandwich.

I had to hear that song. "Preston, I want to go out to your Jeep and listen to the radio. Do you mind?"

He shook his head. "Nah, the keys are in it."

Marcus stood and let me out. I started to walk toward the door, and he grabbed my hand. I turned back to him.

"Are you going to be okay by yourself?" he asked in a hushed tone.

"I need to do this alone," I assured him, and he let me go.

I sat and flipped through a few stations until I found one that I knew would most likely play it often, and I waited. I didn't have to wait long. The moment the guitar began, I knew whose song it was. I had heard those exact chords being played outside while I worked in the garden. Even if this song wasn't for me, he had written it when he had been with me. When he was mine. Because of that, it was special to me. And then his voice joined the music and I got lost.

> "Your eyes hold the key to my soul.
> Your hands heal all my pain,
> and you're everything that makes this boy whole.
> When you breathe, it sends warmth through my veins.
> When you laugh, my body goes insane.
> You're all I need to survive.
> Your body is what makes me feel alive.
>
> "Don't cry. I'm not that strong.
> I can't stand here when your heart is broken.
> How I long to be all you need.
> But instead, I'm everything that's wrong.
> No, no, don't cry. I'm not that strong.
> I can't stand here when your heart is broken.
> How I long to be all you need.
> But instead, I'm everything that's wrong.
>
> "The day you walked into my life,
> I knew it was no sacrifice to let you in.
> I wanted nothing more than to win your heart.
> And once I had it, my poison ruined everything.

*So now all I can do is stand here alone with my guitar*
*and sing.*

*"Don't cry. I'm not that strong.*
*I can't stand here when your heart is broken.*
*How I long to be all you need.*
*But instead, I'm everything that's wrong.*
*No, no, don't cry. I'm not that strong.*
*I can't stand here when your heart is broken.*
*How I long to be all you need.*
*But instead, I'm everything that's wrong."*

"And that, my friends, is Jax Stone's new chart-topping 'Don't Cry.'" The dj's voice droned on, and I reached over and turned off the radio.

It did hurt. The pain was there. But his voice had been like a balm to my wounds. I had something now that would help ease the hurt. It wouldn't make it go away, of course, but hearing his voice was enough to ease the pain, if only for a short time. I could make it from day to day if I could just hear his voice. If I could just hear my song.

# Chapter Eighteen

**JAX**

Sadie's mom had had her baby. Ms. Mary said Sadie was back in school and that she was still working at the job she'd secured her. What worried me was that Ms. Mary had mentioned that she hadn't heard from Sadie in a couple of weeks. She knew juggling a job and school was probably hard on Sadie, and she'd said not to worry about it. She'd check in with Sadie soon if she hadn't made contact.

I'd wanted to ask her about Marcus, but I couldn't. I wasn't sure I could handle the answer. If Sadie had moved on, it would break me. I was holding on by a thread right now. These little bits and pieces I got from Ms. Mary were all I had to live on.

## SADIE

Sam didn't sleep at night. He slept wonderfully during the day while I worked, but in the evenings he stayed awake. Jessica seemed to be in some sort of depression, and when I came in the door, she handed Sam to me and went into her room and cried. Ms. Mary said this was normal. Jessica suffered from the "baby blues," so I didn't worry about it too much, except I wasn't getting any sleep. Jessica slept all night, and if I tried to wake her, she burst into tears. When she cried, Sam cried, so I just left her alone.

He and I bonded during this time. I talked to him about everything I couldn't say to anyone else. I told him about life with Jessica and how he would love her, but how he should not ever expect a normal mom. I assured him that he'd be fine because I would always be there if he needed me. I told him about Jax. I emptied my soul to a newborn baby, but it made it easier to breathe freely again when I talked about Jax. Sam cooed and smiled and kicked. He liked for me to talk, so I did. I made him happy, and it helped me cope.

No matter how special these times in the wee hours of the morning were, it still wore on me. I fought the urge to crawl up in a corner at work and sleep. Some nights Sam slept two hours at a time if I put him beside my bed. The next day I always functioned better having had at least five hours' sleep. Jessica and I didn't talk much. When I came home, she went into her room to cry and listen to eighties music. I always took Sam to her before I left each morning, fed and with a clean diaper and clothes on. I called her from work and reminded her about feeding time because she just didn't seem to have it together. I was starting to get nervous about leaving him at home with her, but I reminded myself she was the mom, not me.

School started back. Marcus had left two weeks before, and I'd stood in the yard and waved as he drove away. At first I'd panicked because I worried about what would happen if I found myself back in the dark blanket. But then I remembered Sam, and Jessica's unstable behavior, and I knew that scenario could not happen. I had someone to take care of now. I couldn't lose it again. My life no longer belonged to me. Sometimes it seemed like my time with Jax had happened in another lifetime. But then the memories of his smile and his laugh reminded me of how close we had been to happiness.

I sighed, grabbed my book bag, and gazed down at Sam, sound asleep. I stood my door open and left him in the bassinet by my bed. I opened Jessica's door, and she turned and stared at me with swollen red eyes.

"I'm going to be late if I don't go. I fed him an hour ago, and he has on a clean diaper. He is asleep in my room." I stopped there and forced myself not to give her any directions on taking care of her child.

She yawned and stretched. "All right, thanks, Sadie. I know

I have needed you a lot lately. I just can't seem to get it together."
She sounded almost wounded.

I nodded and left her there. I didn't know what to say to her, because what I wanted to say was "Grow *up*! You have a baby!" and I knew I couldn't, so I just left.

My bike ride to school was short, and I was there and in the building in plenty of time to find my new locker and my first-period class. People watched me, and a few whispered, but I ignored them and focused on the task at hand. I'd received a top locker this year in the middle of the hall. Apparently, the seniors were given the better locker locations.

"Hey, stranger," a familiar voice said behind me, and I turned to see Amanda.

I hadn't spent much time with her because she didn't hang out with her brother and his friends. "Hey, Amanda, how are you?"

She smiled and shrugged. "Great! Finally a senior!"

I smiled and wished I cared. "Yep, finally seniors," I said, feigning excitement.

Her eyes seemed sympathetic. "I'm sorry about everything that happened and all. Marcus told me some of it before he left because he wants me to watch out for you and call him if you need him."

I couldn't help but smile at her words. "Your brother is very good, and I don't deserve him," I admitted, and turned to put the rest of my books in my locker before I ran late for class.

She chuckled. "Yeah, well, that would be because he wishes you cared about him like you do Jax Stone." She froze and bit her lip when she saw me wince. "I'm so sorry, I . . . Marcus told me not to talk about Jax. . . ."

I shook my head. "No, that's fine. People are going to talk about him, and I'm going to learn to deal with it."

She nodded, but she didn't seem too sure. "Well, I had better get to class. I'll see you around later, maybe. We might have some classes together."

I smiled and nodded. "That would be nice."

She grinned and turned to walk away, but then stopped and looked back at me. "I, well . . . Is, um . . . Okay, I don't know if this is off-limits to talk about, but is 'Don't Cry' about you?"

My throat tightened as I remembered the song I had listened to countless times, curled into a ball as I let the memories wash over me. Lately I had stopped listening to it because it put me in a mood I could hardly escape. Sam needed me, and I couldn't do that to him. I wanted to believe the song was for me, but I didn't know for sure. I knew I had heard him working on the chords when we were together. But I wasn't sure if it had anything to do with me.

I shrugged. "I don't know."

She gave a sad sigh and walked away. I took a moment to compose myself as the words filled my head. I had to get a grip and get to class. After several deep breaths, I turned and went to room 223. I started my day off this year with trigonometry. How exciting.

After two classes of people asking me questions about Jax that I didn't want to answer, the thought of going to a cafeteria where I was going to be the main source for Jax Stone info made me cringe. I stood at my locker longer than necessary, then went to the library instead. I could eat when I got home. I would begin on my homework. I slipped over to the tables and got out my trigonometry book and began working. My eyes, however, had a hard time staying focused, and I had to fight to keep them from closing.

"Sadie! Wake up! Sadie!"

I lifted my head to see Amanda frowning down at me.

"Are you all right?" she asked, reminding me of her older brother.

I rubbed my eyes and nodded. "Yes. I guess I need to get more sleep." I knew I did, but I wasn't going to until I got Sam to sleep through the night.

"Well, come on, you're late for literature, and Mr. Harris almost didn't let me come get you. I told him you thought your next class was Spanish, and he agreed to let me come find you."

I smiled at her imagination. "Thanks."

She picked up my books and tugged on my arm. "Don't thank me now. We may both be in trouble if you don't hurry.

And get rid of the I-just-woke-up stare. It'll blow my cover."

I rubbed my face and nodded. We had to go to my locker first and switch out my books. "Why were you in the library, anyway?" she asked as I grabbed the correct books.

"Because I didn't want to face lunch and everyone's questions," I mumbled.

She nodded. "Well, you were missed. The only reason you were not bombarded in the library was because by the time everyone figured out where you were, lunch was over."

I sighed and shut my locker door. "I want to go back to being invisible," I grumbled, and fell in step with Amanda.

Amanda frowned and shook her head. "Not gonna happen. You need to prepare yourself. The homecoming dance is next month, and you're going to be hit big-time with requests to take you."

That wasn't even an option. I wasn't going to date anyone. I refused to go to any dance.

"Well, help me get the word around that I don't dance," I muttered as she opened the door to the classroom and we went inside. Luckily, Mr. Harris only gave me a stern glare and said nothing. I slipped into the only free desk, behind a tall dark-haired guy whose head blocked my view of the board. I'd leaned over to write the page numbers we were supposed to read for homework when the tall guy in front of me turned around.

"You're Sadie White, aren't you?" he asked, grinning.

I nodded, wishing I could just lie and tell him no. He cleared his throat. "I'm Dameon Wallace."

I gave him a small polite smile and searched for the page we were supposed to be reading.

"Do you speak, or do you have something against me?"

I sighed and glanced up. He must've been unleashing what he assumed was a charming smile. It wasn't bad, really. He was attractive enough. His blue eyes lacked the intensity of Jax's steel-blue eyes. His smile didn't really look sincere. More sure of himself and cocky, maybe.

"I'm just late for class, and I'm trying to get caught up."

He flashed me a crooked grin he also apparently thought was cute. "No worries. You didn't miss much. So, you single again?"

My stomach knotted. I gave him a tight smile and nodded before turning back to my book.

"What are your plans after school? I was thinking we could go get a drink and walk down to the beach." He sounded so sure of himself and his offer that I had to remind myself I was a good person and not mean.

I managed a smile and said, "I work after school. Sorry." I went back to trying to read my page.

"After work?" He seemed a little unsure of himself now.

"I'm sorry, but I have to go straight home and get homework

done and help my mother with my little brother." I wanted to add, *I am not going to be dating anyone, so leave me alone,* but I refrained and went back to reading.

He watched me a few seconds more, and then I heard him sigh and turn back around in his seat. I tried to comprehend what I was reading, but I couldn't keep my mind on the words. I hated feeling like I was an item to be studied on a display shelf. Everyone wanted to watch and see what I would do. Once the bell rang, I grabbed my books and headed for the door as quickly as humanly possible. I needed to get away. Far, far away.

"Hey, Sadie, wait up," Amanda called from behind me. I slowed and turned to see her running to catch me. "What did Dameon Wallace say to you?" she almost squealed in delight.

I frowned and tried to remember our one-sided conversation. "Well, he asked me out, I said no, and that was about it." I kept my eyes on the hallway and didn't think about the people staring at me.

"He asked you out?" she asked with a hushed reverence. I simply nodded.

"OMG, he is the absolute hottest guy in Sea Breeze. You do know he is a quarterback, and not only that, he has several SEC schools interested in him."

I'd had no idea, and I did not care.

I shrugged and opened my locker to get my bag out.

"That's great. Good for him," I replied.

She stood staring at me, openmouthed. "I can't understand how you told him no. No one tells him no. Girls dream about him at night. He's gorgeous. Did you see his arms?" She fanned herself. "Wow," she added for extra affect.

I rolled my eyes. "Really, Amanda, if you like him that much, then you date him. I'm just not interested."

Amanda sighed and leaned back against the locker. "If he would acknowledge my existence, then I would go after him. But until today I have never seen him interested in a girl in this school. He dates college girls."

I slipped my bag over my shoulder. "Well, apparently, he has changed his mind," I muttered.

"He's so cute. I don't know how you turned him down," Amanda droned on.

I liked Amanda, but I wasn't in the mood for this. I wasn't interested in this guy. "I need to get to work. Thanks again for waking me up."

She nodded, and I headed for the exit.

My first day back, and I was already hating school.

If I could just blend in and go unnoticed, this would be bearable.

I looked up to see Dameon headed my way, and I picked up the pace. I wondered how obvious it would be if I ran to my bike. My faster pace apparently tipped him off that I wasn't in the mood to talk, because he didn't run after me. I had to get to work, but first I wanted to call and check on Sam.

The entire first week didn't go very well. The only good news was Dameon had taken the hint and left me alone. However, after falling asleep again in the library during lunch, I realized I was going to have to stop going in there. I forced myself to face the lunch crowd. It really hadn't been as bad as I thought. Amanda saved me a seat by her, and I liked her friends. Dylan McCovey wanted to reminisce about his July Fourth party a little too much, but other than that, it was fine. Most days, I just sat at the table and listened to them talk. Every once in a while someone would ask me a question or attempt to get me to join the conversation, but my social inadequacies mixed with my being exhausted didn't make me a good conversationalist.

On Friday, Dylan had finally worked up the nerve to ask me about "Don't Cry," and I was proud of the way I handled it. I managed to talk clearly through the lump in my throat. My breathing didn't get too constricted. To all outward appearances, I seemed normal and unfazed. I successfully replied, "I don't know who it is about. He never sang it for me," without choking up once.

On Monday, I had made it through my first period without falling asleep, which happened to be a miracle because Sam still couldn't manage to get his days and nights adjusted, not even a little bit. I had even called Ms. Mary and asked her what I should do, and she said we needed to keep him awake more during the day. The problem with that was that during the day Jessica wanted him sleeping so she didn't have to deal with him. I hated to admit it to myself, but my mother was not being a very good mom to Sam. She ignored him mostly, and she still cried frequently. I couldn't explain all that to Ms. Mary because it made Jessica sound bad, and I couldn't bring myself to tear her down in anyone's eyes. She just seemed so fragile.

Anyway, I was still managing to stay awake at school. After fighting my heavy eyelids during a very boring lecture, I headed straight to the bathroom so I could splash cold water on my face to wake up. I had to fight this sleepiness. I wasn't going to get the grades for a scholarship if I didn't stay awake in my classes. I stepped around a group of girls to get through the congested hallway, and one of them pointed at me. I was used to this, so I ignored it and kept my eyes on the bathroom.

However, one turned around. "Sadie White?"

I stopped and considered lying about my name, saying no, I was in fact Ivana, an exchange student who didn't speak good English. But instead, I turned around to see the short redhead whom I'd met at the July Fourth party. I immediately recognized that unfriendly gleam in her eye.

"Hi, I'm Mary Ann Moore. We met at Dylan's house this summer, but I doubt you remember me, after everyone you met that night." She paused as if I was supposed to say something, but I continued to stare at her, awaiting what she wanted with me. "Yes, well, um, I have the new edition of *Teen Follower*, and there's a picture of Jax Stone with his new girlfriend, Alana Harvey. She's going to be in his new music video. . . . You know, the one for 'Don't Cry.'"

I understood what this girl wanted now, and I didn't know what I had done to her to make her hate me so much. My throat was dry and began closing up. So I decided against responding. She smiled as if pleased with my reaction and handed me the magazine.

"Rock stars are such fickle creatures. One never knows who they'll want next. You take the magazine; I don't need it." And with that, she snapped her fingers and the group surrounding her followed after her like a school of fish.

I tried swallowing, but it was no use. I couldn't manage it. The pain returned again, and I didn't have the strength to stop it. I turned to run, and Amanda was there blocking my path.

"She's just being mean to you because of Dameon. Now come with me, and we'll get you all pulled back together in the bathroom."

I followed obediently behind her. "What does Dameon have to do with this?" I asked, holding out the magazine Mary Ann had placed in my hands.

Amanda pulled me into the bathroom, then took the

magazine from me. "Dameon and Mary Ann dated this summer. When she found out he was interested in you, you became her enemy. Even though she knows you blew him off. I think that makes her dislike you more."

I frowned. "Why?"

Amanda wet a paper towel. "Because you're blowing off what she wants so badly. See, the thing is, Dameon dated her this summer, and, well, after a few weeks he dumped her flat. She wants him back, since dating Dameon would make her the most popular girl at the school."

I sighed and closed my eyes. "High school is so stupid," I muttered.

Amanda moved my hand from my face and she wiped my tears with a cold wet paper towel. "You need to get a grip on yourself. If everyone thinks they can get to you by showing you pictures of Jax with other girls, you're going to get hammered by them."

I walked over to the discarded magazine and picked it up against my better judgment. There on the page in front of me was Jax at the Teen Choice Awards, and on his arm was a gorgeous blonde with curly hair. I inhaled deeply and sank down against the wall.

"Dang it, Sadie, what're you looking at it for?" Amanda went to take it from me, but I shook my head and held on to it firmly.

"No, let me read it." I knew the stuff they wrote in these

things wasn't true, but I somehow wanted to hurt myself further.

"No!" Amanda said firmly, and jerked it out of my hands. I let it go. She flipped it over. "Sheesh, at least your curls are natural," she said before throwing the magazine in the garbage.

I closed my eyes against the pain and sat on the floor. The dark blanket seemed to be coming for me, and I knew I was going to have to fight harder to keep it from getting me. There was peace in the blankness, but then I wouldn't be able to take care of Sam if I went into it, and Sam needed me. I shook my head and stood up quickly before it reached me. I focused on my reflection in the mirror and calmed my features until the haunted look left my eyes. Amanda came up behind me and took my arm.

"It was just a publicity picture," she said quietly.

I nodded because she was right. Seeing the picture of him with the girl hadn't been as hard as seeing him so happy in it. I wanted to be happy too. He could be happy—why couldn't I? Because I'd been the one to love too much. It would just take me longer than him to smile so brightly. I needed to work on it. Thinking about those around me who did love me needed to be where I started. And then there was Sam, who needed me. I had to learn to be strong. Once, I had believed I was very strong. Now I had to find that me again.

# Chapter Nineteen

**JAX**

"People are talking. It won't be long before the media gets ahold of it too. Either you're gonna have to snap out of this funk, or just go back to Alabama and get her. I don't see how this is any better than the alternatives." Jason was sitting across from me in the limo, frowning.

I hadn't been in the best of moods the past two months. If it was possible, I was getting worse. Today I'd been supposed to film my new music video for 'Don't Cry' and I hadn't been able to do it. I'd been so frustrated with the blonde they'd picked for the video and her not being Sadie, I'd walked off set and told them all to fuck themselves. I wasn't in the mood.

"You're a rock star. You can get away with acting like an ass. But, bro, you're gonna have to give a little. Go get Sadie back.

Get some of that lovin' you apparently need, and then get your act together. If the media thinks you're heartbroken over her, they will eat her alive. You don't want that."

He was right. I couldn't keep doing this. I didn't want Sadie to deal with any more shit. I was going to have to show the world I was over Sadie, and I had moved on. They had no reason to still follow her or talk bad about her. If they thought she had broken my heart then they would eat her alive. I couldn't allow it. I wouldn't. The problem was, how the hell was I gonna be able to pretend I wasn't completely shattered?

**SADIE**

September would be over in a week, and I knew running on empty fumes would soon catch up with me. My grades were suffering because staying awake throughout class had become impossible. Sam still kept me up all night, with what Ms. Mary said was probably colic. She told me that other than giving him gas medicine, I just had to help him through it. Jessica continued to get more and more withdrawn to the point where I called her from school to check on Sam and make sure she remembered to feed him. Several evenings when I'd come home, he had gone without a diaper change so long a rash had developed. Each time, I cleaned him up and applied the cream I'd found at the pharmacy. I attempted to explain to Jessica that this was not good for him, but she didn't seem to hear me. Sam needed her. I couldn't get her to wake up and face the fact that she had a baby now.

Sam only had me, and I needed to toughen up because I couldn't come crashing down too. The more I thought about college, I realized there would be no way I could go and leave Sam with Jessica. He'd never survive. School took a backseat to work. Formula and diapers cost a fortune. The thought of dropping out of school and getting my GED crossed my mind several nights when I came home to find Sam crying and hungry and Jessica in her room yelling for me to do something with him. My life was spiraling downhill, and it seemed the harder I worked at getting it under control, the worse it got.

I woke up with my head on the kitchen table and an empty bottle in my hand, and Sam crying in his bassinet beside me. I rubbed my eyes to get focused, glanced at the time, and realized I had overslept. I jumped up and fixed him another bottle and fed him. Twice I tried to get Jessica to get out of bed and help me, but once she threw her pillow at me, and the second time she said she had a headache. I managed to get myself dressed and gather my homework that I had scattered all over the coffee table while taking care of Sam all night. I changed Sam's diaper and his clothes, and of course, as on cue, he fell fast asleep. In a way, I was thankful that he slept so much during the day, because if he didn't, I would worry about what Jessica would do to him. I had already witnessed her locking herself in another room away from his crying.

I went to tell Jessica bye, but she was sound asleep again. No point in waking her up. I headed out to my bike, and suddenly the world around me tilted. I stopped and leaned up against the house until the wave of dizziness passed, and then I went and got on my bike. My stomach rolled as if I had eaten something bad. Sickness didn't fit onto my to-do list. I didn't have time for that. I had to get to school. I'd pulled out of the driveway and was headed toward the main stoplight when everything started to go blurry in my peripheral vision. I turned onto Main Street and headed toward school as fast as I could. It was as if I were riding into a tunnel that grew smaller as the world around me seemed to dim. Everything went black with the school in sight.

A sharp pain in my head woke me. I couldn't open my eyes, so I reached up to feel something warm and wet in my hair. Something oozed from somewhere. My arm grew heavy, and I couldn't control it. I let it fall, and my eyes still didn't want to cooperate. Slowly I drifted off to the darkness. I welcomed it because it reminded me of my dark blanket, and I wanted the pain to go away.

I floated through my memories. A painless journey. Jax's face smiling at me filled me with happiness, and I felt the tingling sensation from his nearness as well. I saw Jax bent down in front of the little girl at the grocery store, and my heart fluttered as I remembered her face when he kissed her. Jax bending over his first guitar and singing "Wanted Dead or Alive" made me want to laugh out loud, but for some reason I couldn't. And then Jax was singing to me in the moonlight and holding me in his arms. More memories I had tried so very hard to repress rushed back to me, as well as many I wanted to laugh at, but I couldn't make myself laugh. The heavy blanket made it impossible to move. So I lay there and enjoyed my memories without pain. And just like before, the darkness came, and I floated into it.

Music and a voice I recognized called to me. I tried so hard to move the heavy blanket so I could find him. I knew that voice. The music came from him. His voice sounded sad, but the words belonged to me. It was my song. I fought the blanket, but it remained too heavy, and the darkness washed over me. The song faded away.

My head pounded and my arms tingled. I tried to wiggle my fingers, and it worked. I tried to move my foot, and it moved. The dark blanket had left me. I wanted to open my eyes, but the thought of it hurt my pounding head even more. I didn't think I could open them just yet. For some reason, the darkness had given me a horrible headache. I remembered the warm, oozing liquid, and I wondered if it was still up there causing problems. I lifted my arm, but I only got it so far before it fell back down again. Someone moved beside me.

"Sadie?"

My breathing stopped, and I waited to see if I could hear that smooth voice say my name again.

"Sadie, can you hear me?"

I wanted to speak, but I wasn't sure the words would come out right, so I stayed quiet. A warm hand slipped into mine, and my arm tingled in a familiar way. I knew the hand must belong to Jax.

"Sadie, please, if you can hear me, show me. I saw you move. You can do it again."

It *was* Jax. His voice sounded worried and anxious. I moved my hand in his and tried to open my eyes. The light hurt and I stopped trying.

"You can hear me. Okay, baby, listen. I'm going to get the nurse."

The nurse? What nurse? I didn't want him to go. I squeezed my hand tightly, trying to hold on to him, and then I heard him chuckle, and suddenly the heaviness faded away and I inhaled. My lips formed a smile this time, and his warm breath tickled my ear.

"I'm not going to leave you. I swear it. But please let me get the nurse," he whispered, and goose bumps rose on my arms. He laughed softly, and his hand left mine.

The room became silent, and the darkness started coming back. I wanted to fight it. I wanted to see Jax. I needed to see his face. But the darkness came anyway, and once again I floated into it, unable to control its force.

A soft sound warmed my ears, and I fought to get to it. The closer I got, the clearer the words seemed. They were familiar, but I couldn't seem to get close enough to understand. I fought the darkness and strained to hear the soft words that seemed to send warmth through my cold body. I squeezed my hand again to make sure I could still control it, and it was no longer empty. The words stopped, and I wanted to hear them again. I tried to speak, but nothing seemed to come out. I squeezed again and the warmth in my hand reminded me I wasn't alone.

"Sadie? Can you hear me?"

I wanted to say yes, but instead I only managed to move my head.

"I'm not leaving this time, baby. I'm staying right here. Can you open your eyes for me?"

His voice sounded so anxious and worried. I wanted to reassure him. But the light seemed too bright. I needed to tell him. I focused hard on the words, and then I remembered how to speak. "The lights," I heard myself say in a raspy voice.

"I'll turn them off. Hold on one second." His hand left mine, and then I could see the darkness on the other side of my eyelids. His hand slipped back into mine, and he squeezed it.

"Please open your eyes for me," he begged, and I slowly opened them.

Everything blurred together in the darkness. I blinked slowly, and things began to come into view. I searched for Jax first and quickly found him right beside me. He looked exhausted. His eyes had black circles under them, and he needed to shave badly.

"Ah, there are my beautiful blue eyes," he murmured with relief on his face.

"Hi." I struggled to get the word out of my parched throat.

He grinned, and my heart fluttered as usual. "Hello," he said softly.

"Why're you here?" I asked, but I slipped my free hand up to my throat, and that's when I noticed I had tubes in my hand. I stared at him, confused, because now the fact that he had wanted to get the nurse made sense. I was in a hospital.

"I'm here because the reason I get up each morning needs me as much as I need her, obviously."

I closed my eyes, trying to understand what he meant. "Please don't close your eyes again," he begged softly. I opened them immediately. I didn't understand his urgency and worry. And why he appeared so tired.

"Why'm I here?" I asked, despite my mouth and throat being as dry as a desert.

He sighed and kissed the hand he held. "You exhausted yourself and passed out while riding your bike. You hit your head so hard it cracked your skull. You were not found right away." He stopped and seemed to be struggling with his words. "By the time they got you here, you were unconscious, and they couldn't tell me if you would ever come back to me."

He struggled with the last part, and I squeezed his hand as tightly as I could. "I did."

He smiled and laid his head against our joined hands for a moment. "I know you did, but that doesn't mean I haven't died a thousand times since Ms. Mary called me a week ago."

A week ago? I had been unconscious a week. And then I remembered Sam. I started to sit up. Jessica couldn't take care of Sam for a week. He might be . . . I didn't want to think about it. I just needed up.

"Whoa, what're you doing? You can't get up. I still have to get the nurse in here."

I shook my head, and it began to pound. "Sam," I spit out through my panic. Jax held me firmly in the bed.

"Sam is with Ms. Mary and is just fine. He's even sleeping nights now."

How did Sam end up at Ms. Mary's? I stared at him, needing answers, but my dry throat had about reached its limit.

"Jessica is getting help. She's sick, Sadie. It's called postpartum depression, and she has a very bad case. She is at the best clinic money can buy, and when she comes back to you, she'll be just like new. I swear it."

I sank back against the bed, and I realized my head hurt fiercely. I flinched.

"Hold on, I'm getting the nurse now. Do *not* close your eyes. Please keep them open."

I nodded and watched him walk out to the hall, where he yelled, "She's awake."

He immediately turned and came right back to my side. "The nurses and doctors will probably kick me out in a minute, but I'm not going anywhere. I'm going to stay outside that door, and if you need me, I'll be right there."

I nodded, and my heart raced when he leaned down and his breath tickled my ear. "I'll never be able to leave again. I'm not that strong."

The doors opened and in came faces I had never seen before.

"How long has she been awake?" A large nurse with dark brown hair cut in a spiky style asked as she rushed over to my side.

Jax winked at me. "Um, a few minutes."

She shook her finger at him and said, "All right, pretty boy, that singing of yours must have done some good, but now I want you out of here. Her heart rate is all over the place. What were you doing to her? The girl has been in a coma."

"I said not to use that word," he interrupted in a hard voice that surprised me.

She sighed and shook her head. "Sorry, I forgot. She has been 'unconscious' for a week. She doesn't need you in here making her heart race."

He seemed worried, and I wanted to send the lady away because she upset him.

"Will it hurt her? Is she going to stay awake?"

The nurse smiled at me, then turned back to Jax. "She's going to be fine. Now go."

He looked at me one more time, and then he was pushed out of the room by another nurse coming in.

"Jeesh, I sure am glad you're awake," the nurse continued. "That poor boy is about to drop from exhaustion. Although, I will admit, it was nice having our own little concert around here. We just kept your door open and listened while he sang to you. Sometimes he would spend hours just singing. I swear he sang that 'Don't Cry' song a hundred times."

I smiled at the thought of Jax singing to me.

"Yes, go ahead and grin. If I had a hot rock star singing to me and watching over me like a mother hen, I'd smile too," she teased, and then reached for a glass of water. "Are you thirsty?"

I nodded, knowing my throat was too dry for me to speak. She sat my bed up and instructed me to take small sips. I did for a few minutes.

After I swallowed, I said, "My throat hurts."

The nurse nodded. "You've had a tube down your throat for a while. After you woke up briefly last night, we took it out in case you woke up again and panicked during the night."

I nodded and reached for the cup.

"Remember, slow sips," she warned, and then continued to work over me. She examined my head and nodded. "You're going to be just fine, Miss White. Before you know it, you will be up and going again. However, this time things should be easier for you. That smitten rock star out there seems to be taking care of everything."

My heart swelled when I remembered Jax stood right outside my door.

"You have quite a few other guests. He didn't allow them in here for very long periods of time. I'm sure they'll want to be contacted. You might have to encourage him to do that. I don't know if he is going to want to share you right away."

I nodded and smiled. "Okay."

She took her supplies and opened the door. Jax glanced in at me, then back at her anxiously.

"She's fine. She'll be out of here in a few days." Jax seemed to almost slump in relief. He walked back into the room and closed the door behind him.

"You okay?" he asked, and this time my throat worked much better.

"Yes, I'm fine," I assured him, and he beamed at me.

He pulled his chair right up beside me again and took my hand. "Sadie, I'm sorry. I left you here thinking I was doing what was best for you, and I knew you didn't have a stable home life. I wanted to leave you a car and money and"—he laughed bitterly—"I wanted to leave you everything you could ever need. But I knew you wouldn't take it and you would resent it.

Leaving without knowing you were taken care of was so hard. But I convinced myself you would be better off without me. Ms. Mary promised to get you a good job with good pay. I wanted you to have a safe, comfortable senior year. I had no idea—"

I put my finger over his mouth. "Stop it. Nothing is your fault. You did what you had to do. Your world is different from mine, and I understand that."

He kissed my finger, and I had to catch my breath. "I knew when I caved and allowed myself to be with you that your life was going to be turned upside down, that my world was going to affect you. But I pushed those thoughts away, and I just lived in the moment. When I saw your face all over the television, and I heard you being talked about like your personal life was nothing, I lost it. I wanted to hurt someone, and when I realized it was my fault, I wanted to hurt myself. So I hurt myself in the deepest way possible . . . by walking away from you." He paused and held my hand against his face. "I didn't want to hurt you. I was trying to save you from me, but it was a very bad plan, and I'm so sorry."

I licked my very dry lips and smiled. "Thank you for being here now. I fought the darkness so hard because I kept hearing something. It was music. I remember thinking the sound of it made me warm inside. I fought so hard to get close to it. Now I know it was you. If you hadn't been here singing to me, I don't know if I would have fought at all."

He closed his eyes for a minute, and pain flickered across his face. "I've had a lot of time to think about you and me. I know my life isn't normal, and I can't be the boy who sits behind you in class, no matter how appealing that sounds, but I can't walk away again. I'm not going to." He moved closer to me and touched my face with his other hand. "If you still want me, I'm yours. Your life will never be normal. You'll be put in the spotlight, although I'm going to keep you as safe as possible. But here's the thing, I didn't get to go to high school. I missed out on all my experiences because I was on the road touring. I can't do that to you. I need you to get every experience high school has to offer, and enjoy it . . . for me. I'll come back to my summer house one week out of every month, and any other time I can squeeze it in. I know my schedule is crazy right now with the tour, but I'm going to make this work. I swear."

I lay there trying to comprehend his words and knowing I would do anything to have him back in my life. I didn't care anymore if my privacy was invaded. If I had him, it wouldn't matter.

"What experiences are there for me in high school? I hate it."

He smiled and traced my cheekbone with his finger. "Well, there are football games and dances and being picked on in the hallway. There is bad cafeteria food and field trips and—heck, I don't know. I missed it all. I just don't want you to look back one day and wish you had experienced it. Because if you did look back and feel that way, it would be my fault. I'm asking you to give up so much to be with me. I can't take everything."

I sighed. "But I never do all those things. I never go to football games, and I'm not going to any dances. Sam needs me."

Jax shook his head. "No. When Jessica gets home, Sam's going to have a mother, not a big sister, caring for him. I'm in communication with her doctor, and he says she's much better, but she was in a very bad state."

Relief washed through me. To know Jessica would be returning to her normal self sounded wonderful. Being a mom at seventeen had almost killed me. I needed her to be Sam's mom.

"I still have no desire to do those things."

He grinned wickedly. "How about doing them for me?"

I sighed and closed my eyes, wishing he was asking anything of me but this. Finally I opened my eyes and nodded. "Okay, for you."

He broke into a huge grin, leaned forward, and kissed my lips softly. "Thank you," he whispered before sitting back down.

"Ms. Mary is in the waiting room dying to see you, and so is . . . um . . . Marcus," he finished reluctantly.

I smiled and squeezed his hand. "Marcus has been a wonderful friend through everything."

Jax nodded. "Yeah, he made sure to threaten me with my life if I hurt you again. Then he gave me a very descriptive recap of what happened after I left." Jax swallowed hard and looked away. "Because I owe him for being what I couldn't be, I'm allowing him in here."

I smiled as Jax stood and turned to the door.

"However, if he so much as goes near your face with his lips, all bets are off."

I laughed, and Jax gave me one last sexy grin before walking out the door to get my friends.

Ms. Mary entered first with the anxious frown of a worried mother on her face. "Oh, Sadie, honey, I'm so glad to see those eyes. Girl, you've given me the scare of my life. Lord, if I had known things were so bad, I would have done something." She touched my hand, leaned down, and kissed my forehead.

"I'm fine now. How's Sam?"

She smiled and sat down beside me in the chair Jax had been sitting in earlier. "He's wonderful. I started him on some rice cereal, and he's sleeping all night long now. He is such a happy baby."

"Thank you so much. I don't have to worry about him when I know he is with you. It means a lot that you're taking care of him." Tears stung my eyes.

"I wouldn't have it any other way. Sadie, honey, you're my family now too. I love you just like I do my own kids. Don't you go thanking me for nothing."

At her words, the tears spilled over. I had a family now. It had always been Jessica and me against the world, but now I had others to love and who loved me back.

"Oh, lordy, if Master Jax catches you crying, he's gonna shoo me out of here for good. Stop that now. You got Marcus outside with Jax, and the way they're glaring at each other, it won't be long before we have a fight on our hands. I'm gonna go." She squeezed my hand. "I'm so happy you came back to us, sweetie. You're very loved." She turned to leave.

"Ms. Mary."

She stopped and said, "Yes, honey?"

I smiled through my tears. "I love you, too."

She sniffed and wiped a tear from her eye. "I know you do, girl, I know you do." She walked out of the room.

Jax stepped back inside and frowned at me, concerned. "Are you all right? Ms. Mary is crying, and so are you." He came over and wiped the tears from my face.

I smiled through them. "These are happy tears. Now stop fussing over me and let Marcus in."

Jax nodded but didn't smile, and he went back into the hallway. Marcus came in with a fierce frown on his face. "I swear, Sadie, if you ever scare me like that again, I'm not sure I can live through it."

I grinned. "I don't intend to ever scare anyone like this again."

He managed a smile and sat down beside me. "I didn't get

to come in here but once while you were, um . . . out of it. . . . Jax refused to leave your side, and they only allowed one at a time. Jax let me in once, but he didn't leave. He kept sitting in the seat over there playing his guitar and singing. He has every woman in this hospital in love with him."

He rolled his eyes, and I laughed.

"Don't let it get to you, Marcus. He's a rock star. They would've been in love with him even if he hadn't sung to me."

Marcus sighed and leaned back in the chair. "I don't know, Sadie. I'm a guy, and I'll be honest with you, seeing someone like him in a corner of a hospital room playing love song after love song and refusing to leave your side was pretty touching. I've managed to let go of most of my resentment toward him."

I pictured Jax singing to me, and I wished I had been awake to watch him. "I love him," I whispered.

Marcus nodded. "I know you do. You've loved him about as long as I've known you. It's something I've come to grips with. I never stood a chance. He stole your heart first."

I smiled sadly at the friend I would also always love. He had been my knight in shining armor when I needed one.

"I love you too," I said, almost without choking up.

He smiled at me. "I know you do. Just not the way you love him."

"You're the best friend I've ever had, Marcus. You've been there for me when I needed someone the most. I'll never forget that. But he stole my breath away the moment we first spoke. He's my air."

Marcus stared down at the floor for a moment, and I gave him time. Finally he looked back up at me. "I used to think he didn't deserve your love, but now I think he just may be as in love with you as you are with him. I want you to be happy, and if he makes you happy, then that's all that matters."

"He affects all my emotions. My happiness is connected to him."

Marcus nodded and stood up. "Yeah, I figured as much." He glanced at the door. "He's going to come bursting in here any minute and make me go back to disliking him, so I had better leave before that happens."

I laughed. "Okay. Thank you for everything."

Marcus smiled. "It was my pleasure." He left the room.

I knew he would always be there when I needed him, but in a way I had just set him free.

Jax stepped back in the room, smiling at me. "Can you try to eat something?"

I thought about food, and suddenly I was very hungry. I nodded. "Yes, I think so."

He broke out into a very happy grin, opened the door, and signaled for a nurse. "She wants food."

The nurse stuck her head in and smiled. "You ready to try some Jell-O?"

Jell-O was not what I had been thinking, but apparently I had to start somewhere. "Yes, please."

She nodded and stepped back out of the room. Jax picked up his guitar from the corner and sat down and began to play. He smiled, and the smooth voice that had made him famous joined the guitar.

# Chapter Twenty

**JAX**

I would be completely changed for the rest of my life. I'd never been terrified like that. My world had never felt like it was crashing down around me. I had lived a really blessed life. Things had always come easy to me. I'd expected it.

The phone call telling me Sadie was in a coma had been a turning point for me. All I'd been able to focus on was getting to her. I needed to be near her. I was convinced I could get her to come back to me. That she just needed me near her to wake up. I was also positive that I'd spend the rest of my life in a hospital room by her side if she didn't.

Seeing her smiling at me now as I sang to her made me realize how lucky I was. How much I'd taken for granted and how easily life could change. It could end. Running from Sadie to protect her only hurt us both. Life was short and we had another chance at it. I wasn't going to screw it up this time. Sadie would never feel alone again as long as I was breathing. She'd be taken care of and she would be the reason for every song I sang.

I couldn't change the past. My mistakes had almost cost me everything. But I knew now what was important. The path my life had taken would not control my choices any longer. I would.

## SADIE

I spent another week in the hospital, but I didn't mind it. Having Jax with me all day long made the days go by quicker. Once they allowed more visitors, Mr. Greg came and we played chess. He let me win, and he didn't realize I knew what he was doing. I spoke with Jessica on the phone several times, and she seemed happy and more like herself. She also desperately wanted to see Sam. She was really having a hard time dealing with what she'd done to him. Jax assured me she would be getting help for her guilt as well. Ms. Mary brought me chicken fingers and mashed potatoes and apple pie, which was a wonderful relief from the hospital food. Jax continued to sing to me. The nurses peeked in the door and sighed at the sight of him. I understood. The guy I loved also happened to be the world's biggest heartthrob. I had accepted it.

Jax refused to let me go back to my apartment, and Ms. Mary refused to let Jax take me home with him. So I ended up going home with Ms. Mary. I was anxious to see Sam. He had managed to wedge his little self deep inside my heart. I had to keep reminding myself the role I played in his life every time I began to think about his future and worry over things that were not my place to worry about. Holding him again and letting his chubby little fingers curl tightly around my finger made everything seem right.

Jax sat down beside me on Ms. Mary's couch and looked down at Sam. "He's a cute kid. He has your eyes."

I smiled up at Jax and nodded. "Apparently, Jessica has really strong genes."

Jax touched Sam's nose gently. "Well, fella, you're going to be one of the prettiest guys I've ever seen, then."

I laughed, and so did Ms. Mary.

"All right, you've seen him. Now you need to say your goodbyes to Jax and get some rest." She stared at Jax. "You've been with her for two weeks straight. She needs a break."

I started to argue, but Jax shook his head. "No, she's right. You need some rest. Monday you'll be able to go back to school, and I want you rested up before then."

I didn't think I could be any more rested. I'd been in a bed for two weeks. "Okay, fine," I muttered, and sank back against the couch.

Jax chuckled and leaned down to kiss my forehead. "I have canceled two concerts on my tour, and I need to get them rescheduled. I won't stay gone long. I just need to go home and deal with the thousand phone calls I have put off."

I didn't want him to leave, but I knew he had given up everything to stay by my side the past two weeks. "All right." I forced a smile.

He sighed. "Come on, Sadie, don't look like that. You're making this so hard. You have school on Monday, and I'm going to have to be on a plane to New York by tomorrow evening."

I knew this. We had already talked about his schedule for the next few months. I was not going to make this any harder. I had sworn to myself to make things as easy as possible for him.

"I know, you're right. I won't sulk anymore, I promise."

He laughed, leaned down, and kissed my lips this time. I instantly responded, and he moaned and broke the kiss.

"Come on, don't do that to me in Ms. Mary's house. I'll get all the blame if she catches us."

I grinned. "Sorry."

He raised his eyebrows and smirked. "Sure you are." He stood up and walked to the door, where he stopped and said, "I'm going to be back as soon as I can. In the meantime, sleep, so when I get back we can talk without Ms. Mary breathing down my neck."

I nodded, and he blew me a kiss, turned, and continued out the door.

Our last day together went fast. Before I knew it, Jax was gone again and I was getting ready to go back to high school. I woke before the sun came up and took a shower. Facing high school after being with Jax so much was depressing. By the time I'd dressed and made it to the kitchen, Ms. Mary had a plate of pancakes and bacon on the table.

"You got up early enough. What's taking you so long? Come eat this before it gets cold."

I had never had a hot breakfast made for me before I went to school. I couldn't help but smile at her through my sadness. "Thank you, Ms. Mary. I'm sorry it took me so long." I didn't elaborate.

She turned from washing the dishes in the sink and put a soapy hand on her hip. "Now, I know you miss that boy. I can completely understand it. However, you've done promised him you'd enjoy your last year in high school, and you ain't gonna be able to do that if you're moping around." Her Aunt Bee frown was back, and I nodded.

"You're right, of course. I have so much to be happy about. Starting with you."

Her cheeks flushed and she waved her soapy hand at me. "Oh, you, goin' and saying stuff like that. You're special, girl, ain't no doubt about it."

She turned around and continued washing the dishes.

I ate as much of my breakfast as I could and took it over to the sink.

"Now you go on and have a good day."

I nodded and grabbed my book bag. Sam let out a cry, and I walked over to him, bent down, and kissed his sweet little bald head.

"You be good for Ms. Mary, squirt. I'll see you after school."

His fat arms slapped at the air, and he kicked his feet. It was his favorite pastime. I waved to him on my way out the door.

Kane stood leaning against the Hummer. When he saw me, he glanced down at his watch as if I was late. I had stopped moving, confused as to his presence there. It was then that my phone rang. I reached into my pocket and pulled it out.

"Hello?"

"Good morning, beautiful. Now, I want you to do me a favor and go get into the vehicle for Kane. Don't argue with me. I happen to have doctor's orders that you're *not* to ride your bicycle for at least another two months."

I stood staring at the now grinning Kane. "Doctor's orders, huh? You wouldn't happen to have paid the doctor for the orders, would you?" I challenged.

He chuckled. "Never. Now go get in that Hummer before Kane does what he was instructed to do."

I froze and stared at the giant in front of me. "What were his instructions?"

"To get you in that vehicle no matter what," he countered.

I grinned, shrugged in defeat, and walked to the Hummer.

Kane opened the door, and I had to take his hand to step up into it. "Okay, rock star, I'm in your Hummer."

"Thank you."

I had been expecting him to gloat, so his simple thank you made my heart flutter. "You're welcome."

"I miss you," he said softly.

"I miss you, too."

"I have a concert Thursday night, and then one on Saturday, but after that I'm coming home to you for Sunday at least."

"I'll be waiting."

"Have fun at school today for me, please. Remember, you're experiencing high school for both of us."

I sighed. "I'll keep that in mind when I am being picked on in the halls and eating bad cafeteria food."

He chuckled, and then his voice got very serious. "If anyone picks on you, threaten them with me."

This time I laughed. "Sure thing. That'll help me fit in real nicely."

"I love you, Sadie."

My heart still raced when he said those words. "I love you, too."

"I'm going to let you go because Kane should be pulling up at school."

I glanced outside the window and realized he was right. "Yes, he just stopped. Bye. Have a good day."

"You, too. Bye."

I pressed end on the phone and sighed. I reached for my backpack as Kane opened my door.

Smiling at him, I said, "Thank you, Kane."

He nodded, and I could have sworn I saw him smile. I headed for my locker. I was going to have tons of makeup work. I needed to empty my book bag so it could hold it all.

"Sadie, I'm glad you're back at school. Bum thing that happened." Dylan McCovey had come up beside me. He glanced back at Kane leaving and grinned. "You sure got a sweeter set of wheels now."

I had to try hard not to roll my eyes. Instead, I nodded. "I can't ride my bike for a while."

Dylan laughed. "Yeah, well, I doubt you're going to be riding your bike again ever. The whole town's talking about the way Jax Stone sat in your hospital room and sang to you until you came out of your coma. Then he apparently wouldn't leave you alone for a minute. The boy sounds hooked."

I smiled at Dylan's words, but I didn't respond. We stepped inside the school building.

"I've got to get to class. See ya later, Dylan," I called over my shoulder as I walked away from him. I didn't want to talk about my private life to anyone.

The moment I stepped into the hallway, people stopped and stared. I wanted to turn around and run back outside. Instead,

I forced my feet to walk to my locker. I didn't make eye contact with anyone, but it didn't seem to matter. Before I got five steps, people began to attack.

"I'm so glad you're better, Sadie."

"Sadie, is it true Jax Stone was with you in the hospital?"

"Was that Jax's Hummer that brought you to school?"

"Are you living with him?"

"Is Jax Stone going to move here?"

I wanted to put my hands over my ears and scream for them all to go away. More voices joined in, and people kept asking questions that I didn't want to answer since it was none of their business.

"Move! You all have classes to be at, so I suggest you get to them," Principal Farmer called over the vultures.

They moved away, but they all did so reluctantly. I turned back to my locker and got what I needed.

"Miss White, we're sure glad you're back and doing well," Mr. Farmer said from behind me.

I turned and smiled at him. "Thank you."

He nodded and cleared his throat. "I want you to know, if you need anything or you are having problems like the one I just encountered, you can let me know and I'll fix it. I want your experience here at Sea Breeze High to be a great one."

He had never spoken to me before, so his sudden desire to make sure I was happy was strange.

"Thank you, sir," I said, despite my confusion.

"Yes, well, I also want you to know that if your, uh, boyfriend wants to attend any of our functions here, we would love to have him. He is more than welcome."

It all made sense to me then, and I wanted to burst out laughing. Mr. Farmer was just as star crazed as everyone else. I didn't trust myself to speak, so I nodded and headed to class. I was probably already late.

Lunch in the cafeteria was some sort of tomato and pasta mixture that was hard to swallow. I did the best I could, but after a few bites I just resigned myself to drinking my water. I found Amanda and sat with her. We were surrounded by her friends and people who wanted to know about Jax. I didn't say much. I managed to ignore most everyone's questions, and Amanda worked hard to get them to leave me alone.

"So, who's ready for homecoming this Friday night?" Amanda asked, trying to get everyone's mind on something else.

"I found the cutest dress last week in Mobile," a girl on the other side of Amanda gushed. Several other girls started talking about their dresses and how they planned to wear their hair. I listened, but I didn't have anything to add to the conversation since I wasn't going to go.

"Sadie, are you coming to the game?" Amanda asked me before she bit into her apple.

I started to say no, but then I remembered my promise to

Jax and his wanting me to go to football games. "Um, I don't know," I said over my bottle of water.

Amanda swallowed. "Please come with me. I'm going to the dance afterward with Jeff Garner, but he's on the football team, so I'll be dateless during the game."

That sounded good to me. I could go to the game and tell Jax, and maybe that would satisfy him for a while. "Sure, sounds good."

Amanda beamed. "Great! You can come over to my house after school and we can play around with those amazing curls I'm so jealous of. We'll find a way to style your hair, and then you can help me with my straight-as-a-board head of hair!"

I frowned. "Um, does it matter how my hair looks for the football game?"

She grinned and nodded. "Yes, because you're not going to have time to do anything but change before the dance."

"Oh, well, I'm not going to the dance, so that isn't a big deal."

Amanda frowned at me. "Why not?"

Well, because I didn't want to dance without Jax. I shrugged instead of telling her the truth.

She leaned over and whispered in my ear, "If you want a date, all you have to do is crook your finger and every guy will come running."

I shook my head. "No, that's not it. I just don't want to go."

She sighed. "So you're going to leave me alone. I thought you said that Jax wanted you to take advantage of all high school experiences."

I nodded reluctantly.

"Well, big news flash, the homecoming dance is one of the biggest experiences of the year."

I sighed. She was right. He had said dances. I could come and go quickly. "Okay, I'll show up."

Amanda beamed. "Perfect! You want a date?"

I shook my head. "No, I'm going alone."

She sighed and shrugged. "Whatever. I'm just glad you're going."

We won the homecoming football game, so the dance was a wild celebration. The cheerleaders actually wore their cheerleading outfits to the dance, and the football players wore their uniforms without the pads. They were dirty and sweaty, and I wondered how Amanda was going to dance close to Jeff with him smelling like that. I wrinkled my nose at the thought.

The dj played music the minute everyone walked in the door, and I had already started watching the clock so I could make my escape. Amanda had tried to get me to go shopping with her for a new dress, but I assured her I had one I could wear. She had drooled all over herself when she saw the blue dress Jax had given me. I'd let her play with my hair, since she enjoyed it so much, but in the end I had just worn it down and loose. It was easier this way.

"Sadie, will you dance with me?"

I turned to see Dameon, and he was, of course, in his sweaty uniform. I didn't want to dance with anyone but Jax. Dameon could have been nice and clean and I still wouldn't have wanted to dance with him.

I started to shake my head when Mary Ann walked up and slipped her arm around his. "Well, hello, Sadie. All alone tonight?"

I smiled at her because, really, she was just a very insecure, silly girl. "Yes, I am," I assured her.

She looked at Dameon like she had won some sort of prize. "Once again you seem deserted by your famous friend," she purred, and pulled on Dameon's arm. "Let's go dance."

He stared at me as if he wanted to argue, but I turned away to let him know I wasn't interested. Mary Ann tugged one more time, and the couple walked off. I let out a sigh of relief. Amanda waved at me from the dance floor, and I smiled and waved back.

The clock said I had been there twenty minutes. I had promised Jax I would stay thirty at least. I had ten minutes to go. I turned to go get a drink, and I stopped short when I heard the song coming over the speakers. It was my song. I watched the couples on the dance floor slow their pace and hold each other closer. Hearing his voice made me feel less alone.

"Excuse me, but can I have this dance?"

My heart faltered. I swallowed and prayed I wasn't imagining this. I turned around, and Jax stood grinning at me with his hand held out.

"Jax," I said breathlessly, and then I threw myself into his arms. He chuckled in my ear and pulled me closer. "What're you doing here? How? You have a concert in Detroit tomorrow night!"

He grinned and leaned down to kiss my lips softly. "I couldn't let you come to a dance without me."

I laid my head against his chest and breathed him in. "Why didn't you tell me you were coming?"

He held me tighter. "Because I wanted to surprise you." I smiled. I liked these kinds of surprises. "And I wasn't completely sure I was going to be able to get away. But when I talked to you on the phone this morning, you sounded so sad I decided nothing else mattered. I made a way. You come first, always."

I kissed his chest, and then gazed into his intense eyes. "I've become so selfish. All I care about is that you're here."

He laughed, took my hand, and kissed it. "That's okay. You can be selfish with me all you want. I'm yours."

I sighed and listened to his heartbeat.

He leaned down to my ear. "Come down to the beach with me."

I nodded, and he took my hand. We walked in silence out

across the school parking lot and down the hill that led to the beach.

"I want to hold you a little while longer, away from the audience we had in there."

He stopped and sat down just as gracefully as he had the first time we'd sat on the beach together. I sat down, and he frowned. He pointed to the sand right beside him.

"Come here," he said, grinning wickedly. I laughed and scooted as close as I could get. He lay back then, with one hand behind his head and the other out beside him. "Now lie right here," he said, nodding at his outstretched arm.

I lay back on his arm. He pulled me closer, and then he began playing with my hair.

"This is so much harder than I imagined," he murmured into the darkness.

I sighed. "Being apart from your 'air' is never easy."

He grinned. "No kidding. I've had a hell of a time breathing this week. I want nothing more than to tell you to forget this and leave with me. But I can't do it. I want you to have this. I will be here for everything I possibly can. I want to experience with you all the stuff I missed. I just want you to know there isn't a minute that goes by I don't miss you and think about you and wish I were holding you."

I leaned up on my arm and stared down at him. "When it's over and I graduate, what happens then?" I needed to know.

He grinned. "Then I take you, and I don't give you back." I laughed quietly. His face got serious. "What do you want to happen when this is over?"

I thought about college, and my desire to be more than Jessica had been. I wanted to have a purpose in life. "I always thought I would go to college. But now . . ."

Jax pushed up on his elbows. "College is good, Sadie. There are plenty of colleges in California." He paused. "Or were you thinking of staying close to home?"

I pretended to have to think about it. "Um, well, I guess I could go to somewhere in California. That is, if I get accepted."

He raised his eyebrows. "Have you not figured out by now that I can move mountains?"

I laughed and shook my head. "You're not moving mountains to get me into a college."

He sat up and pulled me with him, then took my face in his hands. "I'll do whatever I've got to do to be close to you. I'm not gonna lie. This year is going to be the hardest year of my life. When it's over, I want to get you close to me."

I wanted that too. My future was Jax. Yes, I wanted to go to college, but I wanted to be with Jax more than anything else. If he could make both of those things happen, I wasn't going to let my stubbornness get in the way.

"I want to be with you." My words brought a huge grin to his incredibly beautiful face.

"You're my present and my future, Sadie. I'll use whatever power I have to make you happy."

He leaned down and touched his perfect lips to mine, and my heart took flight. I would never get tired of his kiss. Jax Stone was my everything.

"I missed you so much," Jax murmured against my lips.

I shifted closer to him, and Jax grabbed my waist and pulled me on top of him until I was straddling his hips. A moan escaped me as his erection pressed against me just where I needed it.

"Does that feel good?" he asked, kissing a trail down my neck. He lifted his hips and I rocked against him. It felt incredibly good. I managed a nod. "Do what feels good. I want to see you get off. God knows I've been fantasizing about how your face looks when you come while we were on the phone at night. I need to see it again."

I felt my face heat up at the mention of our recent phone sex. I hadn't realized that was what we were doing until he called it that the other night. But it made sense. I also liked it a lot. It wasn't as good as having him there, but it was wonderful hearing his voice in my ear as we both found relief.

I did as he asked and began rubbing against him. My dress was pushed up my thighs leaving only the thin fabric of my panties and his pants between us. I was getting braver with Jax. I knew he loved me, and it made it easier to take what I wanted. I wasn't ashamed of what felt good.

"Stop," Jax commanded, and I froze. He had just asked me to do this. Why did he want to stop it now? "Anyone could walk out here and see you like this. I was so consumed with needing to feel you, I wasn't thinking clearly."

I couldn't keep the disappointed look off my face.

Jax chuckled. "Not even that cute little pouty face is going to make me finish this out here. The last thing I want is a picture of this all over the place."

He picked me up and put me beside him, then he stood up. I stared up at him as he held out both his hands to me. "Come with me to the limo. I'll kick Kane out and we can finish this in there. Besides, I think I've had my fill of high school dances. I just want to be with you."

Smiling, I slipped both my hands into his as we walked away from the high school, leaving that part of my world behind.

Marcus may have a broken heart, but find out
what happens when he meets Low!

HERE'S A SNEAK PEEK AT

# because of low

**MARCUS**

Moving back home sucked. Everything about this town
reminded me of why the hell I'd wanted to get away. I had a
life in Tuscaloosa, and I needed that life to escape. Here, I was
Marcus Hardy. No matter where I went, people knew me. They
knew my family. And now . . . they were talking about my family.
Which is why I had come home. Leaving my sister and mother
here to face this alone was impossible. The scandal hovering
over our heads took away all my choices and my freedom. Right
now few people knew, but it was only a matter of time. Soon the
entire coastal town of Sea Breeze, Alabama, would know what
my dad was doing—or should I say, who my dad was doing.
King of the Mercedes car dealerships along the Gulf Coast had
been a high enough title for some little gold-digging whore only

a few years older than me to jump into bed with my dear ol' dad. The one time I'd seen the home wrecker working behind the desk right outside Dad's office, I'd known something wasn't right. She was young and smoking hot and apparently money hungry.

Dad couldn't keep it in his pants, and now my mom and sister would have to deal with the stigma it would cause. People would feel sorry for my mom. This was already devastating to her, and she didn't even know yet that the other woman was barely a woman. My younger sister, Amanda, had caught them going at it late one evening when Mom had sent her over to the office to take Dad some dinner. She'd called me that night crying hysterically. I'd withdrawn from school, packed my things, and headed home. There was no other option. My family needed me.

A knock at the door snapped me out of my internal tirade, and I went to see what chick was here looking for Cage this time. God knew the guy had an endless line of females parading through his life. My new roommate was a player. A major player. He put my best friend, Preston, to shame. I twisted the knob and swung the door open without peeking through the hole.

The surprise was on me. I'd been prepared to tell whatever tall, willowy, large-but-obviously-fake-chested female dressed in almost nothing waiting outside the door that Cage was busy with another one very similar to her. Except a very natural, almost curvy redhead stood before me. Red-rimmed eyes and a tear-streaked face gazed up at me. There were no mascara lines running down her face. Her hair wasn't styled, but pulled back in a ponytail. She wore jeans and what appeared to be an authentic Back in Black AC/DC concert T-shirt. No belly button drawing attention to a flat, tanned stomach, and her clothes weren't skintight. Well, maybe the jeans were a little snug, but they hugged her hips nicely. My appreciation of her legs in the slim-fit jeans stopped, however, when I noticed the small beat-up suitcase clutched tightly in her hand.

"Is Cage here?" Her voice sounded broken and musical at the same time. I was having a hard time digesting that this girl was here for Cage. She wasn't anything like he veered toward. Nothing was enhanced. Everything from her thick dark-copper hair to the Chuck Taylors on her feet screamed "not Cage's type." And the fact that she was carrying a suitcase—well, that couldn't be good.

"Uh, um, no."

Her shoulders slumped and another sob escaped her. One small, dainty hand flew up in an attempt to mute the sound of her obvious distress. Her nails were even classy. Not too long, with a smooth, rounded tip and soft pink nail polish.

"I left my cell phone"—she let out a sigh, then continued—"at my sister's. I need to call him. Can I come in?"

Cage was out with a swimsuit model who apparently had a thing for college baseball players. I knew from the way he talked he didn't intend to come up for air much tonight. He'd never answer her call, and I hated to see her get more upset than she already was. A horrible thought crossed my mind: Surely he hadn't gotten this girl pregnant. Couldn't he see how freaking innocent she was?

"Uh, yeah, but I don't know if he'll answer. He's busy . . . tonight."

She shot me a sour smile and nodded, stepping around me.

"I know the kind of busy he is, but he'll talk to me."

She sounded rather confident. I wasn't feeling her confidence myself.

"Do you have a cell I can use?"

I reached into the pocket of my jeans and handed it to her, unable to argue with her further. She had stopped crying and I wanted to keep it that way.

"Thanks. I'll try calling first."

I watched as she walked over to the sofa and dropped her suitcase to the floor with a thunk before sinking dejectedly down onto the worn cushions as if she'd been here a hundred times. Being as I'd only been moved in for two days, I wouldn't know if she had been here before or not. Cage was a friend of a friend who had been looking for a roommate. I'd needed somewhere to live fast and his place was nice. Preston was on the same baseball team as Cage at the local community college. Once Preston heard I needed a place to live, he'd called Cage and hooked me up.

"It's me. I left my phone when I ran. You're not here, but your new roommate let me in. Call me." She sniffed, then hung up. I watched, fascinated, as she proceeded to text him. She really believed the male whore I lived with was going to call her right up as soon as he got her message. I was intrigued and growing more concerned by the minute.

She finished and handed the phone back to me. A smile touched her splotchy red face and two dimples appeared in her cheeks. Damn, that was cute.

"Thanks. Do you mind if I wait a little bit until he calls back?"

I shook my head,. "No, not at all. You want a drink?"

She nodded and stood up. "Yes, but I'll get it. My drinks are in the bottom drawer of the fridge behind the Bud Lights."

I frowned and followed her into the kitchen. She opened the fridge and bent down to get her hidden drink. With her bent over digging for her so-called drink, the snug fit of the faded jeans over her ass was hard to miss. It was a perfect heart shape, and although she wasn't very tall, her legs seemed to go on for miles.

"Ah, here it is. Cage needs to run to the store and restock. He must be letting his one-nighters drink my Jarritos."

I couldn't keep guessing. I needed to know who she was exactly. Surely she wasn't one of his girlfriends. Could she be the sister Preston had mentioned dating? I sure as hell hoped not. I was interested, and I hadn't been interested in anyone in a while. Not since the last girl broke my heart. I'd opened my mouth to ask her how she knew Cage when the phone in my pocket started ringing. She walked over to me and held out her hand. The girl really believed it was Cage. I glanced down, but sure enough, my roommate had called back.

She took the phone from my hand.

"Hey.

"She's such a selfish jerk.

"I can't stay there, Cage.

"I didn't mean to leave my phone. I was just upset.

"Yes, your new roommate's a nice guy. He's been very helpful.

"No, don't end your date. Get her out of your system. I'll wait.

"I promise not to go back.

"She is who she is, Cage.

"I just hate her." I could hear the tears in her voice again.

"No, no, really, I'm fine. I just needed to see you."

"Don't. I'll leave.

"Cage—

"*No.*

"Cage.

"Okay, fine."

She held the phone out to me. "He wants to talk to you."

This conversation was nothing like I'd expected. The girl had to be his sister.

"Hey."

"Listen, I need you to make sure Low stays there until I can get home. She's upset and I don't want her leaving. Get her one of her damn Mexican soda thingies out of the fridge. They're behind the Bud Lights in the bottom drawer. I have to hide them from other chicks I have over. All females tend to like those nasty drinks. Turn on the television, distract her, whatever. I'm only ten minutes away, but I'm putting my jeans on as we speak and headed home. Just help her get her mind off things, but *don't* touch her."

"Ah, okay, sure. Is she your sister?"

Cage chuckled into the phone. "Hell no, she ain't my sister. I'd never buy my damn sister drinks and call her back when I'm in the middle of a fucking threesome. Low's the girl I'm gonna marry."

I had no response to that. My eyes found her standing over by the window with her back to me. The long thick copper locks curled on the ends and brushed against the middle of her back. She was absolutely nothing like the girls Cage regularly hooked up with. What did he mean, she was the girl he was going to marry? That made no sense.

"Keep her there, man. I'm on my way."

Then he hung up the phone.

I dropped it on the table and stood there staring at her back. She turned around slowly and studied me a moment, and then a smile broke across her face.

"He told you he was going to marry me, didn't he?" she said laughing softly before taking a drink of the orange soda with what appeared to have Spanish writing on the label.

"Crazy boy. I shouldn't have bothered him, but he's all I've got."

She walked over and sank back down onto the old faded green sofa, pulling her legs up underneath her.

"Don't worry. I'm not leaving. He'd rip apart my sister's house searching for me and scare the bejesus out of her if I left. I've got enough issues where she's concerned. I don't intend to unleash Cage on her."

I slowly made my way over to the only chair in the room and sat down.

"So, you're engaged?" I asked, staring down at her bare ring finger.

With a sad smile she shook her head.

"Not in a million years. Cage has crazy ideas. Just because he says them doesn't make them true."

She raised her eyebrows and took another drink of her soda.

"So you aren't going to marry Cage?" I really would love for her to clarify this because I was incredibly confused and more than a little interested in her. She bit down on her bottom lip and I noticed for the first time how full it was.

"Cage was my 'boy next door' growing up. He's my best friend. I love him dearly and he really is all I have. The only person I can count on. We've never actually been in a relationship before because he knows I won't have sex with him and he needs sex. He's also real wrapped up in the whole idea that a relationship between the two of us before we get married will end badly and he'll lose me. He has this irrational fear of losing me."

Did she know the guy had bagged more than three different girls this week and apparently was having a threesome when she'd called? She was so much better than Cage.

"Wipe that look off your face. I don't need your pity. I know what Cage is like. I know you have probably seen the kind of girls he's attracted to, and I look absolutely nothing like them. I don't live in a fantasy world. I'm very aware." She tilted her head and smiled at me sweetly. "I don't even know your name."

"Marcus Hardy"

"Well, Marcus Hardy, I'm Willow Montgomery, but everyone calls me Low. It's a pleasure to meet you."